THE POWER AND THE FURY

EDEN CHRONICLES I

JAMES ERITH

EDEN CHRONICLES I
THE POWER AND THE FURY
First Published in 2013

2018 Paperback - Edition 003
978-1-910134-04-7

Jerico Press

Cover: Tom Moore (tom@beatmedia.co.uk)

THE POWER AND THE FURY is written in UK English.

ISBN-13: 978-1-910134-04-7

AVAILABLE ON MOST DIGITAL PLATFORMS

www.JamesErith.com

To Florence

It started out as a story for my Godchildren:
Isabella, Daisy and Archie.

Thank you:
My wonderful family and friends for their reservoir of support.

Also:
James, Kate and Charlotte Allen for Southwold.
Susan and Joe Swiers for Yorkshire.

CONTENTS

ONE

A DREAM IS GIVEN

A rchie tensed.

No, it was nothing, he thought, *just a gust of wind rattling a loose tile on the roof, or the strange 'yessss!' sounds that his twin, Daisy, shouted in her sleep.*

He took a deep breath. Isabella's last sleep-talking dream was something to do with atmospheric pressure and barometers or some other weird weather-related thing.

Archie smiled and rolled over; who else but his sisters could dream of such odd and opposite things—football and science. Crazy.

He rubbed his eyes and yawned. His heavy eyelids began to close but, just before they locked tight, he noticed something unusual above Daisy's head that forced them open.

A shudder fizzed down his body.

He closed his eyes and counted, very slowly, to three.

ONE.

TWO.

THREE.

Then he opened them just a bit.

It was still there!

But it couldn't be! An angel... when had anyone seen an angel, really seen one?

His brain whirred.

Maybe it was a ghost. But ghosts didn't exist. Or did they?

A cold sweat dampened his forehead.

And now he looked harder, it was more like a huge, strange species of spider covered by a thin, opaque jellyfish that sprayed blue forks of electricity from its midriff.

Archie didn't want to stare but he couldn't help it. He exhaled as quietly as he could, desperate not to draw attention to himself. Now that his eyes were adjusting to the light, Archie could see delicate claw-like contraptions at the end of the *thing's* long slender legs, and they were moving in perfect time with Daisy's every breath.

As if the claws were somehow *feeding* her.

Archie's heart pounded as a flurry of questions crowded his brain:

Does it hurt?

What if it's poison?

What if it comes towards him—what then?

Will it do the same to me, the same to Isabella, Old Man Wood, Mrs Pye... everyone in the house?

A nauseous feeling churned in his stomach.

What if it's an alien and hundreds more are about to drop out of the sky?

Shouldn't he *do* something?

And then another thought struck him and, absurd as it sounded, it felt... possible. Really possible.

What if this creature had a connection with the strange dreams he'd been having? What if it was giving Daisy a dream?

As if hearing his thoughts, the spidery-angel turned its head and stared at him with deep black eyes like cavernous empty holes. Archie froze as a chill rushed into his brain and in the very next moment the creature had vanished.

Gone. Just like that.

Archie stared out into the dark night air as his heart thumped like a drum in his chest.

Gradually, the iciness began to thaw but Archie remained stone-still, terrified that the *thing* might reappear directly on top of him. After what felt like a month, he sat up, shook out the arm he'd been lying on, and wiped the sweat from his brow.

All he could see was the fabric of the large drape, perched like a tent above him, and the outline of the thick old wooden rafters beyond. And opposite lay Daisy, fast asleep, snoring, as though nothing had happened.

Had the spidery creature been in his head, a figment of his imagination—another dream?

He pinched himself and felt a twinge of pain.

So what was it doing to Daisy with those tiny claws on the end of its long legs? Sucking her brains out?

Archie replayed the scene in his mind, as though scrolling through a film. He remembered the way the creature waited for her inhalations and then, as she drew air into her lungs, its tiny claws spun like crazy.

Each time, he returned to the same conclusion; it wasn't *taking* anything from Daisy, more *giving* her something. And whatever it was, she had drawn it deep inside.

Archie flicked on the bedside lamp and a gentle yellow glow filled the attic room. From the far wall, Isabella yawned and rolled over. Archie waited until she had settled, then slipped out from under his duvet.

He tiptoed silently towards Daisy's bed, a couple of wooden planks moaning in protest as he went.

He knelt down and surveyed her.

She was silent and at peace. She looked as pretty as anything with her golden hair tumbling wildly over the pillow, her mouth parted.

He smelt her sleepiness.

Leaning in, his face was just a few inches from hers as he inspected her nose, her chin, her lips, her cheeks and ears.

But there were no odd marks or stains, no bruises, no bleeding, nothing amiss.

Archie put his head in his hands.

Perhaps he had imagined it—perhaps it was just another nightmare.

He rubbed his face and readied himself to go back to bed

when suddenly Daisy gasped as though she'd been stuck underwater and burst through to find air.

She groaned and tossed her head from side to side. Then, without warning, she sat bolt upright as though a massive electric current had smashed into her, her face missing his by a whisker.

Her wavy hair brushed his nose.

Archie's eyes nearly popped out of their sockets. He could feel her breath marking his cheek. He swayed to the side and noted that her eyes were shut tight.

She was asleep!

Now she was mumbling, but he couldn't make out the words. He listened harder.

What was it... "odd", followed by "wo-man?"

She repeated it, this time louder. This time the word "odd" sounded more like "blood" or "flood". And there was something else. Yes, a word like, "a-shunt" before "woman" and then a word like... "bread". That was it.

But what did it mean?

"Blood—a-shunt—woman—bread?"

A car accident?

Again Daisy said these words, again and again, growing louder and louder. And now it sounded like, "flood an shunt woman Fred"."

'Flood an shunt woman Fred?' Archie repeated.

What was she talking about?

In a flash, it came to him.

Archie reeled; he knew he wasn't mistaken. Now he said it with her. The first word was definitely "flood" followed by, "Ancient Woman... dead".

Archie felt the blood drain from his face.

He stood up and stared at his twin, his mouth open.

It wasn't possible—it couldn't be. How could she access his very own nightmare, the exact same dream he'd had over the past few nights; the flooding and the haggard old woman?

Was it a twin thing?

No. Twin things never happened to them.

He noticed tears falling from Daisy's eyes, eyes which were wide open and staring at a fixed point across the room.

Without warning, Daisy screamed.

Archie automatically ducked and covered his ears.

She began to shake.

Then, her hands reached out as though clawing at an invisible figure.

Words spilled out incoherently.

A moment later she stopped, and, with a look of absolute dread and fear mixed upon her face, she spoke, her words faint, like whispers.

Archie leaned in but wished he hadn't, for her next words stabbed him, as though a knife had been plunged deep into his heart and twisted round and round.

'No, no, please don't do it, Archie,' she implored, repeating these words over and over and louder and louder until she was yelling.

'DON'T DO IT, ARCHIE... NOT HER,' she cried. **'PLEASE.'**

And then one final plea.

'PLEASE, ARCHIE ... NOOOO!'

TWO

THE ROUTE TO SCHOOL

A rchie swung the bag over his shoulder. 'I'm going the forest route. Anyone want to come?'

'Not today,' Daisy replied, while staring at her nails. 'Saving my energy for the big match—if I'm allowed to play. It's the announcement in assembly.'

'Oh yeah, of course. *The announcement*,' Archie said, dragging his fingers through his black hair. 'I'm sure you'll be fine.'

'Promise me you won't get covered in mud or torn to bits with brambles,' Isabella yelled from behind her curtain. 'It'll be detention if you do. And I *will* make sure you do it.'

Archie pulled a face.

'I can tell exactly what you're doing, Archie de Lowe,' Isabella said. 'Ten quid says you're making a face.'

Archie stuck his tongue out and waggled it towards her curtain.

Daisy laughed.

'Hilarious,' Isabella said, as she popped her head out. 'I'm on a mission to tidy you up. Up until now you've ignored everyone. But it has to change.'

Archie rolled his eyes and, with a smile where the corners of his mouth curled up mischievously, he winked at his twin, turned, sneaked out of the door and down the stairs to the landing below.

ON HIS WAY OUT, Archie poked his head around the door of the kitchen where Old Man Wood and Mrs Pye were washing up breakfast.

'Just off,' he said, 'see you later.'

'You're going early,' Mrs Pye said. 'Anything the matter?'

'Nah, just fancy a walk, that's all.' He spotted Mrs Pye placing some apples in the fruit bowl. 'Ooh. Can I have one?' he asked.

Mrs Pye gave him a look.

'*Please*.'

Mrs Pye selected one and lobbed it over. 'Now don't you go getting them clothes ripped again or go tripping down any holes or burrows or bigger holes like those badger ones on them slopes. I'm fed up with constantly mending your things and darning your clothes and washing, young Archie, oh, I am.'

Then she smiled, although to most people it would have looked like a grimace.

'But what am I telling you that for, eh? You're quite old enough to know better.' She grimaced, or smiled again.

'Whatever you do,' she continued, 'don't go breaking any of them bones of yours. Understand? It's your football tomorrow and you know how Daisy would be disappointed.'

Archie smiled. He loved it when she rambled on. He grabbed his bags, opened the thick oak door and slipped outside.

He drew in a large breath of air as he watched the first rays of light slowly creeping up over the vale, smearing the base of the thick cloud in a fiery orange glow.

At first he followed the stony path towards the ruin but, before long, he cut along a makeshift animal track that weaved through the long grass before it met the forest and the steep slopes that ran down to the river.

For several minutes he hurdled fallen branches and jumped rabbit warrens and fox holes, untangling brambles from his clothes as he ducked through thickets and bushes. Every so often he would stop and pluck a few blackberries or scavenge for hazelnuts on the ground.

He chewed them as he went, savouring the tastes—be it tangy and sour or over-ripe and juicy—smearing his hands and lips with red berry juice.

In the semi-darkness beneath the forest canopy, he found long creepers dangling down and swung on them, pretending to be a pirate boarding a ship. One gave way in mid-flight and he tumbled to the ground but he picked himself up and brushed his clothes down.

He fingered a tear in his blazer and another in his shorts and shrugged.

Nothing he could do about it now.

He wished Daisy was with him. She loved this kind of thing, even if she didn't like to admit it. She only came out in the holidays—when her friends weren't around worrying about their looks and their make-up and nails and hair, and boys.

When Daisy was out here, she went wild; her blonde hair tangled up in brambles and grass, her face smeared by mud and berries and blood.

She wasn't that into all the girlie stuff. In fact she wasn't into anything particularly, except football.

His thoughts were interrupted by a fly buzzing round his head. Daisy and her passion for football. Strange that, really. A girl up here on the moors playing football with farmers' sons and country boys; she had to be good—and tough.

Yep, he thought. Daisy was equal and better on both counts.

He loosened his clothes as his body warmed up and before long he came to a huge grey boulder three times his height. In his mind's eye, he measured the distance and set off at a sprint towards it. At the last moment, he sprang up and grasped a stony outcrop just high enough to haul himself up onto the top of the boulder where he sat down and gulped in mouthfuls of morning air. Removing his rucksack, he reached into his bag and flipped open the lid of his bottle, grateful for the cooling effect of the water.

The day wasn't hot, just sticky, like a Turkish bath without the heat.

He rubbed the apple on his jumper and took a bite, wiping his lips on his sleeve.

Nonchalantly, he stared out over the valley, his eyes focusing on the buildings of Upsall—particularly the school—perched above the flood plain at the foot of the moors.

Above the school he noted the rugged, menacing, dark forest and jagged rocks that jutted out of the steep slopes like angry faces. In stark contrast were the manicured green stripes of the school playing fields, laid out symmetrically below.

He smiled. *Man's doing down below,* he thought, *God's above.*

He cast his eye along the valley, where weeping willows marked the course of the meandering river at perfect intervals, as though guarding the valley floor like sentries.

From here, Upsall appeared so much grander and more important than it was close up.

At school, there were constant reminders of the its monastic heritage. The quadrangle with its grey stone and red-brick colonnade were relics of an age when it was a vital refuge for those heading north or east over the harsh Yorkshire moors.

The buildings had medieval emblems of security and style. Solid chunks of masonry, a huge circular rose window inlaid with delicate stained glass, a thick oak door and, most obviously, a square tower that soared into the sky.

This must have been a welcome sight for weary travellers as they came off the hills.

Raised on a platform above the river sat a jumble of buildings in varying shapes, sizes and colours. The occasional facade was rendered in plaster but most were finished in grey stone or red bricks typical of the area. And, surrounding the village, the high slopes of the moors protected these dwellings like a shield.

The effect was of chocolate-box charm but with no real order or sophistication.

Old Man Wood often told them that the ruin next to Eden Cottage was far older than the rest. Archie spun to his right, towards the sheer rock face that rose high above him.

A great position for a fortress up there, he thought, hidden away in the forest, but at the same time imposing and bold— as a castle should be—with a view that stretched across the Vale of York.

Today, something was missing.

He searched his mind. Nothing came.

No one really knew about their ruin, not from the school at any rate. Perhaps it was a bit too rustic, or too hard to get to, Archie thought.

Mr Solomon, the headmaster, called it, 'the hinterland', but for the de Lowe children the battlements and ancient earthworks gave endless possibilities for games—and battles.

And then it shot into his brain. He stared at the rock face again. Where were the eagles and buzzards that soared high above? He listened. Not a birdcall in earshot. Not a wingspan in sight.

He checked his watch and groaned.

Archie slid off the boulder and ran along the towpath, over the bridge, across the playing fields and towards the chapel. As he neared the stone steps, he dusted himself off and slipped in through the oak door.

Head down, he sped over the large flagstones until he found his row. Then, he squeezed his way to the middle, where he sat down and caught his breath.

He turned to see Daisy chatting to several of her friends. He caught her eye but she frowned and turned away. What did that mean? Was it about the team?

For a brief moment he experienced a feeling that he was being watched, just as he had with the spidery-angel the previous night.

His instinct was right. On the platform at the far end of

the hall stood Mr Solomon, the headmaster, whose eyes bore into him.

Archie's heart sank. Another inspection.

Those who had even the tiniest scuffs or tears, or buttons missing, were being entered into his dreaded red book..

Archie gave himself a once-over. A shambles, possibly the worst ever.

He felt for his tie halfway down his shirt and pulled it up. He drew up his socks and dragged a hand roughly through his hair, pulling out tendrils of a creeper and a few small strands of grass.

Archie knew he had a couple of seconds to run out. But as he thought about it, a familiar voice boomed through the hall.

'Good morning, school,' it said. 'Please rise.'

And automatically, everyone stood up.

THREE
GOOD & BAD NEWS

'Quiet... please,' Mr Solomon roared, patting the breast
pockets of his coarse tweed suit.

Wasn't it strange how the noise level always
seemed to rise as conversations were rushed to a conclusion?
He removed his glasses from his round, ruddy nose and glared
around the hall.

'Thank you, children. Please, sit down.'

Two hundred and seventy-two pupils sat down on the
hard wooden benches, lined out row upon row, the noise
drifting high into the rafters of the vaulted ceiling.

On either side the walls were lined with large portraits of
headmasters, interspersed with dark wooden panels where the
names of past scholars, captains, and musicians were
remembered.

Above, tall cross-beams supported large chandelier lights
that hung from thick metal chains.

Mr Solomon stared out over the throng, cleared his throat
before peering like an owl through his glasses to inspect his
leather-bound clipboard.

'School dress!'

There was a groan.

Archie felt a strong urge to disappear.

'I see some of you shaking in fear,' Solomon said, his

eyebrows raised as if he were all-seeing and all-knowing. 'And rightly, too,' he continued.

'There has been a marked deterioration in dress standards since the beginning of term. After half term, those who fail to comply with school regulation uniform will be given detention. Now, to show you what I'm talking about, no one is shaking more this morning than Upsall School goalkeeping hero, Archie de Lowe.'

A cheer went up.

'Archie, please stand.'

Archie sat stone-still in disbelief. *Not again.*

He felt a jab in his back and then another from the side.

'Come on, Archie. Up you get,' the headmaster prompted.

Archie stared down at his worn shoes and, taking a deep breath, rose from behind the large frame of his old friend Gus Williams.

Every pair of eyes stared at him. Archie could hear girls giggling nearby. His face reddened, the heat of his blush growing by the second.

He didn't dare look up.

Mr Solomon continued: 'Archie, I hate to make an example of you, but this morning you have beaten your spectacular record of being a complete and utter shambles.'

A ripple of laughter filled the hall.

'In all of my time at this school, your attire is by far the most dreadful I have ever come across. In fact it is almost the perfect example of how not to dress. Your shoes are filthy; you have no belt, which shows off your very splendid and colourful underwear, and your socks are around your ankles because there are no elastic garters to hold them up.'

Mr Solomon paused as laughter pealed into the high ceiling. 'Your shirt has lost buttons; your tie is halfway across your chest, and I'm not sure how this could have happened, but you seem to be wearing the wrong coloured jersey. Please turn around, de Lowe.'

Archie shifted, pretending to slouch like a tramp and in

the process getting a laugh. It somehow made the humiliation feel a fraction more bearable.

'Yes, just as I suspected,' Solomon continued. 'Blazer ripped and, of course, your hair is the usual bird's nest.'

Everyone was laughing.

Archie feigned a smile while trying to pull his attire together. On Solomon's instruction, he sat down.

Isabella would be livid with him; only this morning she'd told him to sort out his appearance and he'd completely ignored her again. It meant he'd not only be faced with more detention, which was bearable, but he'd finally have to go shopping. And Archie detested shopping. He bowed his head and didn't dare look up in case he caught her eye.

Then he turned to see Daisy staring at the floor.

Solomon's tone softened as he smiled, showing his small, tea-stained teeth. 'Let this be a lesson to you, Archie. Today, and only today, you are excused because you're an important member of our glorious unbeaten football team. And this, of course, leads me on to the main item on this morning's agenda.'

With these words the mood in the hall changed and the noise level increased.

The headmaster raised an arm for quiet before starting again.

'Most of you are aware of our situation. As a small school our selection for teams is limited, and I regrettably endorsed that a girl could play in the boys' team. This team has subsequently gone on to great things, to the very great credit of our school. However, I... we... were found out.'

The headmaster pulled out a letter from the breast pocket of his jacket and waved it in the air.

'Let me read you the important parts of this letter I received yesterday from the president of our Football Association.'

He nudged his glasses into the correct position on the bridge of his nose and thumbed his way down the page.

'Ah-ha. Here we are: *Now, what this all means,*' he read, '*is that we would expect boys and boys only, to play.*'

A slightly confused murmur spread around the room.

'*However,*' he continued to read, '*under rule 12.7.1 there is a clause which reads: Any team member who has played ten matches consecutively has the right to appeal for an impartial ruling if a matter of disrepute has been reported.*'

Mr Solomon put the letter down on the lectern and removed his half-moon glasses. He peered around the room.

'What they are saying, therefore, is this: has Daisy played ten matches in a row this season?'

He spied a raised hand from one of the girls at the back.

'Sue Lowden, do you have the answer?'

'I believe she's played in twelve, sir. Thirteen if you take into consideration the friendly against the Dutch school.'

'Thank you very much, Miss Lowden.'

An audible buzz passed around the room.

The headmaster donned his glasses once more and turned back to the letter.

'*It is our opinion,*' he read, '*that Upsall School has seriously abused the goodwill of this league. However not one opposition team member reported or noticed Miss de Lowe's disguise until the information was passed to us by way of an anonymous letter.*'

Several heads turned towards a group of boys sitting on the left side of the room. A hissing noise started.

Mr Solomon continued to read, this time in a slightly louder voice:

'*As this happened prior to the National Northern Cup Final, and Miss de Lowe has played in every round, we have decided to impart the following. Should Upsall School win, then we will recommend, with the full backing of the Football Association, that Miss de Lowe be allowed to continue playing for Upsall School and the rules be changed with imme-diate effect—*'

A roar of cheers and whooping noises filled the air.

'*However,*' Mr Solomon read, raising his hand for quiet, '*should Upsall lose,*' and here, his voice went so quiet that you could almost hear a pin drop, '*then it will be Miss de Lowe's last game for the school.*'

Silence spread over the assembly.

Mr Solomon picked Daisy out of the assembly, peeled off his glasses and spoke directly to her.

'So there we have it, Daisy. I have spoken to the authorities to make sure we are absolutely clear about the situation. You will play in tomorrow's final against Chitbury Town, but with no disguise. Do you understand? It's bitter-sweet, but it's not all over by any means!'

Mr Solomon addressed the children crashing his fist down on the lectern. 'Now, let's make sure as a team and a school that we jolly well win!'

Solomon waited for the noise to settle.

'Kick-off tomorrow is at 11am. There will be no assembly, but there will be a chapel service for those of you who wish to get rid of your sins, so I'm expecting a great deal of you. One final thing. I'd like to see all three de Lowes afterwards for a moment, and prefects, can you ensure that everyone leaves in the usual orderly manner.'

KEMP MOVED QUICKLY to cut her off.

'I can look after myself, Kemp,' Daisy said coolly. 'There's no point trying to intimidate me. As you know, I don't feel pain—'

'I'm sorry,' Kemp butted in. 'What did you say, de Lowe, intimidation, pain?' He laughed. 'We wouldn't do a thing like that, would we boys?' he said, addressing his mates, Mason and Wilcox. 'Not really my style, de Lowe.'

Daisy leaned in towards him, taking him off guard, and whispered in his ear, her breath soft on his cheek. 'Only your foul breath could truly frighten me.'

In a flash she tried to push through a gap but Kemp recovered his wits and, with a big hand, grabbed her arm and twisted it behind her back.

A stabbing pain shot into her shoulder.

'I haven't finished,' Kemp said. 'Now listen up, Daisy de Lowe. My mates at Chitbury are SO looking forward to it, especially the second half.'

'Tell your mates I'm looking forward to it,' she spat, staring him coldly in the eyes.

Taking him off guard, she fluttered her eyelashes, pouted her lips and spoke to him in a high-pitched girlie voice.

'You know what, Kempy-wempy,' she started, 'you really are super macho with your big muscles and your fat lips.'

Wilcox and Mason looked at each other and sniggered.

Kemp glared at them.

Daisy whispered very faintly in his ear. 'Deep down, I think you fancy me, don't you, big boy.'

Kemp looked ready to explode. He twisted Daisy's arm higher up her back.

Daisy squirmed. 'Let me go, loser.'

Kemp put his mouth to her ear. 'Don't even think about it, de Lowe.'

'What? Me and you?' she replied.

Kemp loosened his hold. 'No, stupid. The football. They're in a different league—at least soon they will be, so wave bye-bye to your football career, and hello to mine—'

'Back off, Kemp!' It was the large figure of Gus Williams closing in. 'The de Lowes are wanted by Solomon. Didn't you hear? Or are you deaf as well as dumb?'

Kemp released her. 'You're asking for it, Williams—'

'Fine,' Gus replied, his eyes bulging with excitement. 'Any time, just you and me, this afternoon—'

Daisy had had enough. Without hesitating, she aimed a vicious kick at Kemp's shin.

Kemp howled and hopped up and down rubbing his leg.

Gus flashed his big friendly toothy smile at Daisy and turned to Kemp.

'Kicked by a girl. That shouldn't be painful for a tough lad like you.'

FOUR

KEMP'S STORY

'What was that about?' Archie said, as Daisy joined him at the other side of the hall.

Daisy ran her hands through her hair. 'Oh, nothing, usual stuff,' she said flatly. 'Kemp being a creep, telling me how much of a kicking I'm going to get and Gus, heroic, as usual.'

She sighed. 'Why does Kemp hate me so much?'

Archie rubbed his freckled nose and laughed. 'Because he's a thug and he's jealous of you. Because everyone likes you and hates him.' He frowned. 'And possibly because you— a mere slip of a girl—booted macho-man off the team.'

Daisy shook her head. 'But he was useless—always giving away fouls and kicking people off the ball. And anyway that was last year—'

'But he's like an elephant who never forgets—'

'Well, it's ridiculous,' Daisy complained, 'elephant or not.'

Archie grabbed his sister playfully by the waist. 'Strange thing, the way he looks at you.'

Daisy gasped and a smile lit up her face. 'Yeah, right!'

'He likes you. It's kind of obvious.'

She pushed Archie away. 'Eeeuk! No way! I promise you, Archie. Not in a million years!'

Archie grinned and stole a glance over to the far end of the hall, where Kemp was talking to his friends. They locked eyes for a moment, then Kemp reached into his pocket for his mobile phone.

Archie turned back to Daisy, his face concerned. 'Probably a huge mistake to kick him though; other people feel pain in their legs, even if you don't—'

'I wonder,' Daisy said, staring into the distance, 'would Kemp even know me if I didn't play football? I mean, is there another side to him that's not horrible or gross or stinks like a skunk. How did he end up being such a dickhead?'

Archie shrugged. 'Kemp's alright, he's got problems—'

Daisy's eyes nearly popped out. 'Yeah! You're telling me—'

'No, seriously,' Archie said. 'He told me about it in a boring session of detention last term and made me swear not to tell anyone.'

'Well, go on, then,' Daisy urged. 'You can tell me.'

'Of course I can't, it's a secret.'

'Don't be silly,' Daisy implored. 'He's just tried to break my arm and his friends are going to kick the life out of me.'

'No.'

'Yes,' Daisy insisted. 'For curiosity's sake and because it's often best to know your enemy.'

Archie wavered for a second and then shook his head, even if Daisy did have a point. 'Sorry.'

'*Pleeease*,' Daisy begged.

Archie sighed. 'No.'

'*Pleeease*, winkle.'

'God. OK—as long as you swear you absolutely won't tell anyone. And you stop calling me winkle.'

Daisy wobbled her head inconclusively.

'I mean it,' Archie said, 'don't tell anyone.'

'Alright—I swear.'

Archie eyed her carefully. 'You do realise, Daisy, that if he finds out he'll rip my arms off or suck out my eyes. Or both.'

Daisy flashed him a look. 'Yeah, yeah, I know. Not a soul.'

'OK, so the thing is, Kemp's parents died when he was little—very suddenly—and he keeps very quiet about it. He never talks about it. Now he lives with his aunt, who he can't stand.'

'That's awful,' Daisy said, her eyes wide. 'How?'

'What do you mean, how?'

'How did they die?'

'Oh, I see. A car crash. Something happened up on the hills in the forest towards Dalton.' Archie's voice turned to a whisper. 'The rest is really grim.'

'Go on,' Daisy urged, leaning in. 'You've started so you've got to finish.'

Archie sighed, looked over his shoulder, and saw Kemp heading towards the door at the far end of the hall. 'Apparently, both lost their heads. Their car plummeted into a ravine and blew up. Some charred and disjointed remains were found scattered in the woods weeks later.'

Daisy whistled. 'My God. I can see why he doesn't want anyone to know.'

Archie nodded. 'Shocking, isn't it. And the worst bit is that they only found parts of one body.'

Daisy stared at the floor. 'So you like him, don't you?' she said.

'Yeah, I suppose, apart from when he's a jerk to you two.'

Daisy was intrigued. 'Come on, tell me more, I mean he's probably organising my death right now.'

Archie glanced down the hall and hesitated. 'God. OK. Beneath all that macho stuff he's actually quite soft—it's a barrier he puts up to protect himself, well that's what his shrink says—'

'*Shrink?*' Daisy blurted. 'Kemp has a shrink?'

A few heads turned their way. 'Yes, a shrink, psychiatrist, whatever—keep your voice down.'

'They're not doing a very good job.'

Archie shot his twin a look. 'Tell me about it. He seems to snap in and out. I mean, when he told me all this in detention he cried buckets and went on and on about wanting a normal life with a normal family. And then he thumped me really hard on the shoulder and told me not to tell anyone.

Remember that massive bruise I had when I said I'd fallen out of a tree.'

'Oh yeah, I thought that was a bit odd.'

'I couldn't move my arm for a week. Anyway he's basically sad, bored, and to be honest, lonely. Everyone hates him and he knows it.'

'Even Mason and Wilcox?'

'Those freaks don't really like him. They pretend they're best mates but it's fear that glues them together. Ever seen how they jump to attention when he's around or their heads get cracked together? One moment he's charming and funny, the next he's pure evil. It's as if there's a switch that flicks in his head. And he's really strong for his age, the only person who can match him is Williams—'

'And there were sparks flying between them earlier,' she said. 'So why does he like you?'

Archie smiled. 'Because I don't annoy him, and I'm probably not worth beating up,' Archie raised his eyebrows. 'And because I don't deliberately *piss him off.*'

Daisy thumped him playfully. 'He's a loser, Archie. Why doesn't he try being nice for a change?'

'Apparently it's something to do with offloading emotional pain. That's why Solomon and the teachers leave him alone so he can do what he likes. They're terrified he'll go even further off the rails. Apparently it's pretty common. I mean, think about it. If our parents got killed we'd probably go a bit nuts, although to be fair,' and he pinched Daisy on the cheek, 'you're at least halfway there.'

Daisy smiled, sarcasm screwed on her face. Then she sighed.

'Our parents are never around, so it's almost the same thing.'

Archie was glad that he wasn't the only one who missed them. 'Are you sure you're alright, you know, about the match?'

'Yeah,' she said. 'Thanks, Arch. I'll miss wearing that

stupid wig. It felt kind of lucky—something I could hide behind.'

'Tell you what,' he said, changing the subject, 'why don't I cut your hair, make you look a bit more like a bloke?'

'No bleeding way, winkle. You'd probably cut my ears off—'

'Well they're big enough, and anyway, will you please STOP calling me winkle.'

They both grinned.

'Look, do you remember,' he began cautiously, 'anything about last night?'

'Last night? What do you mean?'

Archie felt himself reddening. 'You were having a bad dream.'

Daisy looked confused. 'Did I wake you?'

'Yeah! You were screaming, for starters.'

'Screaming? Loudly?'

'You probably woke up the whole of Northallerton.'

'Now you mention it,' Daisy began, 'I had this nightmare about being covered in water, as if I was in a huge storm.'

'Nothing else?' Archie teased. 'Nothing about me?'

'Nah.'

'You sure?'

'Sure. Why?'

'Well…' Archie hesitated.

'Well, what?'

'Oh, it's nothing really—just that … you mentioned me, and told me not to do something.'

Daisy turned thoughtfully to the ceiling. 'Sorry. Can't really remember. You know, dreams, huh?'

Archie could barely hide his disappointment and Daisy saw straight through him. The reality was that she'd had a terrible night—one she'd rather forget entirely.

'Actually,' Daisy began, scrunching up her cheeks.

'Daisy, Archie, there you are!' said the headmaster. 'Now, where is that sister of yours?'

'Over here,' said the figure of Isabella heading towards them.

'Just been finishing off some science work with Mrs Douglas. You can't believe how...' and she turned her eyes up as if searching for the correct term... '*loose*, some of her theories are.'

FIVE

A WORD FROM THE HEADMASTER

The headmaster ushered the three of them into the adjoining corridor.

'Look, just a quick word, if I may,' Mr Solomon said as he leaned against the painted stone wall, his voice kind and his manner fatherly, but firm. He looked over them sympathetically.

'It pains me a very great deal to say this, but this morning I received an email from your parents who are somewhere in the Middle East. They will not be back for the football match or indeed for the whole of half term.' He scanned their disappointed faces. 'It appears they have discovered something rather important.'

Archie and Daisy exchanged glances.

'What does it say, what are they doing?' Isabella asked, as she attempted to read the headmaster's notepad upside down.

The headmaster folded the pad into his large midriff.

'Well, it's light on detail—in fact there's hardly any information, which, given the circumstances is the very least you deserve. To be honest I'm not at all happy about this situation—'

'But we've got—' Isabella started.

'Yes, I know you're fortunate enough to have your caretakers at Eden Cottage—but looking at your appearance,

Archie, I have to ask myself, are they up to the job?' The headmaster paused for effect.

'This is the third time I've had to reprimand you in the last two terms. Your parents have an obligation to you and this school beyond the callings of their work and the responsibility of others.'

Solomon hated telling children off for something that wasn't their fault; they'd been deserted by their eccentric parents, and not for the first time.

But at least he knew that their caretakers—an old man and a lady—did their best for the children.

The old man, whom he knew as Mr Wood, had looked old when they first met years ago, and he never seemed to get any older.

The housekeeper, Mrs Pye, was another strange looking creature; large and pale, with a mop of ginger hair that hid a scar on her forehead, though she appeared capable of looking after them.

He made a mental note to schedule a visit to see them in the next few days to make sure everything was as it should be.

Mr Solomon was fully aware of the long and established ties the de Lowe family had with the school and village. Their lineage could be traced back for centuries; at least, that was the claim.

The de Lowes from Eden Cottage even had a large stained glass window in the church in memory of a distant ancestor who was rumoured to have slain a local dragon. Solomon scoured their young faces. That particular gene had clearly died out a long time ago.

His gaze settled on Isabella. 'How old is your Great Uncle, Mr Wood? He must be well into his eighties, if not nineties—'

'He's getting on a bit,' she replied, 'but he's fit and well and Mum and Dad have every confidence—'

'And,' Archie butted in, 'Old Man... er... Uncle Wood's an awesome first aider. He's always patching me up brilliantly.'

'And,' Daisy said, 'Mrs Pye's amazing at cooking things

and washing and cleaning and stuff. She's, you know, super-capable.'

'I am quite sure she is,' Solomon replied, not rising to Daisy's burst of enthusiasm. 'But who is going to get Archie to the shops for school uniform? And what if there's another emergency, like there has been in every holiday period over the last two years? Neither drive and you're two miles up a deep, steep, narrow track that's camouflaged by bushes and brambles. Your house is surrounded by thick forest—it's in the middle of nowhere! Frankly, it'd be a miracle if anyone could find you.'

Mr Solomon raised his eyebrows and peered at each of them in turn. He wondered what condition the inside of the house was in, dotted up there on the hillside by the ruin.

'And what if your helpers were to have an incident, like a heart attack or a seizure or a fall?' he continued. 'What would you do? The place would be swarming with police and social workers and, trust me, they would be considerably less forgiving.'

The children didn't really know what to say so they remained silent and stared at the floor. To them, Old Man Wood and Mrs Pye were nothing but the best, so what was the big deal?

Isabella finally broke the silence. 'Sue's mum is taking us to Northallerton on Tuesday. We'll get Archie smartened up then. Mrs Lowden's brilliant at helping out; I'll ask her tonight.'

'Very well, but before you go, Isabella, I'm going to entrust you—as the eldest—to take a letter back for your parents. Come and collect it before you go from my office. You are to give it to them so that this unacceptable situation is on record and does not happen again.'

Mr Solomon cleared his throat, which signified that the matter had been dealt with. He turned to the twins. 'I have some simple Religious Education homework for you two over the break. It's Genesis; the book right at the very beginning of the Bible. Have you heard of it?'

Mr Solomon smiled. 'Jolly good. The bit I want you to pay particular attention to is where God creates the universe in seven days—with Adam and Eve—remember?'

The twins nodded.

'After creation, one of Adam and Eve's children, Cain, kills his twin, Abel, and is sent away. So God decides they're a pretty rum lot and sends a flood that wipes out everything on the earth apart from their descendant, Noah—'

'Who built the ark and put the animals in it two by two,' Archie finished off.

'Precisely,' Mr Solomon said. 'Now, Daisy, as your academic record is simply appalling, I'd like you to actually read it and then think hard about it—preferably before you dream up some kind of hare-brained scheme that gets Archie battered into pieces. Understand? You may find the chapter a valuable resource for your essay after half term entitled, *Did God create the universe, or did the universe create God?*'

Then, in one movement, as though suddenly aware of the time, Mr Solomon straightened, raised his bushy eyebrows and looked over the top of his half-moon spectacles. 'Now, for goodness' sake, over this half term period, behave yourselves, children; I cannot and will not have the Social Services chasing us around with your parents nowhere in sight. Please do not get yourselves into trouble. Understood?'

'Yes, sir,' the children said in unison.

'Excellent. Very best of luck with the football tomorrow morning. There will be a big crowd cheering you on and some members of the press will be present. The circumstance surrounding this game, and the fact that the final involves our larger rivals, seems to have caught the imagination of the entire region.'

He darted a look at Isabella. 'So, best behaviour please.' He hoped his message was clear. 'Now run along.'

Archie and Daisy scampered off down the corridor, the noise of their footsteps echoing off the old sandstone walls. Mr Solomon looked at his watch, mumbled something about the time and, as he turned, he noticed Isabella lingering.

'Excuse me, sir,' she said.

'Yes, Isabella,' the headmaster said impatiently, 'what is it now?'

'Well, it's the weather, sir.'

Solomon sighed. 'Yes, what about it?'

Isabella hesitated. For the first time in her life she didn't know what to say; it was as if her brain had jammed. 'I've made a barometer, to study the weather,' she spat out.

'Yes, congratulations on your skilful endeavour,' he replied. 'Mrs Douglas notified me. I'm told atmospheric pressure isn't even on your syllabus—'

Isabella ignored him. 'From my readings,' she began, 'there's going to be a simply massive—'

'Storm?' Mr Solomon interrupted with a sly smile. He bent down a little. 'Well, I'm pleased that your readings match up with the area forecast, but I don't believe there will be anything to worry about. A bit of rain and some thunder perhaps. But just as a precaution, please remind your class to take their umbrellas and waterproofs as I mentioned in assembly.'

The headmaster scratched his chin and smiled at her. 'While you're here, let me remind you that it would be a very bad idea to go racing on to the pitch as you have done in the previous two football matches. You must leave events on the games field to the referee and other officials—whatever the circumstances and however difficult.' Solomon smiled in a fake, head-masterly way and straightened.

'I expect nothing less than immaculate conduct, Isabella. There will be serious repercussions if you do it again.' He paused for effect. 'Do I make myself perfectly clear?'

Isabella nodded.

'Good. Now, thank you for your concern but I really must fly,' he rubbed his hands together. 'Geogo test with year eight.'

The headmaster marched off down the corridor, his steel capped shoes tip-tapping on the old stone floor. That girl was one of the finest pupils they'd ever had—bright as a button and eager to learn. He liked that a lot. And she was loyal, with a temper that could flare up like a storm, especially with incidents surrounding her brother and sister.

He chuckled as he thought about his analogy of her and a storm. Well, it was perfectly sweet of her to warn him but he had a leaving party and other pressing things to organise.

Nothing would stop his celebrations; certainly not a little storm and a warning from a pupil with a homemade barometer.

SUE LOOKED up as Isabella opened the door. She noted how, when her straight brown hair hung like a curtain over her forehead, it made her look slightly older. She was frequently told how similar they were and the joke went round that they were more twins than Archie and Daisy, who looked nothing like one another.

They were alike in so many ways: top of the academic pile, both enjoyed intellectual challenges rather than sporting endeavour and their features were remarkably similar: Isabella with straight mousy hair, Sue wavy mousy hair. Both had narrow faces, straight noses and brown eyes, although Sue's lips were fuller and her eyebrows finer.

But Sue's appearance turned heads—she exuded sex appeal—and she looked after herself, her clothes and hair had a sense of style, whereas Isabella had a nerdy more academic air and her clothes often sat on her like cloth sacks. Isabella regarded boys' general infatuation with Sue as a complete waste of time.

What's up now? Sue thought. Isabella's scowl had pulled her brow over her nose as though it were held by an invisible clip. 'Is everything alright?' she said.

Isabella slumped into a chair. 'You won't believe what I did,' she began. 'I told Solomon there was going to be a massive storm.'

Sue gasped. 'You did what?'

'I told him about the barometer.'

'Are you insane?' Sue said, turning a little red. 'I hope you didn't tell him it stemmed from my dream?'

'Of course I didn't!' Isabella said, holding her head in her hands. 'It was so embarrassing—he said he'd seen news of the storm on the forecast. I mean, what was I thinking?'

'I can't believe you did that,' Sue said, draping an arm around her and trying hard not to smile. 'But at least you tried.' Sue ran her hand over the scientific instrument her friend had made. 'Maybe your barometer's faulty—perhaps the calibration's wrong.'

'It's not possible,' Isabella said, frowning. 'Every time I reset it, exactly the same thing happens.'

'Well, please don't spend too long fiddling with it,' Sue said. 'You've got to watch the football tomorrow. It might be Daisy's final game. In any case, I'm required to keep you under control after last week.'

Isabella felt a burning sensation filling her cheeks. 'I know, I know. Solomon reminded me. But I just don't seem able to help myself—'

'Well, you must. You can't verbally abuse the referee and then get yourself manhandled off the pitch, screaming like a loon. And you've done it twice.' Her eyes flashed at Isabella. 'You'll be expelled if you're stupid enough to do it again.'

'But Daisy gets kicked and flattened more than anyone—'

'I know,' Sue said, 'but she doesn't make a squeak. It's a mystery she makes it through week after week and continues to smile as if nothing happened. It's half the attraction—what makes her unique. And the fact that she's a footballing genius.

'You need to do the same and control that temper of yours.'

SIX

STORM WARNING

'The thing is,' Isabella said, 'I've done some calculations and I'm beginning to think that you might be right!'

'You really think so?' Sue said.

'From what you've told me, it's going to be massive. Look, here's some data showing severe weather depression models exactly like—'

'Where did you get this?'

'I pulled it off the web,' Isabella replied, coolly. 'Hacked into the Met Office data bank and downloaded flood sequences and weather system models from around the world.' She ran her finger down the page.

'Can you see the similarities in humidity and cloud density; it's unbelievable—inches of rain—potential for devastation on a huge scale.'

Sue sat down and whistled. 'You're predicting rainwater at a couple of inches every twenty minutes covering a surface area of say ten square miles—based on what I saw in my sleep! According to this, we'll be white water rafting in less than two hours—'

'You told me that the rain was so hard and heavy you felt you could hardly breathe, that it was weighing you down, right? So, I've tried to figure out how much rain that would be and then multiplied it by the area, the potential volume the land can absorb and the capacity of the river to drain it away. Then, I've added in the tidal flow of the river at York, and the increased effects of a full moon—'

Sue was astonished. 'Isabella,' she began hesitantly. 'Let's get this straight. I had a nightmare about you and the twins and a flood here at school. It was very real, sure, but let's remember, it was only a dream.' She looked straight into her eyes. 'All of this,' she waved a hand at the barometer, 'it's great—really amazing, but it's pretty mad too.'

Isabella stared back. 'I'm doing this because I believe you, Sue.'

'You do?'

Isabella drummed her fingers on the desk. 'Yes, of course.' She paused as if wondering what to say. 'If you must know, I've had a similar nightmare.'

Sue nearly fell off her chair. 'What! Why didn't you say something? How similar?'

'Well, most of it was to do with water, but the rest is sort of different,' she said. 'And it's been peeing me off. Anyway, who says you're wrong? The evidence stacks up in your favour, even if the weather forecasters are saying it'll just be a localised storm. I mean, they've got it wrong before.'

'But forecasters screwed up years ago, before they knew what they were doing—before they had satellites and computer models,' Sue said. 'You can't go round with a megaphone and announce that there's a storm coming that's going to submerge the village because of the readings on a homemade barometer and a couple of freaky dreams. No one will believe us. Look how Solomon reacted. We'll be laughed out of school and just imagine what morons like Kemp would say? The humiliation would be—'

'OK, OK, I understand,' Isabella said, rubbing her brow. 'I'll keep my mouth zipped, for now at least, I promise. You sure you're alright?'

'Yeah.' Sue lowered her voice. 'Bells, there is one important thing I need to talk to you about—'

But before she had a chance to expand, the door was

kicked open and smacked into the wall. Sue jumped and then groaned when she saw who it was.

'Aha!' said the voice she least wanted to hear. 'I've found the nerds.'

It was Kemp and his friends, Mason and Wilcox.

'Oh, marvellous!' Sue said sarcastically under her breath.

Isabella straightened. 'What can I do for you, Kemp?' she said curtly. 'Come to break my arm like you did my sister's?'

Kemp went to a desk in the middle of the room, turned a chair around and sat down heavily. 'And what would you do if I did? Run outside and scream and scream and scream and tell me off, like you usually do?' Kemp and the boys chuckled.

'I've got a message from chief nerd, Mrs Douglas. She wants to see you,' he said. 'Seriously, it's a real request and I'm just being friendly.'

Isabella smiled but her eyes were narrow and icy. 'Kemp, thank you. You've delivered your message; now you can leave... we're busy.'

Kemp opened a book. 'I'm fine staying right here for a while,' he replied putting his feet up on the desk. 'I believe I'm allowed to—'

'Allowed to what?' Sue cut in.

Kemp ran his eyes up and down Sue's body. 'Fancy a date, Sue? Take you to the cinema. There's a new action film just out.'

Sue stood up smartly. 'Listen. I will never be interested, Kemp. Besides, you're far too young. Now go away.'

'Woah, no need to be like that,' Kemp said, standing up and grasping his heart as though mortally wounded. He turned to his mates and winked. 'Oh well, worth a try. One day eh, you and me.'

Kemp extended his arm and patted Sue's bottom.

Sue rounded on him, slapping his face, the sound like the crack of a whip. 'Don't you ever, ever touch me you filthy animal, or I'll report you for assault.'

Kemp's happy face vanished and a look of anger flashed in his dark eyes. 'You'll do what? Tell on me? Tell on me...

again,' Kemp fumed. 'Yeah, well big deal! Do you have any idea the number of hours I've spent in detention because of you two—?'

'You deserve everything you get,' Isabella said calmly.

'Forty-two,' he said, ignoring her. 'That's how many. Forty-two wasted hours.' He thumped the table. 'The teachers must think you're making it up, the way you pick on me—'

'Pick on *you*. Get lost, loser,' Isabella said, 'you make me want to vomit.'

Kemp smiled and sat down. 'Well now, speaking of vomit, a little bird tells me you've made a ba-rom-eter?' He said the word very slowly and as he did he felt under the desk and pulled away some sticky tape. He held up a small recording device. 'Hello little birdie.'

Isabella shrieked.

'Brilliant isn't it?' Kemp said, turning the black box around in his hands. 'Superb reception for such a tiny thing. I'll tell you what I'll do,' he continued, rubbing home his advantage, 'just before the football starts I'll announce— perhaps with Coach's megaphone—that there's a big storm on its way which will devastate the whole area. What was it, boys?' he said to the sniggering pair. 'Ah, yes... we're going to enjoy a bit of white water rafting, right?' He looked triumphant. 'And all because you dreamt about it. Isn't that lovely.'

The boys laughed, thickly.

Isabella's face was like thunder. 'That is immoral and illegal—'

He waved her protest away. 'Now, pray tell where this clever barometer thing is.' He took a couple of paces to their desk.

'Christ, is this it?' he said picking it up.

'Don't you dare—'

'A glass jar filled with liquid and a straw.' Kemp seemed genuinely disappointed. 'What a pathetic, useless piece of shite—'

'Put it down!' Isabella demanded.

'Why? If anyone saw this you'd be laughed out of school,' he said, winking.

'Put it down—'

'Give me one reason?'

'Because I asked you to, that's why.'

'Not good enough—'

'Because it's an important part of my module—'

Kemp sneered. 'No, it isn't. It's not even on your syllabus.'

'Please—'

'What will you do if I don't?'

'Put it down!' Isabella roared.

The door swung open.

'Archie,' Isabella gasped, relieved, 'what are you doing here?'

'Oh!' he looked at their faces. 'I'm dropping off a book... what's going on?'

Kemp held the barometer in the air. 'Archie, my friend. Your sister thinks she should tell the world about a huge storm that's coming based on this hilarious scientific instrument. What do you think?' Kemp placed the barometer on the edge of the desk where it swayed for a moment and then righted itself.

Archie frowned. 'Er, I don't know.'

'Well if you don't know, Archie, then I really should dispose of it to save them making complete idiots of themselves—'

'No!' Isabella cried.

Kemp ignored her and raised an eyebrow, 'and of course, to protect the great academic reputation of Upsall School.' Kemp laughed and slapped the desk with his free hand.

'I don't think that's a good idea,' Archie said, trying to read his sister's face. 'Why don't you give it back?'

'What!' exclaimed Kemp, turning on him. 'Don't get me wrong, but I'm the one who's going to decide whether they can or can't have it back. Tell you what,' said Kemp, addressing the girls again, 'if Sue goes out with me, I'll give it back.'

'Never!' Both girls instinctively replied. Sue slid her chair back so fast it fell backwards and clattered on the floor.

'There are rules for a reason, Kemp,' Isabella said, regaining her composure, 'so listen up. Here's what happens. You put the barometer down and leave it exactly as it is, while we go and get Mr Bellwood. Do you understand?'

Kemp scratched his fat nose. 'Bellwood will never believe you—and I've done nothing wrong. Nothing. Your little brother can prove that, can't you Archie?'

Archie shrugged.

The girls gathered up their things and headed towards the door.

Kemp wasn't finished. He winked at Sue and blew a kiss to Isabella. 'Remember, Mrs Douglas wants to see you in the science labs. I'm just the messenger.'

'You'll pay for this,' Isabella yelled, as she closed the door, 'if it's the last thing I do.'

SEVEN

SWEAR ON YOUR LIFE

'Christ alive, Kemp,' Mason said, 'you're asking for it, didn't you hear her? She's gone off to get Bellwood. He'll go mental.'

Kemp smiled. 'You really think so? Well I don't know how it got there—do you?'

Mason suddenly realised what he meant. 'Me neither,' he said, his voice as thick as dough.

'Nor me,' said Wilcox scratching his long chin.

'That leaves only one other person who could have witnessed it.' Kemp turned to Archie. 'So, Archie, tell me. Did you by any chance see who dropped the barometer out of the window?'

'Well, I'm not blind,' Archie replied.

Kemp rolled his eyes. 'I don't think he gets it, lads. I don't think he quite grasps the seriousness of the situation. Look, Archie, all you have to say is that you didn't see anything. Get it?'

'Right,' Archie said, wondering why it was that Kemp was such a massive jerk when Mason and Wilcox were around.

'I won't say a word,' he said, mechanically.

Kemp hesitated. 'I'm not sure that's really acceptable. Swear on your life that you won't tell anyone.'

'Oh, come on. I'm not a kid and I'm not a sneak. You know that.'

'Archie, I need you to promise—on your life—that you're not going to tell anyone, that's all,' Kemp insisted. 'I mean, unlike your sister, you can keep your mouth shut, right?'

'If you didn't want anyone to know, why did you throw it out of the window in the first place?'

Kemp smiled. Wasn't it funny how threatening words seemed to cause Archie no pain and physical beating seemed to cause Daisy no pain either?

He stepped in front of Archie and drew himself up.

'Your big sister hates me. She's responsible for putting me in detention pretty much every week for the last two years. She cannot be trusted. Prove that you're different.'

'Oh, belt up, Kemp, you're just showing off to moron and muggings. My sister doesn't like you because you do idiotic things like throw barometers out of windows and put dead rats in sports bags.'

Kemp chuckled as he recalled the rat incident. When he'd found a dead rat by the river, it gave him one of his best ideas ever—pop it in Isabella de Lowe's games bag, and wait.

And every day he waited, getting more and more excited about the slowly decomposing rat. It remained there for the best part of a week, with everyone wondering what the terrible smell was in the changing rooms. Then, on the afternoon of the school cross country run, as Isabella put on her tracksuit bottoms, out dropped the carcass, dripping in maggots.

Dynamite. He didn't realise Isabella had a vermin phobia and she'd screamed so much and puked everywhere and caused such a scene that eventually one of the teachers had to call an ambulance. They had to sedate her and take her away. She'd spent three hours a week for the next six months in counselling, according to Archie.

But the best bit was that no one suspected him in the slightest, apart from Isabella. The enquiry determined that the rat had taken a nibble of poison and wandered into her bag. But Isabella, he felt, had never forgiven him.

Archie sighed. 'Look, if it means that much to you, I'll do it, but only if *you* swear on your life not to do any more harmful, stupid, bullying things to Isabella, Sue or Daisy. It's got to stop.'

Kemp stuck out his jaw and moved it from side to side while he thought about what Archie had said. At last he nodded his head and said, 'OK, I agree. On the condition that it lasts until she puts me into detention again. Well, come on then, you say it first.'

Archie sighed; it was like being a seven-year-old. 'Do I really have to do this?'

'Yeah. Of course—if you want me to.'

Archie shook his head. 'I swear on my life that I won't tell anyone that you dropped the barometer out of the window,' he said. 'Now you say it!'

Kemp grinned. 'I swear on my life not to harm your sister and not to play any more tricks on her. There, good enough?'

Archie nodded. In his book you didn't swear your life away just for nothing.

'Oi, Mason, Wilcox,' Kemp said in his thuggish voice. 'Go and see if a teacher's coming. I want to speak to Archie 'bout something private.'

Mason and Wilcox sloped out of the room.

Kemp's face seemed to lighten up and his tone was altogether different. 'Yeah, sorry Arch. I know. I've been a bit of a tosser.'

'You're telling me!' Archie replied. 'Why do you do it?'

Kemp shrugged. 'Dunno. Boredom. Can't seem to help myself when I see your sister. Look, do you fancy bringing your rod over at half term,' he said, changing the subject. 'I caught a six-pound fish last weekend. Took me ages to land.'

'Only if you stop being a total moron, everyone's sick of it.'

Kemp rolled his eyes.

Archie ignored him. 'Well, I suppose I've got nothing

better to do. Mum and Dad aren't coming home—more work digging up bones in the middle of nowhere.'

'They're never at home, are they. But at least you've got parents.'

'I know,' Archie said, drawing a hand through his hair. 'It's so rubbish, though. Solomon's getting really worried. He thinks we can't cope.'

'Well, can you?'

'Of course we can. Old Man Wood's brilliant at stuff even if he is the oldest man in the world.'

They both laughed.

'But admit it, Archie, you are the scruffiest person I've ever met. I'm hardly surprised he's worried. I would be.'

'And unluckiest,' he countered. 'I'd been running through the forest.'

'Yeah, but being Bear Grylls doesn't work well with head-masters.'

Archie's eyes lit up. 'Lucky he didn't ask me to take off my jacket. I'd ripped the jumper almost the whole way down the back.'

'Look, come for the day,' Kemp said. 'I'll get my aunt to knock up some sandwiches and you can bring some of that unbelievable apple juice your old man whatsit brews.'

'His name is Old Man Wood.'

Kemp repeated it.

'OK. Deal,' Archie said, 'BUT it's on condition that you keep to your word about my sisters AND you get your aunt to do those beef sarnies; the last lot were awesome.'

'For you, Archie, consider it done. It's the only thing she's good at. Get round to mine on Monday morning—about 10 am?'

Archie had reluctantly begun his fishing trips with Kemp last year and, much to his surprise, away from school, he found Kemp to be a totally different person. Quiet and patient, he was a knowledgeable teacher. Kemp showed none of his aggression and he had genuine skill with the rod and tying flies and reading the flow of the river and where the best pools were.

'But you're not to talk about your sisters,' Kemp said.

'OK. Deal,' Archie said. 'But seriously, are Chitbury really going to kick lumps out of Daisy?'

'I said don't talk about her,' Kemp fired back.

'Quick, Bellwood's coming,' said Mason, as he ran back into the classroom.

'Out of the window!' Kemp suggested.

They ran to the window and pulled up the blind, only to find they were looking directly at Isabella, Sue and Mrs Pike.

'Drat,' said Kemp under his breath, and he smiled pleasantly back at them.

'Kemp,' the old teacher hollered, 'and Archie de Lowe. Well, who would have guessed? What can you tell me about the glass fragments on the concrete floor?'

Kemp opened the window and looked out. 'Glass?' he said innocently.

'The mess, down here,' Mrs Pike replied.

'No idea what you're talking about. Window's been closed all along. Someone must have left it lying there. What is it anyway?'

Isabella shrieked. 'Kemp, you know perfectly well what it is.'

'A milk bottle?' he offered.

Mrs Pike fixed him with cold eyes. 'No Kemp. It's Isabella's barometer.'

'A bar-hom-tier,' Kemp said, thickly. 'What on earth is that?'

'Archie, did you see Kemp with the barometer earlier?'

Archie stared at the floor.

Mrs Pike tried again. 'Archie, why don't you tell us what happened?'

'Dunno,' Archie said, running a hand through his hair.

'What do you mean, you dunno?'

'Dunno,' Archie repeated, reddening.

Kemp looked straight into Mrs Pike's eyes. 'Honestly, there's been no one around.'

'Great!' Isabella stormed. 'Kemp's made you swear not to tell or something equally childish?'

The classroom door swung open. 'What have you done now, Kemp?' boomed Mr Bellwood, striding in.

'Nothing!' Kemp said. 'I was trying to explain to Mrs Pike here that I haven't done anything.'

'Yes, you have, Kemp,' Isabella shouted through the window. 'You were the last person to have it and now it's in bits. It must have been you.'

'Prove it.'

'I shouldn't have to,' Isabella yelled back. 'Archie,' she pleaded, 'all you have to do is tell us what happened—'

Archie shook his head.

'Kemp, you've got history with this kind of mindless vandalism,' Mr Bellwood added, his moustache twitching.

'He should be expelled,' Isabella shouted.

'I haven't done anything—'

'Of course you have—'

'But you can't prove it—can you?'

'I DID IT!' Archie yelled. 'It was me.'

There was a long silence.

'You did it?' Kemp said.

'*You*?' Isabella quizzed.

'Archie?' Bellwood said.

'Yes,' Archie sighed. 'I was fed up with you two always getting at each other, so I thought I'd save everyone the trouble.' He bowed his head. 'I'm sorry.'

Isabella looked confused. This wasn't the sort of thing Archie would do, so why was he taking sides with Kemp?

'What did you say to Archie, Kemp? It's like you've done a pathetic deal or something—'

Kemp bit his lip and stared hard at her, his eyes cold and narrow. Then he spun and marched out of the room.

EIGHT

STORM GLASS

'I don't know what to say,' Isabella said. 'Why would you do such a thing?'

Archie shrugged.

'Right. Gosh!' Mr Bellwood said. 'I think you two need to sort this out for yourselves. There's no point in my hanging around. You're with me in ten minutes, Isabella.'

Isabella smiled in about as fake a way as she could, while Mr Bellwood made his way out of the classroom. The two siblings were alone.

'Why, Archie?' Isabella pressed.

'I'm sorry, but this warfare between you is ridiculous,' Archie said. 'If you stop putting Kemp in detention, he might stop bullying. He's only doing it as a reaction. Don't you see that?'

'But the fact is, Archie, he IS a bully and I don't see why any of us, especially me and Sue, should put up with it. We have to protect ourselves and others. It's simple, Archie. If he stopped being so childish, there wouldn't be a problem.'

She clamped an arm around his shoulders. 'Don't take me for a fool. It's perfectly clear that Kemp did this and you've been put up to it?' Her eyes widened. 'Haven't you?'

Archie kept his head down and refused to say anything.

'Have it your way, Archie. I'm not going to believe you

and I haven't got the strength to argue about it. I just don't understand how you can be friends with him when he clearly causes me and Daisy so much distress. Do you have any idea how painful it is?'

Archie took a deep breath. 'But both of you give as good as you get. Daisy kicked Kemp on the shin earlier. If it had been the other way round, Kemp would be in massive trouble. Give him a break and I'm sure he'll chill. He's not that bad underneath.'

'You know that's not going to happen, Archie.'

He shrugged. 'Well, I'm sorry about your barometer,' he said, raising his eyes to meet hers.

Isabella pressed her lips together. 'Don't be; I just wish you'd be honest with me. To be frank, the barometer wasn't reliable. Actually, I've stumbled on a better idea; I'm going to make a storm glass.'

'Storm glass?'

'Yes. It's an old-fashioned weather gauge. And, as a punishment for your behaviour, you can help me make it.'

Archie smiled. 'Cool. But why the craze about weather stations?'

'Well, if you must know,' Isabella said, 'there's a curious weather system brewing bang overhead—have you noticed how sweaty and smelly everyone is—and,' she hesitated, 'this may sound completely nuts but Sue and I have had a premonition, a dream about torrential rain and flooding.'

Archie was astonished. 'Do you always do this after a dream?'

'No. To be honest, I never really dream. But I've got a strong gut feeling, that's all.'

Archie scratched his head and wondered if he should mention his dream and Daisy's mutterings in the middle of the night. But he heard himself say 'So how does this storm glass work?'

'It shows what's going to happen to the weather—in the liquid in the glass. So, if the liquid in the glass is clear, the weather will be clear. If small crystal stars form, snow is on its way, and when a thunderstorm is coming the liquid will be cloudy and so on. I'll show you later, if it works. But first, I'll need a few ingredients—and this, bro, is where you come in.'

'OK.'

'First, go and bat your eyelids at Mrs Culver and ask for ten grams of camphor, she should have some for flavouring food. Tell her you need some in chemistry to show how a compound can burn without leaving an ash residue. If she starts asking questions, start talking about oxygen. For some reason Mrs Culver can't bear the actual word, "oxygen". Then go and find Mr Pike in the Maintenance Department and ask for some distilled water—fill a large, old, Coke bottle if you can. I know he keeps some to top up his forklift batteries.'

Isabella scratched her forehead thoughtfully, making sure she hadn't forgotten anything. 'So, have you got that? Camphor and distilled water. I'll find some ethanol and the other compounds from Chemistry later on—shouldn't be too difficult.'

As she rushed off she turned. 'The science labs are free straight after lunch, we'll do it then. Meet me there.'

ISABELLA LET herself into the chemistry lab using the spare set of keys that Mrs Douglas kept in a jar outside the biology room. When Archie arrived, Isabella was talking animatedly to Sue. Both wore white lab coats, safety glasses, face masks and Lycra gloves. They reminded Archie of surgeons in an operating theatre.

Sue noted his curious look and threw over a lab coat. 'Got to look the part in case someone comes along,' she said, her voice muffled by the mask.

Archie pulled his ingredients from a carrier bag. He'd had no problem getting the camphor, but when Mr Pike asked him in a most suspicious manner what the distilled water was for, Archie stuttered a little and told him that Isabella wanted it. Without hesitating, old Mr Pike poured out the water from a huge plastic container and handed it over, with no further questions.

In no time at all, Isabella and Sue had measured out the required parts of each of the elements which now sat in glass beakers, neatly labelled, on the desk. Sue lit a Bunsen burner and began to gently warm the water. Isabella waited for a couple of minutes before adding the ingredients, with the ethanol and camphor going in last. When these had dissolved to her satisfaction, Isabella asked Archie to find a large test tube sealed with a cork.

Archie popped it into a holding device as, in silence, Isabella added the liquid until the test tube was three quarters full.

Isabella asked Archie to clean the apparatus in the sink in the far corner and just as he was about to clean it, the door swung open. For some reason he couldn't explain, Archie ducked under the table.

It was Kemp.

'There you are,' he said, with a big smile. 'Been looking all over for you two.'

'GO AWAY!' the girls yelled at him.

'Whoa! Calm down, I've only come to apologise.' He looked down at the desk. 'What's all this then. Doing some illegal experiments are we? That's exciting. Creating a bomb or some poison for me or a tiny bit of chemical warfare—'

'It's none of your business, Kemp. Leave us alone.'

'Come on, I'm offering an olive branch. Anyway, have either of you seen Archie?'

Isabella caught Archie staring at her from behind one of the desks, out of Kemp's eyeline. He was shaking his head vigorously.

'Er, no. Sorry. No idea where Archie is,' she said as she brushed an imaginary speck off her lab coat, her face reddening.

Kemp eyed her suspiciously and then his eyes moved to the test tube on the desk. He picked it up before either girl had a chance to react. 'So, this is your experiment, is it? A test tube full of cloudy potions. Brilliant.'

'Thank you for your interest, Kemp,' Sue commented, 'but to be honest this is a very boring experiment dealing with the creation of crystals using camphor, ethanol, distilled water and a couple of other things you probably wouldn't understand.'

But Kemp was interested like a dog after a scent and his tone changed. 'So, if it's so boring, why are you doing it in break time?'

'As I said, Kemp, it's a simple experiment—'

'I don't believe you.' He stepped closer. 'It doesn't add up.'

'Please go away and leave us alone,' Isabella said, sweetly, remembering what Archie had said.

But her words fell on deaf ears. 'Why won't you tell me what you're doing?'

'Why should we?'

Kemp smiled back. 'Cos otherwise, I'll smash it—'

'You wouldn't dare. Give it back immediately.'

Isabella lunged for the test tube, but Kemp was too fast.

'So, come on, what is it? A lethal poison, a nerve gas—'

'Don't be ridiculous.'

'I'm not the one being ridiculous.'

Isabella huffed. 'Well, if you must know, it's a storm glass—'

'Oh, my God,' Kemp said slowly. 'You're not still going on about this storm, are you? When will you grow up and do what everyone else does. Go and watch the weather forecast. Oh, but hang on, don't tell me—you're so far up in the hills that you haven't even got a telly!'

'Of course we do,' Isabella raged, taking the bait.

Kemp thrust out his jaw. 'You lot are so backward—I wouldn't be surprised if your mum has to shave Neolithic hair off her body. But then we'd never know because she seems to have disowned you.' He cocked an eye at Isabella.

'And that old woman who looks after you has whiskers

coming out of her face like a cat,' he laughed. 'I know! Why don't you make a potion for hair removal. Customers in your own home!'

Kemp was enjoying himself and brushed aside Isabella's howl of complaint. 'Now, let me fill you in. Last night the man on the TELLY,' which he said in a deliberately loud and annoying voice, 'said that there was going to be a storm at some point over the next couple of days—but not a very big one—and certainly NOT one with WHITE WATER RAFTING.'

He marched over to the end of the room where Archie was hiding under the table.

Isabella gasped.

'I tell you what I'm going to do,' he continued, 'I'm going to do you a favour and put you out of your ridiculous weather misery. I'm going to spin this tube thing like a spinning top. You do know what that is, don't you? By the time you get over here, either it'll be smashed to bits on the floor or, by some miracle, you may have grabbed it. But if and when this happens, I'll be long gone out of the door. Then, you can go and do what everyone else does and watch the weather forecast on the telly. You'll find it comes directly after the news.'

Kemp put the test tube between the palms of his hands and drew them quickly apart. The tube span so fast and so true that for a moment everyone in the room was fixated by it.

Satisfied with his handiwork, Kemp headed towards the exit, switched off the lights and shut the door behind him.

The sound of the latch clicking seemed to accentuate the wobbling noise of the glass. Instantly the girls rushed over in near darkness, but in their haste they careered into the side of the desk and caught their feet on the chair legs, sending both of them sprawling onto the lab floor. A huge noise of scraping chairs and upturned tables filled the lab.

As the noise receded they heard the test tube slow to a stop, followed moments later by a crash and a tinkling of glass.

NINE
BROKEN PROMISE

'**O**w! My head,' Sue groaned. 'Isabella, get out of the way.'

'I can't. I've got a chair leg in my face. I'm wedged in.'

'Will one of you please turn on the light,' Archie hissed. 'I'm surrounded by glass.'

After a minute or two, and as the children's eyes began adjusting to the light, Archie could just about make out the shards of glass that surrounded him. Water was everywhere, as well as a warm, sticky substance.

Kemp opened the door and flicked on the light. His face was beaming. 'What's going on here, then?' he said, in a mock policeman-like voice.

He looked around to see an empty room and then, slowly, Sue got up. Her hair seemed to have come apart all over her face.

Then Isabella rose, rubbing a bump on her head.

Kemp was in hysterics. 'Bloody brilliant,' he laughed, as he pulled his phone out of his pocket. 'Smile at the budgie.'

He pressed the button and the camera clicked and flashed. Kemp inspected the image. 'Lovely, you two look gorgeous. Social media here I come.'

Archie stood up, brushing fragments of glass from his jacket.

'Archie!' Kemp exclaimed, his expression changing. 'Where the hell did you come from?'

'I've been here all the time, you idiot.'

Kemp's manner changed immediately. 'You alright?' He pointed at Archie's sleeve. 'Is that blood?'

Archie looked down at his hand—blood was pumping out from a gash at the base of his thumb and covered his hand and arm.

'Satisfied?' Isabella said, as she tiptoed around the larger glass fragments towards him. 'Happy now?'

She held Archie's arm and inspected it. 'Sue, get the first aid box, we need to stop the bleeding. And Kemp, now that you've stopped having your fun can you for once be useful? Go and find a brush and a mop.'

Isabella led Archie to the tap. 'This might hurt,' she said soothingly as she ran the water and placed Archie's hand underneath.

He winced.

There's still a bit of glass in there,' she said. 'I need a towel and tweezers and then we'll need to compress the wound.'

Sue barged past Kemp who stood frozen to the spot.

Archie gritted his teeth as the water ran into his cut, his blood colouring the water from pink to burgundy. Sue was over in no time and Archie shut his eyes tight as she plucked out the fragment before applying pressure on the wound.

When Archie opened them, Kemp was still standing in the same position.

Archie looked him in the eye. 'You SWORE on your life, you wouldn't do this kind of thing,' he said. '*You swore—on—your—life*,' he repeated, his voice hard and accusing.

'I held my side of the deal, but at the very first opportunity you couldn't resist it, could you? It's now totally clear to me that you value your life as pretty much worthless. What would your parents think? Do you think they'd be proud of you?'

Kemp's face fell and the colour drained from his cheeks. 'Sorry, Archie,' he said. 'I... didn't realise ...'

And with that, he turned and fled for the door.

SUE NOTICED something a little strange as she swept the glass into the dustpan. The glass they were clearing up wasn't the test tube with the storm glass experiment in it, but a much thinner glass typical of a large beaker.

In which case, she thought, where was the test tube?

As he watched her expression, Archie's smile had grown until he was beaming. 'I know what you're thinking,' he said at last. 'So you may as well spit it out.'

Sue burst out laughing. 'Archie, you're impossible. One minute you're best friends with that oaf and the next you're...' she sat down heavily on the table top.

'Right, where is it?'

'What?' Archie cried, with feigned shock.

'Where is ... what?' Isabella said. She hadn't clicked.

Sue tutted. 'Oh, come along, come along, Sherlock Isabella. Time to use those famous powers of deduction.'

'Sorry, I have absolutely no idea what you're talking about—'

'The storm glass, silly.'

'In fragments in the bin.'

Sue bit her lip. 'That's beaker glass, isn't it, Archie?'

'Beaker glass?' Archie said, thickly.

'Well it's definitely not the test tube, is it? *You've* got it, haven't you?'

Archie grinned.

Very slowly he moved his gaze towards his trousers and pointed at his crotch. 'It's right here,' he said.

Then, very deliberately and very slowly he began to unzip his fly.

'Don't you dare!' Sue exclaimed. 'If you pull anything out that isn't a test tube…'

Archie reached in and very gently teased it out. 'DA-NAH,' he said, his eyes sparkling.

Sue had gone bright red.

Archie held the test tube up in the air. 'Sorry, couldn't think of anywhere else quick enough,' he said. 'Thing is, I had no idea quite how uncomfortable it would be so when I crouched down I lost my balance and wiped out the beaker.'

Isabella looked delighted but horrified at the same time. 'A storm in your pants, Archie. Now that must be a first. Be thankful the storm glass didn't break down there—or just think where we'd be plucking glass fragments from!'

Archie placed the tube on the holder.

Isabella wagged a finger at him. 'One more thing, Archie,' she said. 'Please give it a clean before either of us has to handle it.'

TEN

A POINTLESS EXPERIMENT

After school, the children walked up the long, steep lane home, stopping, as Isabella had promised, for a swing on the rope that hung off the great branch of the oak tree.

By the time they arrived home it was almost dark, the air heavy and surprisingly warm for the time of year.

They walked into the stone courtyard which was flanked on three sides by stone outbuildings, and waved at Mrs Pye whose head had appeared at one of the two windows in her flat opposite the cottage. Using the dim glow of the outside light, Archie and Daisy immediately set about kicking their football, the scuffing noises of their kicks and the thumping of the ball echoing back off the grey stone walls.

Isabella watched them play and her mind turned back to the conversations with Solomon and Kemp, who had both been so rude about their cottage. It wasn't that bad, she thought, as she studied the exterior.

OK, so it was a bit of a mishmash of a moors farm but it wasn't too unusual, was it? Constructed from local Yorkshire grey stone and old, thick timbers, the roof was covered in moss and lichen, which seemed to hang over too far as though it was in need of a haircut. And just by looking at the black-ened and slightly crooked chimneys it was easy to see that it was old. Very old.

Her keen eye noted how the stones were generally larger than most other farmhouses in the area, and she wondered if they had been taken from the ruin. In any case, Isabella liked the way the occasional stone-free area was in-filled with red brick or exposed timbers.

She reckoned it had a cosy feel, especially with the large wisteria that covered the end of the courtyard wall and with the windows which were squished here and squashed there out of proportion to one another.

It was as if the builder simply slapped it up stone by stone without any plans in the hope that it would turn out reasonably well.

Architecturally, she supposed it was a bit of a deformity, but perhaps these quirky anomalies helped it blend in to the rocks and the forest beyond. Somehow, she concluded, it worked beautifully.

Mrs Pye waddled out into the courtyard. 'You're finally back, come on in.'

They followed her inside, the cooking aromas filling their nostrils.

Soon, Mrs Pye was cutting and throwing a mixture of vegetables into a large pan.

Archie smiled. 'Wow that smells good—what's for tea?'

Mrs Pye tapped her nose. 'Wait and see,' she said, 'be ready in fifteen.'

The kitchen was the centre of the house and drew them in with its feeling of warmth—of being used and loved. On the floor were big worn Yorkstone slabs, which bore a glossy sheen from continual use, and above were huge, old, oak timbers—as hard as iron—that ran in neat lines above their heads like ribs protecting the room. A keen eye might notice that one beam, right in the middle, appeared to be missing.

Fixed into these large timbers were hooks of different sizes which held a range of kitchen assortments and herbal delights, like bunches of rosemary, lavender, thyme, dried meats and fruit.

Although the kitchen was a curiosity in itself, the children would point out to their friends that it wasn't entirely a throw-back to medieval times. Yes, it was large and tall and made predominantly from stone and wood, but it was always bright and snug.

This was helped in part by two old wagon wheels that were suspended from the ceiling by three strong metal chains. On each wheel rim were eight electric candle bulbs—and being on a dimmer, these lights could exude real character.

It was then that Old Man Wood's brilliant stories were truly brought to life, the wrinkles in his old face bursting with a wide range of expression and meaning.

Opposite the fireplace was a large white porcelain sink and above this was a Gothic-style window through which they could see for miles across the Vale of York towards the low peaks of the Yorkshire Dales.

On either side of the window were oak cupboards and drawers capped with thick worktops, like coffin lids, the grain of which Archie liked to trace with his finger. Above these, at intervals, were wall units where discreet lighting shone down from each recess, gently illuminating the work surfaces.

At the far end, on the wall, was the latest addition to the family; a large flat screen telly, which Mrs Pye dusted more than any other item in the house.

Running down the middle of the room was a large, rectangular, dark-brown oak table with an immense richness of depth and shine, and surrounding it were eight matching high-backed chairs that were usually tucked in under the table's edge.

Next to this was a brick inglenook fireplace where the old cooker lived. It was an old-fashioned metal range fired by logs, which Old Man Wood lovingly filled up every day from the store next to the larder.

Knowing Mrs Pye didn't like to be disturbed while she prepared supper, the children slipped out, made their way through the hallway, up the large staircase, along the corridor past the bathroom and then up the top stairs to their bedroom, the floorboards creaking at every step.

'WELL, COME ON THEN,' Daisy said, slinging her bag on her bed. 'Show me this amazing thing that's been in Archie's pants.'

Isabella pulled her books out of her briefcase and stacked them neatly on her desk. Then she changed her top, slipped into a pair of cotton trousers and brushed her hair. Daisy and Archie watched her patiently from the green sofa, knowing full well it wasn't worth rushing her.

'Right,' Isabella said, as she unwrapped the test tube from her scarf, 'let's have a look.' She leant the glass between two books on the table. Three pairs of eyes stared at it.

'Bit foggy, isn't it,' Daisy said. 'So, does that mean it'll be foggy?'

Archie raised his eyebrows. 'Don't be silly, Daisy, this is serious science.'

Daisy giggled and elbowed Archie as they continued to stare at the test tube.

'Ooh,' Daisy cooed. 'Look at those little stars. What do they mean?'

Isabella pulled out her crib sheet. 'I think tiny stars means that it might be stormy.' She read it out loud. '*A cloudy glass with small stars indicates thunderstorms.*'

Daisy coughed. 'Is … is that it?'

'What do you mean, is that it?'

'Well, it's very pretty,' Daisy said, glancing to Archie for support, 'but if you wanted to know thunderstorms were coming all you had to do was look at the forecast on the TV. Are you telling me you've gone to all this trouble to find out something we already knew?'

Isabella stood up. 'That's exactly what that fool Kemp said. If you must know, I think there's going to be a terrible deluge. Sue and I dreamt about it, so I'm trying to prove it scientifically.'

'Don't get me wrong,' Daisy said, picking it up and turning it round in her hands, 'but how will this help.'

Isabella sat down heavily. 'Well, to be honest, I was hoping for something a little more dramatic, like the crystals speeding up or something.'

'But how would that change anything?' Daisy quizzed.

'I don't know. I really don't know,' Isabella said. 'Maybe I'm hoping it will give us a warning or … actually, Daisy, I haven't a clue. I've got such a strong feeling about this. I had to do something.'

Archie took hold of the glass from Daisy. 'This must be the worst scientific experiment ever,' he said. 'If Kemp knew he'd tear you to bits.'

'Please don't tell him.'

'I'll never tell him anything again after what he did today. I don't know if I'll ever forgive him.'

'Children!' Mrs Pye's strange voice was calling them. 'Tea's on the table.'

Four bowls brimming with dumplings in a thick vegetable broth sat steaming on the table. The children slipped into their chairs and began sniffing it as though they had never smelt anything quite so amazing before in their lives.

Mrs Pye pulled up a chair and sat at the end of the table watching them, like a sentry.

'Have you heard?' Isabella said between mouthfuls. 'Mum and Dad aren't coming home.'

Mrs Pye's piggy eyes seemed to pop out of their sockets. 'No. Well, I'm blowed—and I'm sorry for you.'

'Can't you say something to them when they get back?' Archie said. 'It's like they're never here.'

'Don't you eat with your mouth full, little Arch,' Mrs Pye scolded. 'You know it isn't proper for me to tell your folks what they can or cannot do. If they choose to be away, then it's for a good reason. They miss you just as much as you miss them.'

Mrs Pye said this with as much conviction as she could, but she could see the disappointment in their eyes and wondered what on earth it was that so completely occupied their parents' time. Something to do with old relics, something terribly important they'd told her.

She sighed. In any case she loved looking after them and she counted her blessings. Being here at Eden Cottage was the only thing she could remember. There was nothing else.

She only had to raise her left arm above her head or try and touch her toes to get a reminder. By all accounts it was a miracle that Old Man Wood had found her, miles up in the forest, in a heap, on the verge of death, her face and shoulder smashed, her clothes ripped to bits—hardly breathing—and he'd carried her all the way home, singing to her, trying to keep her alive.

Old Man Wood still sang it, though she had no idea what it meant. And over the years she'd picked it up:

O great Tripodean, a dream to awaken
The forces of nature, the birth of creation.
Three Heirs of Eden with all of their powers,
Must combat the rain, the lightning and showers.
In open land, on plain or on sea,
Survive 'till sunset—when their lives will be free.
But the Prophecy has started—it's just the beginning.
And it never seems to end, and it never seems to end.

For several months, Old Man Wood and the children's parents nursed her, slowly building up her strength, giving her every support, trying to help her remember her past. But there was emptiness in her memory as if a blanket covered her previous life.

She'd had to learn everything again, although it was true that some things came to her with little difficulty. She had no name, no address, no family, no lovers, no pets, nothing she could ever recall laughing with or crying at.

The first time she laughed was when the babies crawled to her bed and gurgled in her ear, especially little Archie, who was like melted butter. These were her first memories, and happy ones too.

The authorities had been contacted, but no one had come forward. And after a while she didn't want to go anywhere else and why should she?

She loved the children, she loved the quiet remoteness of Eden Cottage with its big views over the Vale of York, and she felt safe being close to Old Man Wood who, although he came and went, seemed not to have a harmful bone in his body.

And it felt right that she should look after the children. A nurturing feeling ran through her core that was both instinctive and natural.

Besides, after she had been found, her face was not one to parade around the streets of Northallerton. Her nose seemed a little squashed to one side and she had a thick scar on her hairline that made her look a bit like Frankenstein's monster —or so she'd been told by Daisy. She couldn't care less, but she was mindful that her appearance might reflect on the children with name-calling and jibes.

As far as her name went, the children called her after the one thing she was a natural at; baking pies. So she was known affectionately as "the famous Mrs Pie", and somehow it stuck.

The children's parents tweaked the spelling to make it feel right and Mrs Pye she'd been ever since, living in the apartment on the top half of the old converted barn across the grey, stone-slabbed courtyard.

ELEVEN

HEADMASTER VISITS

For such a big man, Old Man Wood moved graciously and unhurriedly like a very large gazelle. He was light-footed, although when he pulled himself out of an armchair he groaned in exactly the same way as any old man. But he rarely complained about his age. He popped his head around the door.

'Evening all,' he said. 'Smells marvel-wonderful.'

Isabella got up and gave him a big hug.

Old Man Wood hugged her back, closing his eyes. 'Now then, little one. I sense all is not as it should be.'

'Correct,' Isabella replied, wanting to burst into tears. 'Everything today has been awful. It's like the worst day in every respect.'

'No one died, though, did they?'

Isabella was a little thrown. 'Well no, of course not. But Archie cut his hand and Kemp's been a total jerk again and smashed my barometer and even Solomon gave us a talking to.'

'Oh dear,' he said kindly. 'Tell me again, what is a *jerk*? I find it hard to keep up with your words sometimes—'

'A moron, idiot, fool—someone who doesn't fit in,' Isabella rattled back.

Old Man Wood rubbed his chin as though absorbing this information. 'Any good news?'

'Suppose so,' she said softly, 'Daisy's playing tomorrow.'

Old Man Wood smiled. 'There. Good for you, Daisy, now finish your tea and then we'll talk about it. Must say, I can't remember such strange weather. Feels as though a storm is brewing right bang on top of us. An appley-big one at that. I can feel it in my old bones.'

Isabella slammed her fists on the table, making everyone jump. 'That's exactly what I've been trying to tell everyone. No one believes me; Solomon, Kemp, you two—'

'Woah! Chill, Bells,' Archie chipped in. 'Your experimentation is a bit... bonkers.'

Mrs Pye piped up, 'That nice man the weather forecaster on my big television said there might be a bit of a storm. Localised—'

'Arrggh!' Isabella cried. 'NO! NO! **NO**! Not you as well!'

Mrs Pye turned bright pink and looked as though she might burst into tears.

'That's enough of that, Isabella,' Old Man Wood said. For a moment there was quiet. Old Man Wood furrowed his brow as though deep in thought. 'What's funny,' he began, 'is that I've been having very strange dreams. Real clear ones about a great deal of rain, flooding, storms. Thing is, I'm so old it could mean anything'

'Really?' Isabella gasped. 'You've had dreams too?'

The children stopped eating and stared up at him.

'Oh yes. More than ever. Shocking stuff too. I should check those apples I gave Mrs Pye—'

'There's nothing wrong with those apples, I'm telling you,' Mrs Pye replied from the end of the table.

'If that's the case, maybe there's going to be a storm and three quarters.'

He grabbed an apple, rubbed it on his jumper and took a large chomp. 'Now, you're old enough to know,' Old Man Wood continued between mouthfuls, 'that once upon a time there was a great storm and then a flood. I'm sure you will have learnt about it.'

'You wouldn't mean the Bible?' Isabella's voice was laced with sarcasm.

Old Man Wood seemed surprised. 'Ooh. Yup. That's the one. At least I think it is. You know about it, do you? With a man they called, now what was his name— ?'

'Noah?' Isabella added as though bored rigid.

'Ha!' Old Man Wood clapped his big hands. 'Just as I thought. Been muddling that one for a while. So you know about it. How marvel-wondrous.'

The conversation was interrupted by a banging at the door. The family stared at each other.

'Who on earth could that be?' Old Man Wood said.

Before anyone else could move, Daisy tore off to see who it was.

'You'll never believe who it is,' she said, as she rushed back in, excitement in her voice. 'It's Solomon!'

For a minute they looked at each other not sure what to do.

'Well, don't you think you should let him in,' Old Man Wood said.

The children headed towards the door.

'Mr Solomon, sir.'

'Hello, Archie, Daisy, Isabella. Just a brief visit—to see how you're getting along. May I come in?'

They led him to the sitting room where Old Man Wood was adding a couple of logs to the fire.

'Mr Wood, how nice to see you,' the headmaster said as he eyed up the old man. He was just as tall, big and wrinkly as he remembered and had the strangest little tufts of hair protruding from an otherwise bald but patchy scalp. In fact, if he wasn't mistaken, the old man looked identical to the first time he'd ever met him twenty-five years ago.

He remembered then thinking what peculiar clothes he wore. His trousers and shirt were made entirely of patches, as though he had never once been clothes-shopping. It made him look like a moving patchwork quilt and he immediately thought of Archie and his curious attempt at school uniform.

Solomon wondered whether these had been stitched together by Mrs Pye, who was loitering in the doorway.

He strode over and shook her hand. 'Isn't that road awfully narrow and steep?' he said as a way of breaking the ice. 'It must be devilishly tricky to navigate when the weather turns. Do those parcel couriers ever manage to find you?'

Mrs Pye froze and turned as pink as a lobster.

Old Man Wood rescued her by moving in and extending his hand. 'Now then, is everything in order? Perhaps I could offer you a glass of something — apple juice, tea, my special rum?'

'How kind,' Mr Solomon said, 'a glass of apple juice will be fine. I can't stay long.' The headmaster rubbed his hands against the fire—for a man his age, his handshake was like iron. 'Could I talk to you, er, in private.'

Old Man Wood turned to the children. 'Children, would you excuse us.'

The children headed out of the room while the men sat down.

'You are aware that the children's parents won't be returning until after half term?'

Old Man Wood nodded.

'As I explained to the children, this is highly unsatisfactory.'

'Rest assured,' Old Man Wood began in his deep, soothing voice, 'the children are in perfectly good health and are super-safe here.'

'Good health, yes, safe, yes—there's no doubt about that —but can you give them the kind of assistance that should be expected if, and I hate to say this, if anything goes wrong.'

'What kind of wrong, Headmaster?'

'Well, if Archie was to break his arm again. How would you get him to hospital? And what if there's a fire? Are you capable of protecting yourselves? A fire engine would never get up your lane.'

Old Man Wood burst out laughing, his rich, deep, joyful voice bouncing back off the walls. 'They are strong children, and are quite capable of looking after themselves, with or without me.'

It had the effect of making Mr Solomon feel rather idiotic. 'With respect, Mr Wood,' he fired back. 'Archie's appearance is repeatedly way below standard. Can you explain this? And can you give me your word that Isabella won't disgrace the school by violently interfering with the officials during our remaining football matches as she has done in the previous two?'

'I am in agreement with you that they are strong and capable, Mr Wood. Daisy shows this with her keen soccer skills, but she hasn't done a stroke of work the entire time she's been with us. She is on course to fail her exams—and then what?'

Old Man Wood didn't know what to say so he simply smiled back.

Solomon wondered if the old man had listened to a word. 'Mr Wood, I'll be frank with you. I have no argument with your family, in fact I am very fond of the children, and Isabella shows exceptional academic promise.'

He removed his glasses and rubbed them on a cloth before setting them back on his nose.

'The school exists on the legacy provided hundreds of years ago by the de Lowe family. Each successive headmaster has granted a generous bursary in favour of the family as set out in the original deeds. But I must tell you this: I am to retire at the end of the term, and I doubt my successor and his governors will be so generous.' Solomon paused and took a sip of his apple juice.

'In each of the examples, the children would have been severely reprimanded and perhaps even expelled.' Now Solomon spoke a little slower. 'And in each case, the bursaries would almost certainly cease. While they may look at the de Lowes as a special case, these are difficult times and there is every chance they won't.'

Old Man Wood nodded his head and scratched an imaginary beard. 'I'll make sure the children's parents understand the situation entirely.'

'Good, thank you,' Mr Solomon replied. He cleared his throat. 'Please don't be offended, but are you fit and well enough to continue in the role as the children's caretaker? I worked out you might be nearing the heady heights of 90 years—'

'I may be old, Headmaster, but body and mind are ticking along just nicely, thank you.'

'I ask these questions for the sake of the children.'

'Mr Solomon,' Old Man Wood chuckled. 'When you are as old as I am, love, health and well-being are the things of importance. It is harder to remember things from one's youth but we are lucky to be in possession of excellent health and are blessed that Mrs Pye feeds us and nurses us. You're right to be checking up, though. We don't have so many visitors up here in the hills.'

Old Man Wood decided to change the subject. 'Have you plans for your retirement?'

'Yes,' Solomon said, relaxing. Perhaps it was the apple juice. 'As a matter of fact, I'm hoping to go to the Middle East to see some of the ancient tombs and archaeology—that kind of thing.'

A little while later, as they got up and made their way to the door they heard scuffling sounds heading off towards the kitchen.

Old Man Wood and Solomon exchanged a smile.

'Children,' Solomon said, loud enough so they could easily hear. 'I have something to say to you, so you may as well come back here.'

They appeared from around the corner, looking sheepish.

'I am leaving Upsall School at the end of the term,' Solomon began. 'I have decided the time has come to retire. Please keep this to yourselves until I have made the official announcement after half term.'

He looked each of the children in the eye. 'I would be

disappointed if any of you were to leave the school before me, so I suggest you work together to improve those areas that need addressing. For example, Archie and Daisy, as I mentioned before, learning the opening stages of the Bible story, the bits where Adam and Eve are ejected from the Garden of Eden.'

He gave them a knowing look over his half-moon glasses. 'I have a suspicion that this may well be the main topic in one of your exams.' He winked theatrically.

'And the other thing is that I would very much like to win the football trophy tomorrow. I don't mean to put any additional pressure on you two, but it would be wonderful to leave the school knowing that we had reached the pinnacle in both sports and academics. So, the very best of luck.'

'We'll do our best,' Daisy said, enthusiastically.

Isabella seized her opportunity. 'What about the storm, sir,' she cut in. 'If it breaks there's going to be a disaster. I just know it.'

Solomon's friendly manner evaporated. 'Isabella, I cannot possibly see how a small, localised storm will make the slightest bit of difference. The river has flooded once in the twenty-five years I have been with the school. They may just have to play in the rain and get a little wet. It's as simple as that.'

He smiled and headed out of the oak door.

Isabella wasn't finished. 'But, sir…' she exclaimed as the door closed in her face.

Old Man Wood drew the bolt. 'What a nice man,' he said. 'I wouldn't worry too much about what he said. You're doing well at school and you're fit and healthy and you're polite and you've got friends. What more could you want, eh? Talented littluns, aren't you. Now, off to bed, the lot of you.'

A rumble of thunder boomed high up in the night sky.

Old Man Wood sniffed the air. 'Something tells me that tomorrow is going to be a big, big day.'

TWELVE

THE DREAMSPINNERS

If the three children had awoken and brushed the sleep out of their eyes and read the clock on the wall it would have told them that it was shortly after two in the morning. But they wouldn't wake, not now, for their sleep was long and deep.

It was the night-hour of dreaming.

Four dreamspinners, like the one Archie had seen over Daisy, arrived in a pinprick of a flash. The flash they made wasn't a flash any human could see, but to the dreamspinners it was a tiny, intense, burst of energy. They had come to see Genesis, the eldest dreamspinner, give the last part of the Prophecy of Eden—the Tripodean Dream—the final part of the most important dream ever created.

Using their eight delicate legs banded with grey, each spider-like dreamspinner picked its way over an invisible grid on the air until they were suspended above the children.

From where their abdomen should have been was a maghole, a round hole in which tiny streaks of lightning radiated in wave after wave of blue and white forks. It was through this that a dreamspinner could invert to any place it wished, almost instantly.

Above this maghole, a wiry tubular neck connected the body to a small head the size of a clear, white orange. On each face were three black eyes the size of quails eggs and in the recess beneath the middle eye—in place of a nose—was a dent, as if a tiny scoop of ice cream had been cut out. There was no mouth, well certainly nothing the children or anyone else would call a mouth, just a tiny slit the size of the edge of a small coin.

If the children had opened their eyes, they would have seen the old oak beams holding up the roof, and the dangling lamp with its musty-coloured shade, and the curtains and drapes that hung across their sections.

And the children would have caught the gentle noises of the night outside; the rustle of leaves or the scurrying of a mouse but never, ever would they hear, or see, a dreamspinner.

Genesis had spun dreams every night since the beginnings of modern humans, but she knew her time was up.

But why now? Why had her invisibility failed when she was in the midst of delivering this vital dream?

Was this the cruel way in which elderliness announced itself; by failures in routines, failures of body functions? She touched the burn marks where the boy's eyes had looked upon her.

Failures, that could ruin everything.

Genesis counted her blessings that it hadn't happened a moment earlier, for she was the only one who knew how to knit-and-spin this special dream; the dream that revealed the Prophecy of Eden.

Now all that remained was the final part and the gifts, and then the Prophecy would be told.

Genesis studied each of her eight delicate legs one by one, as if paying homage to them for their service. For the first time she noted the wear; the way so many had turned grey where once they were bright white, how her knuckles and joints were worn down to slivers of hardened bone.

As she seamlessly morphed each leg from needle to duster to pincer and claw, she was filled with a sense of deep foreboding.

What if the Heirs don't understand?

Nature would never allow them to survive, she knew that much.

And what if Cain reappeared?

Putting these thoughts aside, she sent out a communication via the tiny vibrations of her legs to the waiting dreamspinners, Gaia, Janana and Asgard.

'You are here to witness the last part of the Tripodean Dream, for there must be no doubting it. Their sleep pattern is deep and flowing. I am ready.'

Genesis moved her spidery frame deftly through the air as though walking on top of invisible threads. Dropping her head and two slender legs into her electrical middle—her maghole—she pulled out microscopic-sized granules of powder.

Momentarily, she was mesmerised by them. Fragments that hold so much power, she thought, realising that power was the wrong word. These were more than that; these were the opportunity of life itself.

Genesis positioned herself so that four of her long, opaque legs dangled down either side of Isabella's sleeping head like anchors, holding her steady for the dream she was about to deliver. Her other four legs sat by Isabella's lips, ready, waiting.

With ovate, jet-black eyes, Genesis stared at the girl. Instinctively she began to feel the rhythm of her breathing.

'Child, interpret this dream as best you can for all our sakes. Try to understand. Try to make the right choices.'

Then, at exactly the moment Isabella inhaled, two claws spun at amazing speed, releasing a fine powder directly into her mouth, the dust being drawn deep into her lungs.

Genesis plucked more blue, red and yellow powders from within her maghole and then, at exactly the right moment and in precisely the correct amounts, the dreamspinner lowered her silky legs towards the child's mouth and once again filtered the dream powders to the sleeping girl.

Genesis stopped and gauged the girl's reaction for she

understood every frown and flicker, every twitch and groan. And then she'd make tiny adjustments to the rate of powder in proportion to the volume of air being drawn in.

So far, so good. Already she tosses and turns. The dream powders have entered her mind. She begins her lucid and vivid journey. Nothing will wake her.

Genesis hovered across the dark room and settled above Daisy, where she repeated the procedure, scrutinising every movement, looking for signals, making sure that everything was perfect.

Finally, it was Archie's turn.

Genesis had noted the strong, intense reactions of the boy, similar perhaps to those of the Ancient Woman. But his haunting, wailing cries were like those of someone else. Someone she'd hardly dared make the comparison with. Was he really so like Cain?

Genesis studied the reaction of the children, noticing that the noises they made were not just the anguished cries of their previous dreams. These were sounds that exuded certainty and confidence; Daisy laughing, Archie smiling, Isabella's face beaming with happiness.

Maybe the final part of the Tripodean Dream was a reassurance that it would be worth the trouble ahead.

After all, she thought, there must be hope as well as fear.

Genesis, tired and aching, climbed into the middle of the room and addressed the dreamspinners, her legs flicking with subtle, silent vibrations.

'As you also know,' she said, as she floated towards Isabella, 'the Tripodean Dream comes with a gift—a special gift—for each Heir of Eden.'

She dipped two sylph-like legs into her maghole and withdrew them, studying the ends. 'These crystals were passed to me before my mother died, as once they were handed to her. Their purpose? To assist those who seek the rebirth of the Garden of Eden.'

She felt a strong vibration from Asgard but ignored him. 'If the Heirs of Eden succeed in the tasks set before them and open the Garden of Eden, the stock of spider web dream powders will be replenished. Wondrous dreams may begin afresh for all life on Earth. However, if Eden is not reborn, the dreams of hope, wonder and creativity, the dreams that offer a spark of life, will vanish—'

'Why do we meddle?' Asgard snapped, his legs moving quickly, the vibrations aggressive and powerful. 'If the Tripodean Dream had not been spun, who is to say that life would not continue? Besides, the Tripodean Dream has been given to mere *children* of man. These riddles were made by Adam when he was strong and powerful, a wizard at the height of his powers. Children are not equipped to tackle what lies ahead; the storm will tear them to pieces, they will not survive. Furthermore they do not seek, or even know of the Garden of Eden—'

'This is not the time to argue the rights or wrongs of it,' Genesis interrupted, her vibrations overriding his. 'The time has come for change. These children are the Heirs of Eden whether they like it or not, marked by their blood and their birth.'

She stretched out two legs and slowly drew them in. 'It is up to the Heirs of Eden alone to interpret the dreams that I have given them. And when the sky bursts and the thunder-bolts rain down upon them, our lives and the lives of every living thing are in their hands, whether they like it or not.'

Genesis let her words sink in. 'The Prophecy tells that if they fail, rain will fall for forty of their days and forty of their nights. It will rain with such purpose that few will survive.'

Genesis shifted uneasily. 'To succeed, the Heirs of Eden must outwit the storm and seek out the three tablets of Eden. By using their minds, their strength and their skills they will prove that mankind is ready for a new time. It is our role to herald in this new cycle of life. It begins now with these gifts.'

Genesis' silvery-grey, ghost-like body now sat directly above Isabella's sleeping face, her maghole spraying blue shards of light over her.

There was a deep silence, broken only by the child's gentle breathing.

Quietly, Genesis began:

'For the eldest, yellow spider web powder—for hands and feet.
Hands that guide, heal and protect.
Swift feet for running.'

She transformed the claw-end of one of her legs into a needle so long it was like a slither of pure ice melting into nothing. With it she injected a tiny yellow speck into the soft flesh between thumb and finger on each of Isabella's hands.

Moving down Isabella's body, she repeated the action on her ankles, the needle entering the tender skin by her Achilles' heels.

As she withdrew the needle, Genesis noted a buzz of electric-blue energy that flowed through and over the girl's sleeping body.

The gifts are undamaged by time.

Without hesitating, Genesis walked across the night air and was above Daisy, moving directly over her face. As she extended her legs she signed again, the vibrations clear to the onlookers:

'Blue spider web powder, for eyes to see when darkness falls, and ears to hear the tiniest of sounds.
With eyes so sharp and ears so keen, she will understand what others do not hear or see.'

A minuscule blue crystal fragment sat at the very tip of the needle. With astonishing precision she injected it through the delicate tissues of Daisy's closed eyelids into the retinas of her eyeballs. Then, with two of her other legs anchoring her abdomen, she carefully slid two needles down Daisy's ear canals and pushed the crystals directly into her eardrums.

On the withdrawal of the needle, Genesis noted again

that Daisy fizzed momentarily with the strange electrical current.

So skilful was her technique that other than the gentle rise and fall of their chests, Isabella and Daisy did not flicker a muscle.

Now, it was the boy's turn; the one she dreaded most. She sensed other spider legs vibrating nervously nearby. She stretched out a limb and drew it slowly back in.

'Dreamspinners,' she announced. 'The first of his gifts is to his heart. When the needle leaves it will trigger a reaction that will herald the start of the quest to open the Garden of Eden. From this moment forth, the clouds will deepen and build with rain. We do not know what will happen.'

Her vibrations were like a whisper. 'There must be absolute quiet.'

Genesis stood above Archie's chest, which heaved in front of her with his every deep breath.

A roll of thunder drummed high above them as she steadied herself and recalled the previous gifts.

'Yellow for hands and feet,' she said.
'Blue to hear and see.
But red is the one—for heart and mind—for strength—and under-standing what may be.'

With her limbs aching, Genesis galvanised herself for one final effort.

'Red spider web powder, a gift of power, when strength is needed.'

And, on the word "strength", Genesis thrust her claw with the needle high into the air.

She paused and steadied herself, marking the exact spot on his chest where she would thrust it in.

She shut her eyes.

The needle swept down and pierced the boy's heart. His

body fizzed. Genesis held it as long as she dared, making sure every last little speck of spider web powder was injected.

As she withdrew the needle, a terrific thunderbolt rattled the cottage.

Genesis trembled. Nature had awoken.

A sign from one of the other dreamspinners confirmed her suspicions that his sleep waves were changing. But a strange feeling filled her. A feeling of exposure, a feeling she had felt only once before. 'No!' she cried out, 'not my invisibility!'

She concentrated hard on the boy. *I must finish this.* She dipped her leg into her maghole and withdrew her final gift.

'Red spider web powder.
The first for strength—another for courage.'

A minuscule red fragment flashed into the tender flesh beneath Archie's chin. But before she could complete the task, she heard a gasp and felt a movement.

A burning pain seared into her.

Instantly her legs retracted as she looked up. There, on a face contorted by fear, were Archie's large, brown eyes staring back at her.

A SHORT WHILE AFTER THIS, candlelight filtered in to the corridor and a soft light spread through the door into the attic room. In rushed Mrs Pye, out of breath, her flame-red hair hanging down to her waist, her small sharp eyes accentuated by the glow of the candle.

'Goodness me! Oh, my little Arch,' she said rushing over to him, 'I never heard such a terrible scream in all my life. I thought you might have died.' She looked over him lovingly, wiping away the sweat on his brow.

'I... I had the strangest dream, Mrs P. I swear I was about to be stabbed by... by a terrible eyeless, ghostly monster—'

'Is that right?' Mrs Pye said softly, 'and eyeless as well?'

'It had a blue hole in its middle—'

'Well, well, I never. Now, I think you're old enough to know better than to be troubling yourself with all that bunkum.' She helped him back to bed. 'Come now. Get yourself back to sleep.'

Mrs Pye sat on the edge of his bed and cradled him. She stroked his cheek tenderly as Archie closed his eyes. Then she lowered his head onto his pillow.

A gentle, faraway tune that blended with the rhythmical sounds of sleep came to her—the song that had once been sung to her by Old Man Wood—and she hummed it quietly, the music soft and soothing.

Before long, Archie's breathing slowed and he returned to a deep slumber.

Mrs Pye kissed the young boy on the forehead.

What was it, she thought, about this funny young boy; so scruffy, so underrated, so sensitive. And yet with a strange toughness.

WATCHING FROM THE CEILING, her invisible status functioning once more, Genesis the dreamspinner was relieved that the final dream had run smoothly, even if the boy might have missed out on the final part of his Gift of Eden.

If the children failed, would the blame be levelled at her?

Only time would tell.

Genesis drew her legs together and took comfort in the warm glow of electrical current that sprayed over her abdomen and nursed her burns where the boy's eyes had seared into her.

She wondered about the Tripodean Dream. Maybe Asgard was right; maybe the whole thing was foolish. And although she dared not admit it openly, she knew perfectly well this undertaking had never been designed for the children of man.

Perhaps *she* was the fool. At least she was wise enough to know that nature's wishes cannot be resisted.

And what of the old man—there to guide and help? He had forgotten everything. Time had taken its toll, but was he now—in a curious twist of fate—*a liability*?

She dipped her claws into her maghole. She would make sure he was given a dream every night that would somehow, *somehow*—however hard, however shocking, however desperate—stir him into action. Something had to click, it just had to.

With these thoughts, she inverted into her maghole and vanished into thin air.

THIRTEEN
CAIN'S LUCK

T*he Tripodean Dream is doomed.* Asgard fumed. *Children, simple, pathetic children, have been tasked to save the planet! Absurd! They have no chance, none whatsoever. The world of man has slipped into the sort of decline that was talked about from the outset. They deserve to fail.*

And Adam? Pah! He is a bumbling old fool who has forgotten his mantra. Time has got the better of him.

There will only be one winner in this shambles, Asgard mused, *and that is Cain, the Master of Havilah. A ghost like Cain has enough tricks to see off these children one hundred times over. He used to have a talent for this type of occasion. But why does going to Cain sound so right, yet feel so horribly wrong?*

Asgard tried to remove any niggling doubt. *What are the alternatives?*

The dreamspinners' fate worried him more than anything. *Did dreams still have a place in the world?* he pondered. *Was there a need for inspirational, insightful, magical dreams from Eden that elicited love, and joy?*

Maybe—maybe not, Asgard thought.

He cleaned a couple of legs by flicking and rubbing them rapidly. *So long as we dreamspinners keep spinning dreams — any dreams — then we will never become extinct.*

This is our opportunity.

77

Asgard worked out the chain of events:

The children are killed by the storm. Earth falls to the rains. Dream-spinners harvest dreams from the spider webs across Havilah until the Garden of Eden opened again.

So what if the dreams we give are nightmares. At least we dream-spinners will survive.

And then another thought came to him. *What if one of the heirs joined with Cain? Perhaps Archie, the boy heir. He might dilute Cain's power.*

He toyed with it. *How would it be possible to separate the boy from the other Heirs of Eden, when all three heirs needed to survive the storm?*

Asgard could suddenly see a plan forming. The more he thought it through, the more excited and fearful he became.

But he'd made his mind up. He would take sides and align with Cain. After thousands of years, the dreamspinners—the most ancient and lasting species of them all—would no longer be neutral.

'But it must be done,' he said into the dark night sky, 'for the benefit of all dreamspinners.'

Asgard's maghole expanded as the enormity hit him. He felt for Cain's vibrational energy field and, moment later, he was locked on, ready to invert to that old devil, Cain, across the universes in Havilah.

IN NO TIME, Asgard was walking through the massive library in Cain's palace. Asgard remembered how grand it once was; the golden ceiling, the diamond chandeliers that sparkled so brightly they could almost blind, the windows made from cut jewels and shining floors made from complex patterns of coloured stones. Now it was covered in thousands of years of dust, a veil of grey smothering it like a blanket.

The dreamspinner walked through the air, wondering where the ghost might be. Cain's vibration was strong but ghosts could be hard to find. He found himself facing a huge piece of furniture with hundreds upon hundreds of drawers lined out row after row in neat columns.

Suddenly a drawer opened and its contents tumbled to the ground. It was Cain, searching as he always did for his branchwand.

Asgard readied himself to inject the ghost of Cain with a substance that would enable them to communicate by translating his signing into words.

Asgard jabbed at him, his leg shooting in and out so fast that Cain barely felt it.

'Who's there?' Cain called out. 'Which rapscallion of a rascal is it? Because I'll have you. I'll have you good and proper when I find my branchwand.'

Another drawer crashed over the floor.

Asgard materialised into the air above Cain's head.

Cain sensed it. 'Who are you and what do you want? I may be blind but I see things perfectly. Do not underestimate me.'

'I am Asgard the dreamspinner.'

Cain seemed to think about this. 'A dreamspinner, is that right?' he said at length. 'Well, well, well. Then it is lucky I am blind so I cannot look upon your ugly body.' Cain sniffed the air. 'You want to tell me something, don't you?'

'I come with news and a proposition,' Asgard began. 'The Tripodean Dream has been given, Master—'

Cain seemed to slip. 'The Prophecy of Eden!' he yelled. 'The dreams! You lie!'

'No. Clouds are building, the sky is preparing for rain—'

'And the Gifts of Eden? Have they been given too?'

'Indeed.'

Cain roared. 'While I am stuck here in this empty hole, Eden will be reborn and will inflict more useless creations on the worlds. It is infernal.'

Several drawers flew out and smashed onto the floor. 'Who are the heirs, are they strong, are they blessed with power and magic? Huh, tell me, dreamspinner.'

'They are children, weak sons and daughters of Adam. They have no magic and little sense of nature.'

'*Children?* You jest. It cannot be. Are you sure?'

'Indeed.'

Cain seemed to mull this over. 'Then they will not succeed. The tasks require immense strength and cunning. They may not make it past the storm.' Cain's voice petered off into the room. 'And what of the old man?'

'He wallows in self-pity. He remembers nothing. His time on earth has mellowed him. He may prove more of a hindrance to the Heirs of Eden than a help.'

Cain groaned, a noise of deep frustration. 'So, ugly dreamspinner, why are you here?'

'I may be able to help,' Asgard answered.

'You have my ear, dreamspinner, but there is the small problem of getting away from this damnable place.'

'I believe I have found a way of transporting you to these Heirs of Eden,' Asgard began.

'Yes, yes, yes, dreamspinner,' he said, his voice rising until it was booming. 'Don't you think I haven't tried *everything in my power* for the last however many thousands of years to get out of here? Now go away.'

Asgard let the echo die down. He had some explaining to do. 'Dreamspinners move freely throughout the universes— we go wherever we choose—on the feelings of vibrational energy. If a solid being goes through our maghole, our middle, perhaps we will die.'

'What's your point?' Cain shot back.

'You are not a solid being,' Asgard responded calmly. 'You are a spirit, a ghost. Therefore it should be possible for you to travel anywhere I designate.'

'Are you saying that I could go through you, to other places?'

'Indeed.'

'My word, foul creature. It is brilliant! Cain roared as he realised what the dreamspinner meant. 'Utterly brilliant!' But after a few moments his tone changed. 'Why?' he asked. 'Why would you do this for me? What is the benefit to you, dream-spinner?'

Asgard paused and then signed rapidly, his claws flashing in the air. 'Like all dreamspinners, I am concerned with giving dreams. I do not worry where they come from, only that there are dreams to spin and that dreamspinners survive.'

'Clever, very clever,' Cain said. 'And this is on the under-standing that the Heirs of Eden will fail?'

'Yes.'

Cain's enthusiasm dampened. 'But, I am a ghost—I cannot do much with what is left of me. I have no eyes for magic, nor do I have a great physical presence.'

Asgard had been waiting for this. 'Yes. But what if you were to absorb the body of a man.'

'Tell me, dreamspinner, how would this be at all possible?'

'If a being were to freely and willingly offer its body to you, you may join with it—in partnership. It would give you substance. You would be able to move with more purpose and have strength.'

Cain suddenly saw what he meant. 'Get a human to blend into me? Is this possible?'

'Of course. Though it cannot be forced. Perhaps, as the storm approaches, you might form an alliance with one of the Heirs of Eden.'

'Even cleverer, you clever, vile, little dreamspinner,' Cain replied, astonished by this huge stroke of luck. 'But surely it would harm you in your movements across the worlds, dreamspinner?'

'I cannot say,' Asgard said. 'If it was a child of man, it might not dominate your spirit, so movement may be possible.'

Cain chuckled. 'An Heir of Eden with me in harmony. My, you have a seasoned plan, dreamspinner. It is an opportu-nity I cannot afford to miss. Hear me out though: if your transportation fails, will I remain a spirit in another place?'

'You would be on Earth. Permanently'

'I understand.' Cain dropped his voice, 'Do other dreamspinners know?'

'I am alone, for now,' Asgard said. 'I believe others may join me when they learn what I have done.'

'Indeed. You are bold coming here,' Cain clapped his hands together, although being a ghost it made no noise. 'Strange creature, I am willing to try your plan. You will be properly rewarded if this turns out as you suggest.'

Asgard shifted uneasily. Rewards were not what he wanted. 'Time is moving, Master,' he replied. 'On Earth the storm breaks in the morning when the sun is high in the sky and the heirs are in open ground. One of them is a boy named Archie. One of his Gifts of Eden… failed.'

Asgard hesitated knowing he couldn't be absolutely certain. 'His "courage" will not be with him. Now, the boy sleeps, but he will wake shortly. He has seen the Prophecy of Eden in his dreams and he has seen the murder of your mother. You remember?'

'It has preoccupied my time for too long,' Cain replied. 'What do you suggest, Asgard?'

'Use her murder to manipulate the boy. He does not understand it. It confuses him—he is only a child.'

Cain guffawed. 'Excellent thinking. Hardly a stone unturned. But how will the boy believe a spirit? What if he does not comprehend the afterlife?'

Asgard hadn't foreseen this. 'It may not be enough if you are invisible. Can you wear a cloak?'

'I can—but not for long—an hour at a time.' The ghost scratched his non-existent chin. 'There is a long, but light, overcoat which I use to spook my subjects with. I'll see if I can find it.'

Asgard called after him. 'Hurry, Master. Make sure it is bland so that it will fit in with human tastes on Earth. Bring anything else that you may require.'

Cain drifted away, his invisible presence marked only by the swaying movement of dust and papers lying on the floor. Shortly he returned wearing a trilby hat, a scarf and a long overcoat.

Asgard realised Cain had acquired a sixth sense of knowing where and what everyday objects were.

Cain sensed his thoughts. 'I have learnt to find things by understanding the energy within objects,' he said. 'It is amazing what you can see if you can't actually see, and what you can hear even if you can't actually hear.'

Asgard stretched out a leg so it was touching Cain. 'Hold on to my leg—you will feel its energy.'

Cain pushed out an arm.

'I will pull you towards me,' Asgard said. 'On my word, crouch down and dive horizontally, as though into a pool of water. Do this as fast as you can—understand?'

Cain felt a tingle fizzing through his ghostly frame. 'I feel you, it is powerful.'

'Good,' Asgard said. 'Now lower yourself and I will open myself up.'

Cain did as he was asked.

Asgard began the countdown. 'One, two, THREE!'

Cain thrust himself forward, like a diver off a high board. A mild burning sensation coursed through him and, following that, he found himself on a soft floor.

Cain picked himself up and began to dust off his coat. His face beamed with excitement.

'You do not have much time,' Asgard said as he turned invisible. 'You must do the rest alone.'

'Where will I find the boy?'

'Make your way up the stairs. The heirs sleep at the top of the house in a room in the shape of a cross. The boy is on the left side. I must go—other dreamspinners may be around. Return to the fireplace at the bottom of the house when you are done. Hide in the chimney. I will be back before dawn breaks, before the old man stirs.'

Cain stood up and prepared to go.

'Remember,' Asgard called after him. 'Make an ally of the boy. Play on his fear of the murder of the Ancient Woman. Arrange a place and time to meet him before the storm breaks. Go now! Go in haste.'

FOURTEEN
ARCHIE MEETS CAIN

Archie woke, his sleep disturbed. He lay in bed, wide awake, as segments of his dreams flashed back to him like flickers on an old movie reel.

His heart raced as though he'd been running hard. He stared at the ceiling, trying to piece the events together in his mind. Then he closed his eyes.

The images of the murder of an incredibly old and haggard woman came to him vividly in a sudden burst. Why was it always so graphic, so shocking? And then he'd had a feeling of drowning, of gasping for air, of swimming for his life.

He exhaled loudly, opened his eyes and looked out into the blackness of their room.

Was there someone at the foot of his bed?

'Daisy? What d'you want?' he slurred.

A windy chuckle returned. Archie shuffled into a sitting position, yawned, stretched his arms out and searched the room. Before long, he thought he could see a figure, a human figure, masked by a long coat and a trilby hat.

Archie started to slip under his duvet, but then, for some strange reason he stopped. 'Who is it?' he called out.

'Ah! Hello. I didn't see you there!' a voice said, huskily.

Shivers raced up Archie's back.

'Now, are you the boy or one of the girls?'

Archie was baffled by this strange question. He remained silent as his eyes gradually adjusted to the light.

'What can I... er... help you with?' Archie stammered at length. He could make out a long coat and a hat.

His stomach knotted. Were they being robbed?

'Ah! Forgive me for waking you,' said the voice. 'But there is something important I need to share with you.'

The man approached and raised his head.

Archie gasped. Underneath his hat, there was nothing there. Absolutely nothing. He could see straight through.

'You see, boy, I need a favour—'

'Oh God, it's another weird dream.' Archie blurted out.

'I tell you what,' the ghost said, whipping out a tiny dagger the size of a penknife. 'Is this one of your dreams?'

The knife floated fast through the air. Moments later, Archie received a sharp nick just under his chin and he worked the oozing blood between his forefinger and thumb before it turned sticky.

Archie sidled quickly down his bed.

The ghost advanced inspecting his handiwork. 'Goodness me, a little human blood—I haven't seen any of that for years,' he said, coldly. 'You do believe I exist, don't you?'

Archie's body rattled.

'Good. Let's be quite clear about this straight away,' the ghost said. His tone turned softer. 'You, boy, are on the threshold of something rather extraordinary. There are mortal challenges you must face. I am sure you know of them through the images that have been given to you.'

'The nutty dreams?' Archie stuttered.

'Precisely,' the ghost chuckled. 'Nutty dreams.'

Archie shivered. 'But I don't understand them.'

The ghost sucked in a mouthful of air. 'You've heard about the Garden of Eden?'

Archie's brain fizzed. If it wasn't Solomon or Old Man Wood banging on about the Garden of Eden, it was a deranged ghost. I mean, the place didn't even exist? OK, so it might have done six thousand years ago! But even so.

Archie kept as still, and as quiet as he could, hoping like mad the spirit would say his piece, not mutilate him further, and go away.

The ghost seemed to stare at Archie for a few moments as if trying to gauge his knowledge of the subject. 'Eden's where life began, you must know this. But more recently it's been, how should I put it, on... standby. The thing is, there's a slim chance it may operate again, which would mean terrible things must happen to my mother.'

The ghost paused, taking stock. 'Everything clear so far?'

Archie couldn't think, let alone try and understand what the ghost was talking about.

'Good. Now this forthcoming event is known as the Prophecy of Eden and it involves you, my boy. I would like to help you.'

The ghost leant in.

'And, in return, you, boy, can help me. You know, a tit-for-tat arrangement.'

Archie tried to remember to breathe. His eyes were straining to remain in their sockets. He blinked several times over. How on earth could this ghost know about his dreams which were still rattling around in his mind?

Archie sensed that the ghost was smiling thinly at him. 'If the time comes, I will need you to take good care of the Ancient Woman—see that no harm comes to her.' His voice trailed off as he searched Archie's face. 'You do know about the Ancient Woman?'

Archie's face betrayed him.

'Well, you see,' the ghost continued, 'she's my mother and she's a sad old woman hanging on to life. But she'll never see it again because she's blind, like me.' The ghost paused solemnly as if remembering her. 'To cut a long story short, Archie, she took the noble but worthless step of sacrificing herself in order to keep a spark alive.'

'A spark?' Archie quizzed, barely able to squeeze the words out. 'A spark of what?'

'A spark of life, I suppose.'

Archie thought he'd better play along and said weakly, 'And if you save your mother, will it mean you stop being a ghost?'

The ghost was thankful Archie couldn't see his face as he was barely able to control himself. What a naive thing to say, the boy didn't have a clue. 'Of course not,' he sobbed trying to hide the laughter in his voice. 'My body is gone, but my spirit is forever.'

'But it will mean I'll stop having dreams about... about killing her.'

'If you help me, then I promise that is exactly what will happen.'

Archie was confused. 'What do I have to do?'

'In due course, you must protect her, no matter what,' the ghost said quietly. 'That is all. There are some that would want her dead. These people may think they are right, but rest assured they are mistaken. You must protect her from harm—do you understand? I'm asking so very little.'

Archie breathed out a sigh of relief. In the event that this entire conversation hadn't taken place in an unknown part of his brain and in lieu of his appalling dreams, looking after this Ancient Woman had to be the right thing to do. So, maybe the ghost was on their side, even if it was a bit knife-happy. Perhaps ghosts were like that.

Archie nodded, hesitatingly, but it was a nod.

'Very good,' said the ghost, whose gaze lingered over Archie for rather too long.

Cain hovered into the middle of the room. The boy has no idea what is going to happen, he thought. He has found no meaning in his dreams. Did people of Earth not understand them anymore? Asgard was right—these children would never survive the storm. Now, time to put in place Asgard's plan.

Cain floated back to Archie's bedside. 'There is another way,' he began.

Archie didn't move a muscle.

'I want you to consider joining me—physically—as my flesh and blood.'

Tiredness swept over Archie. He yawned. 'Join you?'

'Not right now, of course, I'd like you to think about it. But joining me will save your life.'

Archie had no idea what the ghost was gabbling on about. 'Sure,' he said, wearily. 'Whatever.'

'Good-good, I'm thrilled... delighted,' Cain said, as he felt the weight of his coat. 'I am sorry about the knife,' he continued. 'I don't have time to explain things in great depth, so occasionally it pays to use... other means.'

'But, Mr... sir,' Archie said, summoning his nerve, 'if I did this joining-thing, er, what's in it for me?'

'What else, for you, Archie? Ah yes!' the ghost was thinking on his feet. 'What's in it for you - apart from saving your life? Of course, how silly of me!'

The ghost drew himself up as best he could and faced Archie. 'I hold the secrets of ages past, Archie. I will offer you strength and courage, young man, so you are feared and respected. You will have the strength of a horse and the courage of a lion. I give you my word that these rewards are genuine. All you have to do is meet me tomorrow morning— somewhere safe, where I can be with you alone. Then I will show you more. When you know the facts you will choose, freely, to join me.'

The ghost made this sound so easy—so obvious. But his voice turned darker. 'There is a terrible time coming, Archie, but I alone offer you salvation.'

Archie muffled a yawn. 'Yeah, sure, OK.'

'Excellent! Then you will meet with me in no more than nine hours and no less than eight,' the ghost demanded. 'Think of a place where no one will see us.'

Archie found himself saying 'There's a back alleyway above the bank of the football field, near the school,' he said.

'You'll know you've found it when you see two houses leaning in on each other. If you go up there it's normally pretty quiet.'

'Very good,' the ghost gushed. 'Make sure you wear a long overcoat like mine and a scarf. Do you have one?'

Archie didn't, but he said he did.

'And do you like sweets, Archie?'

'Yeah, a bit,' Archie replied. What a curious question from a ghost. 'Old Man Wood's the sucker for sugary things. He's always dipping his fingers in the sugar bowl and getting told off by Mrs Pye.'

The ghost, invisible though it was, seemed to flinch. 'Is that so? Yes, I had forgotten.'

Archie felt a little stupid.

A groan from the bed nearby signalled that Daisy was stirring.

'We meet in a few hours in the alleyway,' the ghost whispered as it drifted slowly to the door, struggling to keep the coat on top of him. 'Now remember, tonight's chat, young man, is our very own secret. Any tongue-wagging and the deal is off.'

Archie caught a glimpse of the knife.

As the ghost reached the door he was almost bent double. 'See you tomorrow, Archie. Be in no doubt that your life will change forever a few hours from now—the strength of a horse and the courage of a lion—you will never regret it. Now not a word to anyone, including the old man.'

'What... what's your name?' Archie asked.

'Ah yes. I forget—the finer, little details.' His invisible eye sockets bore into Archie who felt as though his heart was briefly being sucked out.

'I am the ghost of Cain, son of Adam and Eve, brother of Abel. Maybe you've heard of me, maybe you haven't.'

Cain stopped as if an idea had popped into his head. 'You have a cup of water?'

Archie pointed to the table just behind him.

Cain dropped something in which fizzed a little. 'You will

need this. Drink and it will give you great strength. Until tomorrow, Archie.'

And with those words, Cain slipped quietly out of the door.

ARCHIE FELL BACK on his pillows, rubbed his eyes and wiped the beads of sweat off his face. What was that all about? What a dreadful, dreadful night; nightmare after nightmare.

In the back of his mind he wondered if this ghost was *the* Cain as in 'Cain and Abel' in the Bible story. Wasn't he the son of Adam and Eve? Crikey. Properly bonkers. Didn't Cain kill Abel or something and then get turned away? He'd have to look it up.

Archie was so tired he felt it was almost impossible to know what was real and what wasn't. Anyway, the one thing he was sure of was that he wasn't going to meet the ghost. No way.

He studied the clock. Three thirty-five. He did a quick calculation. Eight hours from now and it'd be bang in the middle of the football match. Nine hours and the game would just be finishing.

He chuckled—a classic timetable clash. Well, at least the problem was sorted; there was no way he was missing the game and certainly not for a deranged ghost.

He smiled, relieved by his fortunate scheduling, closed his eyes and drifted back to sleep.

GAIA THE DREAMSPINNER HAD A FEELING—A vibration—that Archie was awake. She arrived in the room to find the ghost talking with the boy. From the corner, she listened in.

She was astonished. Firstly, that it was Cain, the Master

of Havilah himself, forever banned from leaving Havilah, who had somehow found his way to the Heirs of Eden's bedroom only hours after the last part of the Tripodean Dream had been given.

This was beyond comprehension.

Secondly, Cain knew about the children's dreams and was aware of the Gifts of Eden. Thirdly, Archie had no idea about his own gifts—but Cain knew enough to exploit him.

It was astonishing. Cain was clever and manipulative, but how was it possible?

Gaia thought it through. One of the dreamspinners must have communicated with Cain. It was the only way. But dreamspinners were honour-bound to be neutral in all things. They did not meddle; this was engrained into their very fabric.

There were only four of them who had seen the dream and gifts given: Genesis, Asgard, Janana and herself. The most senior dreamspinners.

Genesis? Was she bitter about coming to light in front of the boy? No, it didn't add up. What about Asgard? He was the one who objected to giving the Gifts of Eden to children, but he was also the most passionate dreamspinner about dreams. Or Janana, the quiet one. Yes, Gaia thought, maybe it was her.

And then another thought whistled into her mind. Cain was a spirit so perhaps he had travelled... through a dream-spinner?

Gaia reeled. In which case, a dreamspinner must have forged a pact with Cain.

But why?

Gaia looked down on the boy who turned his head on the pillow. The children had no idea what was about to happen. She moved in close and administered a deep space dream in the hope that the meeting with Cain might feel like it never happened. Whether it worked was up to Archie's subconscious to decide.

FIFTEEN

HAVILARIAN TOADSTOOL POWDER

C ain could feel his overcoat bearing down on his body, but he had an idea, an idea so brilliant he was determined to carry it out even if it meant he had to let the coat slip to the floor.

While searching through his cupboards, he'd stumbled upon a jar of grey powder. Cain pulled the jar out of his pocket and inspected it—wondering if the contents were still alive.

Havilarian toadstool powder was a lethal poison, designed to kill or reduce to nothing those who originated from the Garden of Eden. And there was enough powder here to reduce the old man to a ghost just like himself—several times over.

Cain reached the hallway. No Asgard. Good, he thought, better the dreamspinner doesn't know.

Cain cursed as his ghostly frame struggled under the weight of the coat. He let it fall and searched the vibrations of the objects in the room. Soon, a map appeared in his mind's eye.

He sensed a room with a table in the middle. He could feel the resonance of plants and foodstuffs that hung from the ceiling. A little to the left were strong vibrations of a smouldering fire—a cooker perhaps. Good; he was in the right place.

As he moved about, he could feel the energy of the cupboards. He thought hard about sugar. Cain felt a surge of energy. There, -near to the cooker, nestled in a bowl exactly as Archie said.

Cain grinned. Easy to see, he thought, when one has had eons of time to master the energy that surrounds us. With considerable effort he opened the jar and poured the contents into the sugar bowl. As he did, he could hear tiny squeals coming from the powder.

Cain chuckled. Double luck. The Havilarian toadstool powders were most definitely alive.

Cain replaced the items and drifted out of the room back to the fireplace. He felt for the vibrations of the spider. Nothing. Damn.

Upstairs he could hear the yawns of the old man stirring in his bed and his feet padding on the ceiling above.

Come on, Asgard, where are you?

A moment later, the stairs began to creak very loudly under the old man's weight.

Cain didn't want to hang about. He knew he couldn't be seen but he absolutely didn't want to be sensed. He didn't want anyone to know that he had left Havilah, and was in the house of his father—the house of his greatest enemy.

As the footsteps got louder he heard a tiny noise. 'Master, it is Asgard. Dive now. Do nothing else.'

'About time,' Cain snapped just as he heard a small cough and the shuffle of feet of Old Man Wood entering the room. Without waiting to be prompted, Cain knelt down and dived.

'You cut it fine, dreamspinner,' he snapped.

'I cannot pretend it was easy, Master. One of the dream-spinners is suspicious. I must go. There are dreams to give and other dreamspinners to talk to. I cannot be found in Havilah.'

'Find me in eight hours as the storm breaks,' Cain said.

'With luck, I will get the boy. You know there will be no hiding place for you, dreamspinner, if this is the case?'

Asgard signed. 'That is why I must go.' He inverted, leaving Cain in his great ballroom.

Cain gasped as a terrible realisation struck him; he had left the coat behind with the dagger in the pocket! But his shock soon turned to glee and then laughter.

Ha! The cut on young Archie's chin might be explained by a bump in the night but the coat will prove I was there, he thought. The boy *cannot* ignore it. Archie will see it and take it. Cain thumped the air. Oh, to see the look on his face! And now he will come to me, like flies to sugar.

Enjoying an image of a bowl filled with Havilarian toad-stool powder, sugar and flies, Cain threw his invisible head back and roared with laughter, the noise echoing eerily down the passages and through the rooms of his huge palace.

SIXTEEN

SIMILAR DREAMS

D aisy could feel the intensity building in her head.

A sharp noise rang in her ears. Then the flashing started. Snapshots of skeletons, serpents, and torrents of water combined with the feeling of drowning and then eerie darkness.

She shivered as a nausea grew, and her eardrums thumped, and her eyes ached as if the lids had been smeared in hot wax.

And then there was the murder in cold blood.

Her sobs filled the room. 'Ancient Woman!' she cried out.

Why was it always the same haggard old woman?

ISABELLA RAN across the room and closed her arms around her. 'It's me. Are you alright? You look terrible.'

Daisy burst out crying 'Why?' she sobbed, hiding her head under the duvet.

Archie joined his sisters. 'Daisy, it's me,' Archie said, trying to sound as supportive as he could. 'What's up?' But his question was met by an even louder outpouring of tears.

'Now look what you've done!' Isabella said, turning on him. 'This is so your fault.'

'But I haven't done anything. I didn't touch her—and anyway, it was you that set her off in the first place.'

'Nice try, Archie. The last time Daisy was this traumatised was when you put dog poo in her slippers three years, two months and sixteen days ago. So what is it now? Another one —or is it something else equally as vile?'

'Don't be ridiculous, you're completely over-reacting—'

Isabella faced Archie. 'Listen, Arch. This is a girl problem —so please, please can you give us a couple of minutes?' she smiled thinly at him. 'Be useful—go and see if you can get us a cup of tea or something?'

Archie rolled his eyes and walked off.

With Archie out of the way, she turned to Daisy and looked lovingly into her eyes. 'Right now,' she said, taking a couple of deep breaths, 'you look like you need a huge dollop of sisterly love.'

ARCHIE TRUNDLED down the creaking corridor, his face burning like molten lava. *No one gives a damn how I feel. No one ever asks me what's been going on in my head. And why is it always my fault?* He thrust out his chin and felt the sting of a cut. He froze. Cloudy images of the previous night rushed back at him. Before he knew what he was doing he had dashed into the bathroom and was looking in the mirror. It was a small incision, just as he suspected.

Archie couldn't believe it. Ever since he'd woken the words of horse and lion had reverberated in his head. What was it again: 'The strength of a horse and the courage of a lion?' He shook his head. Nah—ghosts didn't exist, did they? But why was his memory so foggy and why did the meeting he'd had in the middle of the night feel so wrong, but yet so right?

Archie put his head down, deep in thought, and headed towards the kitchen.

Mrs Pye, who was ploughing through a huge pile of washing, looked up as Archie came sloping in. 'You taking an elephant for a walk?' she said.

'Uh? An elephant?' he repeated. Archie realised what she meant and tried desperately hard not to break into a smile.

Mrs Pye leant against the sink. 'What is the matter with you lot?'

Archie coughed. 'Bells and Daisy had a bad night. They're talking about some, er, girlie things, you know…' Archie mumbled. It was the first thing that had popped into his head.

'Periods?' Mrs Pye blurted out. 'Daisy becoming a woman now, is she? About time, I suppose.'

Archie went bright red. Was this what was meant by "girlie things"?

He thought he'd better change the subject. 'Er, my throat's really sore, Mrs P, and my head hurts; feels like some-one's tightened a clip around my neck.'

'Come here and I'll have a look.'

Archie sidled over to the sink and Mrs Pye took his head very gently in her hands. 'What's this cut on your chin? You been playing with your knives again?'

'No. Of course I haven't,' he said, weakly. 'I fell out of bed and bashed it on something.'

Mrs Pye looked at Archie suspiciously. 'I won't tell—you know that. I know you like to disappear off to the potting shed and practice your throwing, though Lord only knows why.' She took his hand, and then felt his forehead and then the back of his neck. 'It's your sister who doesn't approve.'

Mrs Pye had finished her medical. 'You is a bit sweaty, young man. Could be a fever coming on. And what with all that noise in the middle of the night—well, I don't know what to make of it.'

She rubbed her chin, thinking what might be the best cure. 'I reckon you need a couple of…'

'Apples?' Archie said.

Mrs Pye raised her eyebrows. 'Yep, how do you guess?'

Archie forced a smile. 'Just a lucky guess, that's all.'

ARCHIE HEADED upstairs to break the news. 'Can I come in now?' he yelled, from the top of the stairs.

Isabella opened the door. 'Sorry Arch, been a bit of a funny morning. Any luck with the tea?'

'Even better,' he beamed, as he stepped inside. 'Huge breakfast en-route—thank you very much.' He looked rather pleased with himself and then he started to go red.

Isabella noticed. 'What have you done? You look ridiculously guilty!'

Archie pulled a face. 'I told Mrs P that you were having, er, girlie problems—you know, like, er, periods. It just popped out.'

Daisy exploded into laughter. 'Periods? You? OMG, hilarious,' she said, slapping him on the back. 'Winkle, that's a classic.' Her mood instantly lifted. 'Archie, I'm already a woman.' Daisy stood up, posed and strutted around the room. 'The person you see here is ALL woman.'

Archie laughed. 'You could have fooled me—'

Daisy ignored him and grabbed his hands, 'Wo-man, woman,' she said in a low growl which she hoped was cool and sexy. 'I am ALL WO-MAN.'

In no time the twins were dancing a kind of strange waltz in the middle of the room, occasionally tripping over each other's feet and crashing to the floor and laughing and singing, "WO-MAN!" over and over again.

Typical Daisy, Archie thought: one minute scared to death, the next it was quite forgotten about.

Mrs Pye rapped on the door. 'Give us a hand will you!'

Isabella rushed over, opened it, and her eyes nearly popped out of her head at the massive tray. It must have weighed a ton. On it were an array of plates and cups and dishes with poached eggs, bacon, mushrooms and tomatoes. A full rack of toast stood neatly in smart rows and pots of marmalade and Marmite were squeezed on top. Finally, there was a large pot of tea with a jug of milk.

Mrs Pye set it down on the table, drew in some large gulps of air and straightened up. 'Now then, which one of you has the girl problems?' she announced.

At which, Daisy fell about laughing as if it really was the funniest thing in the world.

AFTER THEIR UNEXPECTEDLY ENORMOUS BREAKFAST, and now that Daisy had calmed down, Isabella felt it was time to question her. 'Daisy,' she began quietly, 'earlier you called out, "Ancient Woman". Can you tell me why?'

Daisy took a couple of deep breaths to compose herself and as she did a shadow seemed to fall over her face. 'It was another nightmare,' she began, hoping she wasn't sounding completely idiotic. 'I've had three now,' she said, scratching her chin nervously. 'All totally disturbing, but last night's was the best... and the worst... and the weirdest.' She looked at her sister for support. 'They've been so real—I could smell things, understand everything; birds, trees, plants. They talked to me—properly talked! It's just so complicated, I don't really know where to begin.'

Daisy scrunched her face up and ran a hand through her hair, getting her fingers temporarily caught in a knot. 'And then—then there was this old woman telling me about a wonderful, beautiful place and... also, yes, also there was a terrifying storm—a sort of endless hurricane that felt like it was after me. It had the lot: lightning, mudslides, tons of water beating me to death. I was drowning ...' she tailed off leaving a silence in the room.

'What is it, Daisy?' Isabella prompted.

'I dreamt I reached a sanctuary—and only then was I safe from the storm. It was like... Heaven.'

Isabella couldn't believe it. Daisy's dream sounded so similar to hers. She had to find out more. 'Daisy, what happened to this Ancient Woman.'

'Well, I'm pretty certain this haggard old woman was trying to tell us something. You see, in each dream she died—'

'Are you sure?'

'Oh yes,' Daisy said, her eyes wide. 'Really violently and every time in a different way. It was like being there—I could feel myself actually screaming—but I couldn't tell who'd done it.' Daisy buried her face in her hands.

She took the silence from the others as a green light to continue. 'Look, I know it sounds nuts, but this "Ancient Woman" knew about us... she knew *everything*... even though we were in a completely different world.' Her eyes searched her elder sister's, begging her to believe her. 'It's terrified the living daylights out of me.' Her bottom lip began to tremble and tears welled in her eyes. 'Every time I think about it, I think I'm going mad.'

ARCHIE STARED lovingly at his twin sister. He loathed her for ignoring him when it suited her and for being better at sports and for her ridiculously carefree nature. But he loved her quirky manner and her honesty. If only he could muster the courage, like her, and say what he felt. If he did, perhaps everything would be clearer.

Then, without warning, tears began to well up in Isabella's eyes.

'Oh no. Not you as well!' Archie said.

'Me too!' Isabella cried, tears streaming down her face. 'Same—exactly.'

Archie's eyes nearly popped out of his head. 'But that's crazy—'

'I know—it's totally bonkers.'

Archie was confused. 'Just like Daisy's? Are you sure?'

'It's the truth,' Isabella insisted. 'I swear it. Three intense dreams like Daisy's: clear as glass—but making no sense whatsoever. I've never been so amazed or happy or terrified, and what's more, just as Daisy said, it always ends in death.'

She burst into tears. Daisy handed her a tissue and she dabbed at her eyes before continuing. 'It's like flying into a cloud and every now and then, as you get used to it, you find yourself back in the cloud, trying to figure out what's going on.' She grabbed another tissue. 'And I keep seeing rain, torrential, terrible rain and lightning—you know how I've been going on about this deluge, well it's terrifying me... it's as if this stupid storm targeted us alone.'

Daisy nodded in agreement.

Isabella touched Archie's shoulder tenderly. 'And I'm sorry I was grumpy with you, Arch,' she said, as she raised her eyes and offered him a quick smile. 'It's just a bit overwhelming and confusing.'

It was now Daisy's turn to ask the questions. 'What did you make of this "Ancient Woman"?'

Isabella thought for a moment. 'Well, she'd been stuck somewhere, as if abandoned, I think. She's a really sad, horrible looking thing, waiting for—'

'For what?'

Isabella shrugged. 'I don't know. Something. And her eyes had been gouged out so she could never be sure where she was—'

'That's it!' Daisy agreed. 'Exactly how I saw her. No eyes, but really nice and kind and full of love.' She pulled a bit of a face. 'She was disgusting to look at though, all shrivelled up, like one of Old Man Wood's prunes. I've never seen anything like it.'

'Probably more crinkly and withered,' Isabella added with a thin smile. 'It was very hard to believe how she was still alive. It was as if she held the key to something, something amazing, but I can't remember what it was.' Isabella frowned. 'Why are dreams so weird? Why can't I remember?'

Archie had become noticeably quiet over the past few minutes. As if by instinct, the girls turned on him.

'What about you, Archie?' they said at the same time.

Archie sat with his head against the window. He didn't dare tell them about the odd spidery kind of thing he'd seen hovering over Daisy, or the ghost of Cain. He turned and faced the girls, his face ashen.

'Yeah,' he said, shakily. 'I've dreamt of this flood and this Ancient Woman on three occasions—just like you.'

The girls gasped.

Archie stared at them, his eyes red and brimming with tears. Then he dropped his head.

'Thing is, in each of my dreams, it's me who kills her.'

SEVENTEEN

OVERCOAT

'Look. I know it's odd, really odd, but they are only dreams,' Isabella said. 'They're just part of our minds worrying about stuff in the night. They're not real—however extraordinary.'

'But if you don't think there's any truth in it,' Archie said, 'why did you go to such lengths to make the barometer and the storm glass? I mean, you must have believed there was something to it.'

Isabella thought for a moment. 'Sue had had a similar dream and it sounded like mine and I wanted to try something—anything, I suppose.'

'So, if this is a coincidence,' Archie said, 'do you think there's a storm demon out there putting dreams in our heads?'

'Don't be silly. Of course I don't, Archie. I never said that.' She drew her fists up to her temples. 'I don't know what to think. It's just a stupid dream.'

Daisy, who had been pretty quiet, suddenly piped up. 'Why don't we look at the storm glass? Maybe it will tell us something about this rain we've dreamt about. Where did you put it?'

Isabella stood up and plucked it out of the grate of the

old Victorian fireplace. She placed it against the wall on top of the mantelpiece.

The children stared at it, as though it held the answers to their problems. 'It's still cloudy with loads of little stars,' Archie said, his voice a little glum.

'But is there any change from before?' Daisy continued, now focusing more intently on the glass tube. 'Blimey, those little stars are moving quickly, aren't they? What does it mean?'

'Daisy,' Isabella sighed, 'the thing is, I don't really know what it means or what it's supposed to show. I don't know enough about it.' Isabella went back to her area and began to gather her things.

Daisy concentrated hard on the storm glass and, as she stared, she could see hundreds of tiny stars darting around at high speed. 'Just out of interest,' she said, 'for simple-minded people like me who never saw it before, what was it like when you began this mad project?'

'Cloudy,' Archie said.

'Thanks Archie, very helpful. Well, as far as I can tell, it's pretty zooming,' she said. 'It's way more than cloudy.'

Isabella strode over and stared at the storm glass. 'Nothing there,' she announced. 'Come on you two; time to get your things. You've got this big match to play, or had you forgotten?'

The twins returned to their areas and grabbed their sports bags.

'And we need to get a move on,' Isabella said, looking at her watch. She picked up the storm glass and slipped it into her pocket. 'My guess is that we're being freaked out by this strange weather and our brains are picking up some sort of random signal that's making us react oddly.'

Daisy frowned at Isabella. 'I realise I don't know about these things, but if I were you, I'd keep a close eye on that stormy glass thing-a-me.'

They filed down the stairs and found Mrs Pye at the bottom. 'Good luck you lot,' she said, giving each of them a hug. 'Goals galore for you, pretty Daisy, saves for you, brave Archie. And as for you, Isabella, just make sure you don't go running onto the pitch beating up the umpire—you heard what that headmaster said.' She gave her a nudge. 'Now, away with you—and I expect to hear heroic tales when you get back.'

THE CHILDREN HAD BARELY STEPPED out of the door when the familiar voice of Old Man Wood stopped them short.

'Best of luck today, little ones,' he called out. 'There's one heck of a big dark cloud over our heads. If lightning starts, remember to run for cover. You understand?' He was quite sure they weren't paying him the slightest bit of attention. 'Do you recall that ditty we used to sing about different types of cloud? Now, how did it go? Ah yes:'

High and light, no need for flight.
Low and grey—stay away.
Grey and round—rain around ...
But black with a crack ... is the devil's smack.

'So I'll see you early afternoon. Best of luck, Daisy. Your school is relying on you, you heard what Solomon said.'

The children waved.

'His stupid poems,' Daisy said quietly.

'Oh, *wait!*' Old Man Wood exclaimed, almost forgetting himself. 'Did any of you leave a coat? Found it on the floor of the corridor.' A large overcoat dangled over his arm. 'Nice coat too, with an interesting pattern on the lining. Sure I've seen it somewhere before—reminds me of something.' Old Man Wood scratched his head and then pinched his nose while he tried to remember.

Archie missed a step and stumbled, just righting himself before his head hit the floor.

Old Man Wood saw. 'Is it yours, Archie? Looks a touch big for you, mind. But you might have mistakenly brought it home last evening.'

Archie doubled back, his body trembling. Without looking at Old Man Wood he inspected the coat and ran his hand inside one of the pockets. His hair almost stood on end.

'Back in a second,' he yelled behind him as he flew up the stairs.

Archie ran into the attic room and spied the glass of water on the side. It was tinged slightly blue—exactly as he'd left it. In one movement he grabbed it, and in the next and in one gulp, he drained it. He wiped his mouth with his sleeve, and ran down the staircase.

'Everything alright, Archie?' Old Man Wood asked.

'Fine,' Archie answered, gulping as though a burp was about to burst out. 'Forgot something, that's all.'

'Jolly good,' Old Man Wood said. 'Your coat?'

'Oh, yeah, it belongs to a friend. Must have taken it by mistake.'

'Big fella, is he?'

'I suppose,' Archie said, as casually as he could.

Old Man Wood handed him the coat. But as he did so the ruby-encrusted knife slipped out of the pocket and fell with a clatter onto the paving slabs.

'A knife, Archie? You know you shouldn't carry one of those around with you at school.'

Archie's heart skipped a beat. 'Don't worry. It's only plastic—a stage knife, you know... for acting,' he smiled badly. 'The bloke who owns the coat is the lead part, I think—in the school play; Macbeth or something.'

He bent down, narrowly beating Old Man Wood to it.

'He certainly has an interesting taste in knives,' Old Man Wood commented, raising his eyebrows at Archie. 'Well on you go, young Arch, and remember to save those footballs.'

Archie smiled and ran on, not a full sprint, but not a jog either, to catch up with the girls. As he ran, his heart was thumping like a huge bass drum and his head buzzed with a mixture of dread and excitement.

Old Man Wood waved at the children until they had slipped away down the track out of eyesight. Now wasn't that funny, Archie behaving like that. That wasn't a plastic knife, not a bit of it, not in a million years. He knew how to tell a cheap knife from a proper knife, because he knew all about knives. How, he didn't remember, but he felt it in his bones.

He'd certainly taught Archie about them, how to make one, the different shapes and handles and what they were used for and what certain carvings and notches meant. Not only that, but he'd shown him how to throw them as well, how to understand the balance and how the weight would determine the revolutions and power in the throw.

He mulled this over, wondering what light might develop in his brain on the subject. No, nothing there again—just a deep penetrating feeling, like toothache. But the instant he saw the knife drop from the coat, he knew it was a beauty; a knife worthy of a powerful man with a large hand. And from the clinking noise it made on the floor, he would have bet a trinket or two it was made from silver and hard steel and, from the way the light reflected through the stone and diffused onto the Yorkstone slabs, he'd have taken another wager the knife's stones were special—most likely rubies and pink diamonds. Plastic, never. He shook his head. There was no way in the world it was plastic.

So what was Archie doing with it—and what was it about that funny old coat with the curious markings?

Old Man Wood turned his head up to the sky and breathed in deeply. How dark was that cloud? Too dark by his reckoning, and growing. It now filled the sky from the moors to the dales like a great swollen bladder. It reminded him of Archie's horrid, swollen, purple and black eye from the beginning of the year when a fishing hook caught him on the flesh just beneath his eyeball.

He had a bad feeling about the cloud from deep in his gut, and this feeling hadn't been helped by the images from the infernal nightmares he'd been having—every night—for the past week.

He rubbed his chin. If he wasn't mistaken, they were about his past, fragments from years ago. Stuff he could never remember, not at his age. Things like flooding and a desperate old woman, ghosts and odd spidery creatures that looked like jellyfish with blue flames in their bellies. And a cave? Now that one had seemed more familiar but … the problem was, there were just so many "buts".

Old Man Wood brushed a speck of dust off his coat. Nothing I can do about it now, he told himself, whatever it means.

He shut the door and his mind wandered back to the knife and the coat, as if the subject wanted to spend a little more time in his head.

What had surprised him was his reaction to the pattern on the lining of the coat. It had taken his breath away. Why? Was it the pattern? No, it couldn't be. He'd seen thousands and thousands of patterns of snakes and trees or snakes slithering up poles and the like all the way through his long life.

But why did this particular one send such a shiver up his spine? Why did it make him feel a little weak and thrilled at the same time? Was it was something to do with the fabric? Maybe that was it.

He replayed his memory to the moment he saw the lining for the first time. There it was—that curious feeling again. It was as if the snake had actually moved, had slithered up into the tree right there on the fabric itself. He shook his head, stood up and paced uneasily around the room.

And he'd noted the buttons too, with a matching crest of a snake winding through the branches of a tree.

Suddenly, an idea shot into his head and it filled his entire body with a bolt of electricity as though in some way it was inspired by a greater power. 'My goodness me,' he said. 'But it can't be.'

He made his way into the sitting room and sat down in his large, rather worn armchair which faced the fire. He cupped his face in his large, leathery, old hands and stared at the embers.

'What if the fabric isn't actually from Earth?'

He felt dizzy. Now this was bringing back the past. He'd never seen a fabric that had the ability to change shape before here on Earth, but if he remembered correctly this could be something from one of those other places. And if it bore the marks of the snake and the tree, then could it possibly be from the Garden of Eden?

A surge of energy coursed through his body, making him feel strong for a second or two. He hadn't felt this for years. Another thought hit him. Perhaps it wasn't the Garden of Eden. What if it was the other place—the place he'd deliberately cast out of his mind?

Old Man Wood stood up, narrowly avoiding cracking his head on one of the lower supporting beams of the house.

'Time to study those old carvings,' he said, as he headed up to his bedroom.

EIGHTEEN

KEMP TRIES TO MAKE UP

Today was the last day before the long half term break. Not only was there the excitement of the big football match but the school had laid on exhibitions, a concert, and a play so that almost half the children in the school were, in one way or another, involved in the celebrations. Aside from their earlier worries, the girls had a spring in their step as they headed down the steep track.

At the top of the hill, the banks at either side of the track gradually increased in height. As the children descended, it was like a steep gully, as if the lane had been cut out of the hillside by a giant digger. Overhead, the tree branches provided a thick canopy of leaves, like a covered tunnel, all the way from the top to the bottom.

On a clear day, sunlight flickered through, and when that happened, it was as if glitter was sprinkling down upon them. Today it was almost pitch black and the tree roots that supported the bank twisted through the rock and soil, reaching out at them like the arms and legs of decaying corpses.

The children were used to it; after all, it was their everyday walk to school. So the idea of it being in any way scary was beyond them. But Sue called it "the big graveyard ditch" and she was petrified of it. She was right in one respect; it took the water off the hill and even in the driest summer a constant trickle dribbled down from the moors at the top, to the river below.

As the children walked down the hill, the girls asked Archie about the coat.

He shrugged and told them that it was Kemp's dad's old coat—he must have got it muddled up in the cloakroom. But his heart was thudding in his chest and his brain worked overtime as he tried to remember what had happened during the night.

The girls didn't bother to question him further. For someone as disorganised as Archie it was quite believable that he might have picked up the wrong coat. He was often turning up in strange woolly hats or with pens and pencils that he'd mistakenly pocketed.

A third of the way down the tree-covered lane they stopped by a vast old oak with a huge bough that leaned over the road. Daisy climbed nimbly up the steep, high bank using the large roots as hand grips. At the top she uncoiled the rope that was tied around the middle of the huge branch and tossed down the slack.

Although he didn't feel quite in the mood, Archie went first. He ran up the hill and, as he took off, he climbed up the rope until his feet settled on the large knot at the bottom. Then he swung rapidly backwards and forwards, the wind rushing through his hair. It was exhilarating. As the rope slowed, he climbed down, running to a stop.

Isabella went next. Her way was to sit on the knot and swing gently through the air. Finally it was Daisy's turn. She climbed up the rope and asked Archie to pull her up the hill as far as he could. She soared through the air, her hair flying behind her, until she was almost horizontal with the bank and crashing into the canopy.

She flew backwards, screaming in delight, and then she soared forward before bashing into the bank on the left and twisting to the one on the right. They laughed at her recklessness.

Daisy desperately wanted another go, but Isabella put her foot down. 'We'll be late. But I promise we'll have a go on the way back.'

'Oh sure,' Daisy said, sulking, as she tucked the rope through and around a protruding root. 'I bet we'll forget, or you'll be too tired, or it'll be too dark or some other rubbish excuse.'

'Daisy,' Isabella replied, 'it isn't possible for *you* to forget the rope swing.'

When they came to the rickety wooden bridge, they peered over the railings at the water beneath that had journeyed from the heart of the moors.

Archie was determined to see a fish but was dragged away by Isabella who pointed out how, in the strange light, the school tower to the left looked quite enormous compared to the tiny wooden boathouse at the foot of the hills by the river. She wondered if the boat in there was still sound and made a mental note to enquire about it with Mr Pike. It would make a great trip out before the weather turned.

The children skipped across the lush velvety green football pitch with big, bold, alternating stripes and tattoo-like fresh white markings burnt into the turf. Down each side were posts with safety ropes attached to keep the spectators at bay. On each corner, slightly recessed, was the headmaster's pride and joy, the moveable floodlight towers in a crisscross of metal thirty feet high. They were the first school in the North (as Mr Solomon often repeated) who played football when they liked and cricket when they liked.

Daisy ran ahead, pretending to do skills and dummies, commentating about the goals she was going to score all the way to the steep set of steps up to the school buildings.

AS ARCHIE FOLLOWED Daisy into their brightly lit form room, the rows of incandescent lights glaring down upon them, Daisy immediately rushed over to join a group of girls at the front. Archie noticed Kemp sitting quietly at his desk, reading a book. Let sleeping dogs lie, he thought, especially unpredictable dogs. So, without any fuss, he made his way to his desk at the other side of the room.

Archie draped the coat over the back of his chair, sat down and put his head in his hands. He desperately tried to remember what the ghost had said: a meeting, something about the strength of a lion and the courage of a horse and, after writing it down, he realised that it had to be the other way round. This, and that he'd be saved, but saved from what?

Hadn't he agreed to join him or enter into a partnership or something nuts like that? It didn't make any sense but, and it was a huge BUT, he was in possession of the ghost's coat and dagger, here, in this very room. So it couldn't be *that* nuts.

He pulled out a piece of paper and nibbled on the end of a pencil. "Possible options for the meeting place", he wrote.

Was it down by the boatyard or up by one of the big willow trees? He wrote both down but shook his head. No. Neither of those options rang true. He wondered if it was the alley above the football pitch and he wrote that down as well.

He underlined it a couple of times and leaned back in his chair. Yes, that one rang a bell. But, what on earth was he going to do about it?

His thoughts were interrupted by a friendly, but slightly painful, wallop on his shoulders. It was Gus Williams who had bounced into the room. 'Morning Archie. You're not by any chance writing a "to-do" list, are you?' he said, with a laugh that showed off his extensively large teeth.

Archie smiled. 'No, don't be ridiculous.'

Gus read the list. 'Lost something?'

'Nah. Just trying to remember a dream.'

'Oh, well that's OK,' Williams said, cheerily. 'So long as it wasn't a very big and complex dream?'

'Well, as a matter of fact, yes, it was.' Archie looked up, smiling. 'Now go away and leave me to think.'

'News alert!' Williams announced to the room, his grin

almost completely covering his face. 'Archie de Lowe is thinking! Give him plenty of room, oxygen at the ready.' Gus leant down again. 'Next you'll be telling me Daisy's caught the same bug,' he whispered. 'Good luck!'

He smiled and sprang off like a big, energetic, happy puppy to his desk at the back of the room.

Kemp had been listening to Archie's conversation with Gus with great interest. He smiled. Archie was completely hopeless at organising himself; he would bet money Archie had forgotten something again. And by the looks of it, it was more important than usual.

He stood up quietly and headed over to him. 'Morning Archie, everything cool?'

Archie groaned. First Gus, now Kemp. What did *he* want? 'Not really, Kemp,' he said, coldly. 'I had a very, very bad night.'

'Oh yeah?' Kemp replied as he perched on his desk.

'Yes. If you must know, I had a couple of very odd experiences. But I can't remember either of them.'

Kemp burst out laughing. 'Want to talk about it?'

Archie stared at Kemp's face and noted what a big nose he had and his ridiculously square jaw. 'I told you; I'm not talking to you after what you did yesterday.'

Kemp sighed. 'OK. You win. Look, I had a think, and last night I decided that I'm going to change. No more jokes on people. I promise—'

'You said that before—and immediately let me down. In fact you lied to me. Christ, Kemp, I had to own up for your stupidity and you made me feel like an idiot. Lucky Isabella didn't believe me.'

Kemp sucked in his cheeks. 'Look Archie, I've told Mason and Wilcox I don't want to be part of the gang. When I'm with them, I act like a... like a moron. I don't know what comes over me and, bottom line is that I don't want to hang out with them anymore.'

Kemp noted Archie's look of disgust. 'If you don't believe me, go and ask them,' he continued. 'Go on, they're over there in the corner, playing on their phones like two happy little bunnies. Seriously, I don't want to hurt anyone anymore. I really don't.' He dropped his voice and briefly stole a look over his shoulder. 'I want to be your friend.'

'Blimey, Kemp, this isn't the time. Right now, I've literally got a nightmare on my hands. And anyway, you're going to have to prove it. I'm not going to trust you until I know you mean what you say.'

'What do you want me to do? I promise I won't be nasty to either of your sisters. I'm going to put that behind me. I won't even speak to them if you don't want me to.'

'But I bet you've already arranged with your Chitbury mates that Daisy's going to get a kicking—haven't you?'

Kemp winced. 'Well, there's not much I can do about that now, is there?'

'And the only reason you're being Mr Nice about it is because if they kick her out of the game we'll lose and she won't play in the team after half term, leaving room for someone else. And that person will probably be you.'

Kemp's expression had changed. 'You know what, Archie,' he spat. 'I meant what I said. Just throw it back in my face, why don't you.'

On hearing raised voices, Mason and Wilcox instantly towered over Archie. Wilcox, with one huge hand, picked him up by his collar. 'Back off boys, let him be,' Kemp ordered. The muscle sloped reluctantly back to their desks.

The classroom had fallen silent but Archie wasn't finished. 'See what I mean, Kemp,' Archie fumed. 'If you want to be my friend you've got a long way to go. I swore on my life that I wouldn't tell anyone about the barometer and I kept my word. You... well, frankly, you disgust me.'

Archie was pretty astonished the words had spilled out of his mouth and for a moment the classroom stopped and stared at him.

NINETEEN

ARCHIE SPILLS IT OUT

The spell was broken by the bell and, moments later, the upright figure of Mr Bellwood came striding in, twiddling the ends of his moustache.

'As you know,' he boomed, 'there is no class-work today.' He stared around the room. 'Gosh,' he continued in a softer voice. 'Silence! Oh, hallelujah!'

The classroom remained silent.

'Have I missed something?' Bellwood continued, as his eyes flashed from pupil to pupil trying to make out what had caused this unusual lack of noise. 'No? Very well.' He peered at his notes. 'Our school day looks like this; footie for those playing footie. Can I have hands up for those who are likely to be watching.' The whole class except for Kemp, Mason and Wilcox thrust their hands into the air.

'Excellent. I take it you have other things to be getting on with, Mason?'

Mason grunted an unintelligible response.

'You know, you three aren't the best advert for this school and today is what we like to call an "open day".' Bellwood said.

Kemp stole a glance at Archie, who was still looking troubled. Just beyond him was Williams who was smiling his big toothy smile straight back at him and raising his eyebrows.

Was Williams trying to provoke him with his eyebrows? He put his hand up.

'Yes, Kemp.'

'Actually, I'm watching the football as well.'

'A change of heart, huh, Kemp.'

'You could say that.'

'Well, I'm glad to hear it. So, Wilcox and Mason, just you two. Correct?' They nodded dumbly. 'In that case, you will report to Mr Pike in the Maintenance Department. There are leaves to sweep up and fences to paint.' On cue, the class burst out laughing. Mr Bellwood waited until the noise was bearable. 'Come on. Simmer down. Mr Pike is expecting you to be ready for work at kick off time, which will be at eleven o'clock precisely.'

Mr Bellwood stuck his nose in the air and twitched his moustache. It was a signal that he was going to say something profound. 'Now, about the weather. There is a rather large cloud brrrewing right above us,' and as he said this he rolled the 'r' rather dramatically and then repeated the word, 'brrrewing.'

'To put your minds at rest, our headmaster has been in touch with the Met Office to find out if this might be a cause for concern. I am happy to report that, as far as they know, there are no serious worries. This morning and this afternoon, there is a high chance that we may get a little wet, indeed there may even be a possibility of a heavy downpour. Nevertheless, all school activities are to go on as scheduled.

'Daisy de Lowe, please remove that lipstick from your desk. Now remember, class, just in case lightning strikes, what would be the best course of action to take? Anyone. Ah, yes, Alexander?'

'Put up your umbrella, Sir.'

'No, you do not, Alexander. And stop laughing. And Allen will you desist from flicking paper balls at Daisy please.' He glared at the boys, 'Umbrellas, as you know perfectly well, are for repelling water. I'm talking about lightning strikes.'

Bellwood raised his eyebrows in anticipation. 'Kemp, what would you do?'

'I'd get the hell out of there before I was shrivelled to a burnt crisp.'

The class laughed.

'Well, it's better than holding up an umbrella, but where would you go?'

Little Jimmy Nugent put up his hand.

'Yes, Nugent.'

'I've been told that if you get in a car the rubber tyres would earth the strike, wouldn't it, sir?'

Mr Bellwood clasped his hands together. 'Very good, Nugent, and you're absolutely correct. Either get indoors or hop in a car—'

'My granddad,' Nugent continued, 'got killed by a bolt of lightning in 1983, while walking his bull terrier called Plank—'

'Did he, Nugent?' Mr Bellwood sensed one of Nugent's stories coming on. 'How very fascinating. Perhaps you wouldn't mind telling me about it after half term.'

He turned back to the pupils. 'Now, class, do the best you can today and make us all proud, and have a safe half term. You are dismissed.'

THE PUPILS instantly divided into several small groups, except Archie who remained in his chair twiddling his pencil.

Kemp wandered over. 'Come on, Archie, it can't be that bad.'

'You have no idea. Really, you would never, ever believe me.'

'Try me.'

Archie exhaled loudly. 'OK,' he began. 'If you really want to know, I was visited in the night by something that, as far as I could tell, was a ghost.'

'A ghost?' Kemp chuckled. 'Really?'

'I knew you wouldn't believe me.'

Kemp eyed him suspiciously and raised his hands. 'Sorry. Don't worry about me... carry on.'

Archie rubbed his forehead. 'Well, this ghost promised me stuff if I met up with him.'

'Yeah? What did you say?'

'I kind of agreed. I mean, what would you do?

'I'd probably agree too,' Kemp said. 'Was it a nice ghost or a nasty ghost?'

'Bit of both, I think, although it was wielding a knife, but at the same time I'm pretty sure it wanted to help.'

'Well, that's alright,' Kemp said, sounding like an authority on the subject. 'So, it had a knife and it didn't kill you. That's a start—where were you going to meet up?'

'That's the problem, I can't remember. I thought it was a dream, so I agreed to everything, and said the first thing that came into my head.'

'So, what makes you think it wasn't a dream?'

Archie pointed at the coat. 'This.'

Kemp looked at it. 'An old overcoat! Bleeding heck, Archie.' Kemp wondered if Archie hadn't entirely lost his marbles.

'I know,' Archie said, realising it must sound idiotic, 'but I swear it's the same coat the ghost was wearing. Look at those buttons with the snake slipping up a tree.'

Kemp thrust out his jaw and furrowed his brow. 'How do you know it isn't Old Man Whatshisface's?'

'Old Man Wood,' Archie said. 'His name is "Old Man Wood".'

'Yeah right, chill your boots.' Kemp held the coat up in the air. 'I mean it's pretty big—about his size—are you sure he wasn't... giving it to you? You know, offloading it before he took it to the charity shop.'

'No, definitely not. Old Man Wood doesn't have that many clothes, certainly not an overcoat like this one. Anyway, there's more.'

'More? Great.'

Archie turned his head and indicated the cut on his chin. 'Look at this.' Kemp leant in. 'It's from the blade of the knife I was telling you about—'

'From the ghost?'

'Yes.'

Kemp inspected it. 'Nah, I don't believe you, you could have got that from a bramble or a branch when you ran to school yesterday.'

'Honest to God, it definitely arrived in the middle of the night.'

'You one hundred percent sure?'

Archie nodded.

'Ghosts don't carry things like knives or hit people,' Kemp guffawed. 'Everyone knows that.'

'This one did,' Archie said.

Kemp was trying not to laugh and only just managed to restrain himself. 'Don't get me wrong, Archie, but it doesn't stack up. Why would a ghost want to harm you?'

'To prove it was real, I suppose.' Archie felt in the coat pocket and slowly withdrew the knife, shielding it from prying eyes with his hands.

'Look.'

Kemp's eyes fell to the gap under the desk where Archie held the knife and he swore under his breath. 'Blimey Archie, that's a beauty.' Kemp could hardly prise his eyes away. 'So what did this ghost say?'

'That's where it gets a bit blurry,' Archie began. 'He said he was on a mission to save his mother, that she was going to die and that I had to help protect her at all cost.'

'Epic. Sounds good to me. I'd do anything to protect my mother.'

Archie realised he'd hit a raw nerve. 'Sorry, Kemp. I didn't mean—'

'Chill, Archie, I know you didn't. So what's in it for you?'

'Well, as I said, a partnership of some sort. I told you, I can't really remember. I'd find out at this meeting but,' Archie laughed and turned a little red. 'Thing is I think I said I'd meet him bang in the middle of the football match—not that I'd go anyway.'

Kemp chuckled. 'Your planning skills are very poor, Archie.'

Archie ignored him. 'Somewhere along the line, he was banging on about power and strength or something equally crazy. Oh, I can't remember.' He thumped the desk. 'Maybe it's a lack of sleep?'

Kemp was intrigued but also a little worried about his friend. It might be madness and completely made up, but you had to hand it to them, these de Lowes were nothing less than interesting.

Archie studied Kemp's face, and quickly reached a conclusion. 'You think it's bollocks, don't you?' He nestled his head in his hands. 'I've been suckered in, haven't I?'

'Probably your Old Man thingy playing a joke or something—'

'Or perhaps a hallucination from one of his strange apples—or another nightmare?' Archie added.

'Yeah,' Kemp said, as though it was perfectly normal. He'd heard about the old man's curious apple collection. 'Probably one of those—can't believe you didn't see it all along.' He slapped Archie on the back. 'You ought to be getting along, don't want to miss your warm-up.'

Archie cocked his head and looked at his watch. 'RATS! Is that the time?' He started gathering his bits together. 'Hey, Kemp, thanks for the chat—please don't think I've turned into a nutter—and promise me, you won't tell anyone about this?'

'You de Lowes are all nutters. But you, Archie, are the only one worth their salt.'

Archie noted the look in his eyes had gone cold. Maybe he was bored or had turned his thoughts to Daisy.

Archie ran to the door. 'See you later.'

'Yeah. Sure.'

KEMP SHOOK HIS HEAD. Those de Lowes are properly crackers. There's something distinctly odd, unsettling and eccentric about them. If it wasn't strange scientific experiments or an infatuation with ghosts or girls being brilliant at games designed for men, it was some other random thing, like extraordinary disorganisation, or manic recklessness.

Mr Bellwood re-appeared. 'Time to lock up the classroom,' he said. 'Please gather your things as it won't re-open until after half term. Make sure you take everything you need.'

Chairs scraped against the floor as the remaining students stood up. Kemp slipped into his overcoat and gathered the contents of his desk, dropping them haphazardly in his bag. He tucked in his chair and headed towards the door with the others.

'Kemp,' Mr Bellwood called out, 'haven't you forgotten something?'

Kemp looked puzzled.

'Your coat?'

'Oh. Yeah. Sorry, wasn't thinking.' It was a little odd that Bellwood hadn't spotted he was wearing his own coat in the first place. Oh well, he'd take it for Archie, and give it back later. He returned to the chair, picked up the coat and put it on over the one he already had on. Then he saw the slip of paper on the desk in Archie's scrawny handwriting. Kemp scanned it for a second and noticed the underlined location. It must be where he was meeting this so-called ghost. Kemp read it again, folded it up and put it in his pocket.

'Jolly good,' said Mr Bellwood running his hand over his chin. 'Now, let's go and watch that football match, shall we.'

TWENTY

A STORM IS COMING

A rchie tore around the corridor when he almost collided with Daisy. She was talking with her girlfriends.

Archie reddened. 'Daisy, er sorry, but shouldn't we be getting ready?'

'Oh, I thought we had plenty of time.' She studied her watch. 'It's only just gone ten—we've got at least half an hour, haven't we?'

Archie reddened even more and shook his wrist. Stupid watch. 'Yes. Sure. Right, yeah—of course, er... whatever.' It wasn't going well. Why did he feel so intimidated around groups of girls? Individually they were fine but a pack of them scared him to death. 'Look, I'm going to see if I can find Isabella. Want to join me?'

'No. Not really.'

Archie's face went purple. 'Please,' he squeaked.

Daisy caught his eye, turned and addressed the girls. 'OK, ladies,' she said, 'I'm off to do battle with those big, bad, beastly boys and kick the house down.' They shrieked their approval. 'Wish me luck.'

Each of the girls made a big play of kissing her on her cheek and then broke into a chant;

'GO, GO Daisy de Lowe!
GO, GO Daisy de Lowe!
GO, GO Daisy de Lowe!
Go Daisy! Go Daisy! GO Daisy!'

Daisy put one hand in the air as she waltzed away, her other fluffed up her wavy blonde hair and she wiggled her hips.

Archie put his head down, trying to ignore his sister, although it was virtually impossible. How would anyone believe Daisy was such a talented footballer when she hung out with the "chicks" and did idiotic dances like this?

As the twins turned the corner the chanting changed to the old *Queen* anthem:

'D-D-L,
D-D-L,
D-D-L
SHE WILL, SHE WILL ROCK YOU!'

'You coping, Arch?' she said. 'You're very glum-faced.'

'Moron-faced, more like.'

'Oh no, what have you done now?'

Archie groaned. 'Oh, Daisy. I think I've done something insanely foolish. I told Kemp about my nightmare. He must think I've totally lost the plot. I don't know why I did it. He'll probably tell everyone, like he usually does.' Archie caressed his temples with his fingers.

'Yup. It's social suicide.' Daisy pinched him playfully on the cheek. 'When will you ever learn? He's a jerk and you're best off keeping well away.'

They found Isabella in the physics lab with Sue, running over an experiment, their heads buried in some calculations.

Daisy was full of bounce. 'Ready to go, girls?'

Her jollity didn't really have the same effect on the science students.

'Daisy,' Isabella said, in her most serious tone. 'I want you to wear these, on your boots.'

Daisy looked at her in amazement. 'On my bits?'

'Don't be so stupid. Your football boots.'

She fingered the rubbery, gooey material. 'What is it?'

Isabella peeled off her lab glasses. 'In short, it's a de-energising unit we've created.'

'A what-erising-humit?' Daisy said. 'Lord above, why?'

'Just in case, that's why.'

'I don't understand?'

'Just do it, will you,' Isabella demanded. 'One for each boot. You too, Archie.'

Archie studied it. 'What's it for?'

Isabella squealed. 'In case either of you gets hit by lightning. It might help, that's all.'

Archie stuck the strips to the soles of his boots. 'Aren't you're taking this a bit far—'

A huge roll of thunder shook the building. The windows rattled and the children's hair stood on end. They looked at each other.

Isabella raised her eyebrows. 'We're not, Archie. These could save your life—'

'Where's that storm glass thing?' Daisy cut in, her tone serious. 'I want to see what it's doing.'

'It's next to Isabella's desk,' Sue replied.

Daisy picked it up, studied it and quickly put it down again. 'I don't mean to sound rude, sciencey nerd folk, but have you analysed this lately?'

Isabella marched over as though it was a complete waste of time. 'What?' she snapped.

'This test tube. Have any of you noticed a) how hot it is, and b) that it's literally crammed full of crystals moving very, very fast.'

Isabella grabbed it, stared at it for a moment and laid it down on the bench. 'I have no idea what you're talking about, Daisy. Yes, it's a little warm—but so what? As I said, I'm not sure how it works.'

'Well, you two know what you're doing. But I'd keep an eye on that if I were you.' Daisy stretched out the gooey strip. 'Can I put this in my hair?'

'Please, Daisy,' Isabella said. 'It must be on the bottom of your shoe. Attach it on the underside of your boot using the Velcro.' Isabella sounded a little irritated by the intrusion. 'Now go away—run and get changed or you'll be late.'

Daisy skipped off, singing to herself and punching the air.

As her footsteps receded down the corridor, Archie picked up the storm glass. Immediately he put it down again. 'Woah! It really is hot, seriously. Touch it.'

'I've just done that,' Isabella said.

Sue put her finger to the glass. 'OW! Scorching!' she sucked her fingers. 'Bells, it's steaming.'

'A mild expulsion of water vapour, that's all,' Isabella said, nervously.

'You think so?' They started backing away.

'No, not necessarily.'

The test tube was beginning to glow, steam pouring out of the top.

'Has anyone added anything to it?' Isabella asked.

Archie and Sue shook their heads.

The activity in the test tube increased. They could hear the crystals popping against the glass.

'Get out!' Isabella yelled. 'Crickey. It's going to blow!'

They ran for the door and shut it firmly behind themselves and threw themselves to the floor. Seconds later, the storm glass exploded, sending fragments to every corner of the room.

Sue shivered. 'What does it mean?'

'It means we were right all along.' Isabella's voice quaked. 'For, here above us, beginneth the storm from hell.'

'It couldn't be a mistake, could it?' Sue said, desperation in her voice.

'Possibly,' Isabella replied, as another roll of thunder boomed and shook the walls. 'But I very seriously doubt it.'

'RIGHT!' Isabella said, as she barged past Sue. 'Out of my way!'

'Where are you off to now?'

'To see Solomon and have it out with him. This time properly.'

'Oh no,' Sue said remembering the last time she'd seen Isabella like this. She'd torn into Mrs Douglas, the science teacher, and ended up being severely reprimanded—and very nearly expelled.

As Isabella marched off, her eyes hard and her chin up, Sue had to run alongside to keep up. They wove through the maze of old school buildings, up worn stone stairs and down dark corridors, until they reached a large, dark brown, studded wooden door that sat below a striking Gothic arch. Opposite this was a small, elegant courtyard with a fountain, like a bird bath, in the middle.

Isabella thumped on the door, the noise echoing back at them. 'He must be in,' Isabella said. She turned the handle of the door. It creaked.

'You can't just let yourself in,' Sue whispered.

'Watch me—I'll wait for him inside. Then he can't get away from me.'

'You're being ridiculous—'

'Now then,' said the familiar voice of Mr Solomon as his head appeared around the door. He pulled it open and peered over the top of his glasses. 'Isabella, Sue, how nice to see you.' He smiled a thin and rather fake smile as he studied their faces. 'Is everything alright—what can I do for you?'

Inside, Isabella saw books piled up on tables and crammed into shelves from the floor to the ceiling and stuffed into every nook and cranny of the room. Old reading lamps offered light to large leather armchairs and exercise books with piles of marking were stretched out across the floor. Curiosities and portraits of headmasters dotted the walls.

This room of learning had the immediate effect of dampening her temper.

Solomon caught her staring and invited them in. 'Can I get you both anything—a cup of tea, perhaps?'

Isabella hesitated. 'No, thanks.' She turned to Sue as if for encouragement. 'I'll, er, get straight to the point if I may. You have to call off the football match.'

'Whatever for?' the headmaster replied. 'You're not still worried about this storm?'

Isabella reddened a little. 'Yes, sir. I'm not only worried about it; I'm petrified about it. You see, I ran some programmes on global weather data with specifics exactly like those we have above us, and then I did another experiment which confirmed my suspicions—'

'How fascinating,' said Mr Solomon with a plastic smile. 'Tell me about it?'

'Well, I built a storm glass—and it has just blown up—'

'A storm glass?' Solomon interrupted. 'A 17th century version of the weather forecast?' Solomon laughed dryly. 'I haven't heard of one of those since I was a student. In fact, I'm sure we had one here once upon a time. It was in a cabinet—as a curiosity. I'll have to dig it out.'

Isabella frowned. Solomon knew about storm glasses. She felt a rush of uncertainty.

'You're concerned about this horrid cloud again, aren't you Isabella,' Solomon said, gently, noting that he'd unsettled her.

She nodded.

'Well, rest assured. I am too.'

'You are?'

'Indeed. In fact I have just this very minute put the phone down from a conversation with a senior forecaster at the Met Office. According to them, there's little to worry about. It's a localised cloud—at worst we may hear several growls of thunder and see a few flashes of lightning and perhaps experience some heavy rain, but nothing unusual for the time of year. And they assured me that it was unlikely to break until this afternoon. Satisfied?'

'But—'

'There you have it, Isabella. I'm afraid there's nothing more to say about the matter. The match is on and the other performances will continue as planned.' His tone changed. 'I am particularly busy at the moment organising today's celebrations before the start of the match, so please don't pester me with this again. You should know by now that I have everyone's best interests at heart. Safety, as you are well aware, is my number one priority.'

Isabella stared at the headmaster. He wasn't telling the truth one bit—she could smell it. 'Can I ask who you spoke to at the Met Office, sir?'

Solomon paused and glared at her. 'If you must know, it was a man by the name of Mr Fish.'

With that he ushered them out of the door and shut it firmly behind him.

Solomon leant on the oak door and listened as their footsteps receded down the corridor. Then he let out a sigh. Had she believed him? He couldn't be sure. It was hard to read her expression, although he noted there was more of a frown on her face than before.

Why did she keep coming back to him about the storm? Did she really believe there was going to be a disaster? If she did, he thought, it was very over the top.

Solomon picked up his schedule folder and sat down in one of the leather armchairs. Her persistence was admirable, even if it was misplaced. No, no. Nothing was going to stop today going ahead, not a big storm or even a few drops of rain.

Goodness me, he thought, this is Yorkshire, the finest county in all of England—God's own county they called it— where thunder and lightning went hand in hand with the rough landscapes of the moors and dales.

These kids were getting too soft.

He chuckled to himself. Met Office? He couldn't think

what had made him come up with that nonsense. He simply knew that the only way he'd be able to stop her in her tracks was to throw something scientific back at her.

But why Mr Fish? It was an implausibly good name for a weatherman. In any case, he had a busy morning ahead; press turning up, television and newspapers, new parents and old, and this was his big—and last—chance to showcase everything he had done over the past twenty-five years. The crowning day of his headship.

He busied himself sorting out the place names for the banquet later on in the old school chamber. It was an evening he'd anticipated for years—and wouldn't it be sweeter still if they won the football.

How he hoped like mad that sister of hers, Daisy, would play her heart out again. What a player! He'd never seen the like. She was George Best and Pele and Ronaldo blended into one slender pop-tart of a girl—brave as a soldier, tough as leather and as quick and slippery as a salmon.

He sighed and shook his head before returning to the matter of wondering who he should sit next to. Geraldine Forbes. Yes, perfect. The star of Summerdale, the TV soap actress famed for her gritty Yorkshire one-liners, but in reality she was a delightful, attractive lady, who had simply the most beautiful green eyes he'd ever seen and lips as full as cushions.

He pictured it in his mind; the hall decorated to the nines in the school's light blue and scarlet colours, bright candles accentuating the Gothic arched windows and the trophies and cups in gold and silver from the vaults sparkling in the light. Magnificent!

And afterwards, he'd make his speech of retirement and receive warm, generous and heartfelt thanks from those whose lives he had touched. Yes, he mused. It was to be his swan song and nobody, certainly not Isabella de Lowe, was going to stop it.

And then he laughed even harder, his mood turning from happy to jovial. Mr Fish. Ah yes, he thought. There really had been a weather forecaster called Mr Fish. Wasn't he the one who told the nation there was no storm coming shortly before the devastating storms way back in the nineteen eighties?

Solomon laughed out loud and wiped his brow. Now won't that be hilarious if Isabella rings up the Met Office and asks for Mr Fish.

Whatever will they think?

TWENTY-ONE

ON THE WAY TO THE GAME

'Sue, we need a plan,' Isabella said. 'Solomon clearly doesn't want to know, so we're going to have to either disrupt the match or figure out how to get away—'

Sue couldn't really face direct action. 'Away would be best—'

Isabella was on a roll. 'If I can get Arch and Daisy over the bridge, then I think we'll be fine. When we get to the lane, the canopy of the tunnel will protect us. It's you I'm worried about.'

'*Me?*'

'Yes, you.' Isabella confirmed. 'How are you going to get out of here? You'll need to get home fast. Have you ever driven a car?'

'No. Stop being ridiculous—'

'I'm not. You could steal one.'

Sue glared at Isabella who shrugged back. 'Look, Bells, I'll think of something, OK.'

'Well thinking isn't good enough,' Isabella snapped back. 'You need a plan. Why don't you come back with us!'

'I can't. My mum wants me home.'

'Well, in that case, start engaging that brain of yours.'

As the two girls trudged slowly back from the science

laboratories in silence they could feel the buzz of the crowd making its way down towards the bridge.

'Why do I feel so edgy about this match?' Isabella said as a couple of boys ran past nearly knocking her over. 'What if Daisy gets a huge kicking and can't run and they lose and then the storm breaks and she can't get home? And what about Archie? His mind seems to be all over the place, have you seen him? He looks sick, poor boy. I'm worried he won't save a thing—he seems even more scatter-brained than usual.'

'Well it is the final—'

'I know that,' Isabella said. 'It's just that I've got an awful feeling deep inside me that everything's going to go wrong.' Isabella closed her eyes and shook her head. 'You know, I'm not sure I even like football—'

'Rubbish. You love it,' Sue replied, 'you're just a little jealous of Daisy like everyone else. Just look at Kemp. He's dying to play, but he sees Daisy as his barrier. He simply can't accept that girls can be superior in what is essentially a man's game. And Daisy's a babe too, so it's kind of doubly awful. And that, basically, is why he hates her so much.'

'But that still doesn't mean I like football—'

'Sure, but as you're her sister and sporty as a mole, it's natural for you to want her to do well.' Sue looked up at the sky and her heart seemed to skip a beat. She whistled. 'It really is the biggest, blackest, purplest, most evil-looking cloud I have ever seen, Bells. Even Solomon's hilarious floodlights are on. Every time I look up, my whole body starts shaking like a jelly.'

Isabella laughed nervously; she had the exact same feeling too.

Sue inspected her watch, 'We've got five minutes.' She slowed and grasped Isabella's arm as if setting herself up to say something important. She stared earnestly into her friend's eyes. 'Listen Bells,' she began, 'I've been meaning to tell you something important—'

'Really?' Isabella noticed that her friend had gone a little pale. 'Did you put the wrong mix in the storm glass—?'

'No. It's not about the storm glass... it's about—'

'So you DID—'

'Bells, I haven't touched it. In fact I'm quite sure it did what it did perfectly naturally.' Sue added. '*It's about you.* It's personal.'

'Me?' Isabella's mind whirled. 'You've got a boyfriend and you haven't told me—'

'For goodness' sake, you know full well I haven't got a boyfr—'

'OK, someone out there fancies *me*—'

'NO. Listen, Isabella—it's got absolutely nothing to do with boys—'

'You sure?'

'YES.'

'Good, they're such a waste of—'

'It's about *you*,' Sue said.

'Me? OMG. You... fancy... me?'

Sue shrieked. 'For crying out loud, Bells, NO! *Will you just let me speak.*' She took a deep breath trying to control herself. 'It concerns YOU, in fact it concerns all of you de Lowes. You, Archie and Daisy. All those things I told you about in my dream, well, there's more.'

'More?'

'Yes! The storm—the rain. You see, I'm pretty sure that in some way you're linked—'

Isabella was a bit confused. 'Us, linked?'

'Listen! SHUT UP, just for a minute.' Sue tried to compose herself. 'What I'm trying to say is that—'

Sue heard the long shrill of a whistle and the roar of the crowd. She followed Isabella's eyes towards the floodlit football pitch.

'OH NO! We're late!' Isabella cried and smacked her hand on her forehead. 'Your watch must be slow.'

Sue tapped the face of the dial and compared it to the clock on her mobile. 'Oh help! Sorry.' But already her friend had gone.

Isabella tore off down the track. 'Come on, keep up!' she

yelled over her shoulder as she took off down the shingle path. She felt Sue draw close. 'Look, tell me later! I mean it's not like it's life or death, is it?'

'But there are things you absolutely … must … know,' Sue said, her voice trailing off as she watched Isabella fly away from her at a simply extraordinary speed. In fact she couldn't remember seeing Isabella run faster in her whole life.

Sue felt sick, the moment lost. Everything in the last hour had started to confirm that what she had seen and heard and felt was going to come true. And if there was even the tiniest chance of this happening, then she absolutely had to tell Isabella everything.

She gritted her teeth. Why was it that every time she tried to say something to her, it never seemed quite the right time —as though there was some kind of force preventing it from happening?

Because the thing was, it really was about life or death.

KEMP REACHED into his pocket and pulled out the paper with the scribbles Archie had made. He wondered if what Archie had said had any truth in it. Nah, even though Archie banged on about it—as though it really mattered—he was probably nervous about the football or something.

Kemp dismissed it.

Then he wondered if it was an elaborate set-up for a fight with Gus Williams; the work of one of those girls—Daisy or Isabella de Lowe. He could smell them all over this.

Kemp leant against the stone wall outside the school hall and held the paper up. If that Old Man Wood, or whatever his name was, was old enough to play a prank on Archie and give him this old coat to wear, then what were the others capable of?

Maybe that's what they did up there in the hills; they dreamt up hilarious jokes because they had nothing else to do apart from tell stories and get freaked out by ghosts or the weather. He glanced up. It was ridiculously dark and it was a ridiculously huge cloud. He wondered if Isabella's experimental madness with barometers might have some foundation.

Kemp's eyes returned to the paper. He looked at the middle option, the one which was double-underlined. It read:

'Alleyway behind kissing houses.'

Kemp thought about it. It was a good choice. If he was to meet a knife-wielding ghost in a quiet spot which not too many people seemed to know about—but wasn't too quiet—AND with the advantage that you could get out of both ends —AND close enough to the playing fields for a quick getaway, it was a very good choice. He nodded. Clever old Archie, not just a scruffy little boy.

Then he clenched his fist. It was also the perfect place for a fight.

He remembered the look on Williams' face. He wanted a battle; he could see it in his eyes. Kemp twisted the fabric on Archie's coat; at least it was nice and strong—and light too. Another layer of protection—just what he'd need if Williams came at him.

Kemp sucked in his breath. That was it. They would fight —him and Gus Williams, the two of them—and he'd show him who was the strongest.

Yeah. Finally, Gus Williams was in for a beating like he'd never had before.

TWENTY-TWO

KEMP'S FIGHT

From the road above the football field, Kemp could see the crowd that lined the entire perimeter of the pitch. In places they stood four deep from the touchline. How could so many turn out for a silly game of football? But it was a hollow thought for, deep down, Kemp ached to be part of it—to have them cheer *him* on.

Anyway, he'd never play alongside that girl. That annoying, self-contented, plucky, idiotic Daisy de Lowe. It made him feel like puking just thinking about her, even if she was Archie's sister. That was unfortunate. Archie was kind of cool —laidback and easy. She was a show-off and she got under his skin like a pus-filled boil.

Anyway, his friends at Chitbury would have the last laugh with Daisy de Lowe in the second half. That was the plan.

He kicked a loose stone on the ground which skipped across the raised pebbles and smacked a small boy in the knee with a sickening thud. The boy collapsed in agony on the path as Kemp clenched his fist. Nice shot, he thought, wishing it had been de Lowe's knee.

Kemp looked down on the illuminated pitch. That's what they need out there, strength, leadership and character: me.

He walked further up the slope towards the houses which sat above the playing fields, slowly passing the crowd by until he was on his own high above the pitch. As he walked, he thought about how he could occupy himself over the break with his dreary aunt. Last time, he'd nearly died of boredom, being dragged around endless museums, antiques shops and flea markets. All he ever seemed to do was look at dead things; stuffed animals, bones, and fossils.

Sure, his aunt was kind and nice and tried hard for him, but she was almost too nice; too wet, too soppy.

The very thought of her made him cringe. He wondered whether, if his real parents had still been alive, they would have done things which were more fun—things he'd actually like, stuff they could get stuck into together, like sailing or mountaineering or holidaying abroad.

He smiled as he imagined a camping trip by the side of the river next to a large, warm fire and looking at the stars, his mother singing—her notes filling the air in a sort of magical way in time to the crackle of the burning wood. His father smiling at him proudly.

It was a fantasy, of course—the idyllic family life he'd never have—and every time he thought of it, it brought a tear to his eye. He couldn't remember if his mother used to sing to him or not and he had no idea what his parents looked like, but it felt right.

But how the reality hurt.

A long booming rumble distracted him. He spied another round pebble and took a mighty swipe with his heavy, black boot, connected sweetly—delighted with the way it flew through the air—skipped a couple of times and then, on the last bounce, it lifted quickly and seemed to whistle past the head of someone lurking by the lamppost near to the alleyway.

Oh hell! What was an old bloke doing standing over there in the first place? And he didn't even flinch. Bloody weirdo, probably missed him—must have missed him or he'd have been knocked out cold.

Kemp put his head down and sauntered on as if nothing had happened. He leaned against a tree. Maybe it was

Archie's ghost. He shook his head. Nah, more like a lucky escape.

A few paces on and Kemp noticed a figure just inside the entrance to the alleyway where moments earlier he was sure no one had been there.

His heartbeat quickened.

Kemp studied the person while pretending to read Archie's bit of paper. It was the same figure of a hunched old man, shrouded in a long, dark cloak, a thick scarf wrapped round his chin and nose and a kind of loose-fitting trilby hat pulled over his head in such a way that he couldn't make out a face. The figure was leaning on a stick just like a blind man.

Maybe *this* was Archie's ghost.

A roar rang out from the football pitch. Kemp turned his attention back to the game. He picked out the chant of 'Daisy de Lowe, GO, GO, GO'.

He smacked his fist into his hand. Typical. That idiotic girl must have scored.

Kemp watched as Chitbury kicked off and mounted another attack but after a couple of passes a shot flew high over the crossbar of goalkeeper Archie.

He reached into his pocket for his phone but, as he did, his hand touched a waxy piece of paper, like a sweet wrapper. With a frown on his face he tried to work out how it had got there. He smiled. Of course—it was from one of the packs of Haribos he'd stolen from Poppy—one of de Lowe's girlie friends—at break. He'd stuffed it in his mouth and nonchalantly tossed one of the wrappers into the headmaster's rose garden, where it stuck rather comically on a thorn and flapped in the breeze. But how come this one was folded?

Out of curiosity, he pulled it out, opened it up and stared at it. The sweet paper was covered in random scribbles like a pile of spaghetti plonked on a plate.

Just as he was about to trash it, a few of the lines looked familiar.

They're... faces.

Kemp scanned it and turned it sideways and round again.

And then three figures came out at him, like a "magic eye" puzzle revealing itself on the wrapper.

Then it struck him. It was the de Lowes! Absolutely, definitely, them; all smug and cheerful and ghastly. But, as he studied it, their faces seemed to melt away into the paper, like slush dripping through a gutter.

The next time he blinked, he was staring at nothing. Not a damn thing.

He turned the sweet paper over. It was blank.

Kemp felt a surge of excitement run through him. Was he seeing things? Was this some kind of joke?

He slapped his face and rubbed his eyes. Then he tried hard to remember what Archie had said, and scoured the area for a mysterious old man.

He looked at the wrapper again. It was changing gradually from white through grey to almost black, like the colour of the vast cloud above them. And then the words "HELP ME" started to appear in the form of tiny molten streaks of lightning on the paper, as if burning the words into it. He crumpled it up and thrust it in his overcoat pocket.

Kemp's heart beat so fast that for a moment he felt as if he would vomit.

Instinctively, he started walking, faster and faster; as if walking might make it go away.

A few minutes later, he skipped up the series of wide York-stone steps to street level and tentatively made his way towards the houses that leaned in as though they were kissing. He peered down the dark alleyway but as far as he could tell it was empty, save for the black wheelie bins guarding it like sentries.

As he took his first step under the buildings, he noted how the oak-beamed houses on either side all but touched each other as if challenging one another like fighters. It reminded him of his duel with Williams.

He spun towards the football pitch below him as he heard a groan from the crowd. He tried to figure out what was happening. Had Chitbury won a penalty? Certainly it looked as if there were bodies lying all over the pitch. And was that Archie staring up at him? He almost felt like waving.

Then Kemp turned and headed into the alleyway.

Halfway down, he slowed. He sensed something creeping up behind him.

His heartbeat quickened. There was no doubting it, someone was definitely there, someone really quiet. But who? This was strictly out of bounds—how would he explain himself? Was it a teacher? Nah, unlikely. They'd be watching the football match or making last minute plans for the performances later on. In any case they'd have said something.

Kemp thought quickly and it came to him: Williams. He almost said his name out loud. It must be Williams. It had to be. He was free this afternoon and it was exactly his style to creep up on people.

Kemp curled his fist into a ball and very precisely said, 'Williams, if it's you, I'm warning you. Stop, and walk away, NOW.'

There was no reply.

He could feel him coming closer.

Kemp bent down, pretending to tie his boots. His pulse raced. He readied himself. He sensed the person behind him was now only a couple of paces away.

'I've been waiting for this,' Kemp said, and in one movement swung around and threw his biggest punch.

But it wasn't Williams, it was the old man.

His momentum carried him forward, his fist unstoppable. But instead of connecting, the arm careered straight on and propelled him on to the hard grey stone.

Kemp's head cracked the paving as he went down. His left leg and arm throbbed.

'You don't have to do that, Archie,' said a gravelly voice from behind the scarf. 'We're on the same team now.'

Kemp was struggling to get to grips with what had happened.

'Believe me, it is excellent news that you have arrived on time.' The old man moved almost directly above him, his face covered by the scarf and hat. 'And I sense that you have brought my coat. Very well done; did the old man find it?'

Kemp was horrified and for a moment simply didn't know what to say. 'Yes, he gave it to me,' he lied.

'Are you ready to join with me, Archie de Lowe?'

Kemp's skin crawled. Everything Archie had told him was completely true. He needed more time. 'Join you?' Kemp said, scuffling backwards, trying hard to keep his face hidden. 'Er, can you remind me again? I was very tired last night.'

The ghost hesitated. 'Well, let me put it this way. I've got what you want.'

'What I want?' Kemp repeated. No wonder Archie was freaked out. 'What do you mean?'

The old man moved to one side and appeared to look up towards the sky. 'Why me, of course.'

'You?'

'Yes, me,' said the ghost. 'You see I'm the only one here who can help you escape from this place. And you have only about fifteen minutes in your time to decide.'

Kemp's brain went a little fuzzy. Fifteen minutes? In *your* time? Decide what? Kemp stole a look down the alley.

He needed to get away, fast.

The old man sensed his unease. 'You see, in a very short time the skies will open and it will rain for forty days and nights in a way you cannot even begin to imagine—'

Kemp looked confused. 'What... forty days and nights?'

'Yes. That's what I said, forty days and nights—'

'Forty days and nights—?'

'Yes!'

'What … like Noah's Ark—?'

'STOP repeating what I say and listen!' the old man spat.

The words seemed to smack Kemp around the face. He lost his footing and slipped.

'If you think what I'm saying is any way over the top,' he said, bearing down on him, 'I can assure you that in a short while, all of this—everything here, everything—will be destroyed.'

The ghost gestured, almost triumphantly, Kemp thought, towards the playing field.

'Archie,' he continued, his voice mellow once more, 'there is a shift happening, a shift in time, a shift in the way of the universe and it is happening right here, right now. You are part of this, Archie.

'The wheels are turning and they cannot be reversed.'

TWENTY-THREE

THE GAME

S hortly before the whistle blew for half time, Isabella dashed down the touchline and found Sue.

'Sue, thank God I've found you,' she said. 'What's up with you? We're on drinks duty in the catering cart, or had you forgotten?'

'Ah,' she said. 'You're right. My watch …'

They rushed over to the old Volkswagen Combi ice cream van, known by the children as the "catering cart", which acted as the half time refreshment centre and mobile sweet shop.

Isabella and Sue and a couple of others pulled out a few tables and lined out paper cups for jugs of orange squash. As they did so, a steady stream began queuing to buy drinks or chocolate bars or crisps.

Sue took the money while Isabella handed out cups, but Sue could barely keep up.

Isabella was working at an astonishing speed, darting here and there, handing out confectionery and drinks and talking to everyone about the score or Daisy's brilliant goals or the curious weather or who was next. It was an orderly, efficient operation.

'How did you manage to serve all that in ten minutes?'

Sue said, as she squeezed a few more cups into the over-flowing bin bag. 'We must have made a killing.'

She wiped her brow and breathed a sigh of relief. It had been a welcome distraction and with no rain thus far perhaps Solomon was right. Maybe the cloud would break later on that afternoon. And anyway, with everyone chatting and milling around and surging towards the orange juice and chocolate bars, she hadn't had a moment to think about her predicament, and it was some time after the whistle had sounded for the start of the second half that she focused her attention back to the pitch.

From inside the van she looked out over the scene. The crowd was still three or four deep the entire way around the pitch and she could just make out the steep rise of the bank on the far side that led up to the village.

The floodlights shone down onto the pitch, giving the players a strange quadruple shadow. If it hadn't been nearly midday, there would be no reason to suspect that they weren't playing a night match.

'Isabella,' she called out. 'Get a place left of the halfway line. I'll join you in a minute. I'm going to cash up.'

THE VERY FIRST attack after the break, Chitbury scored. Isabella stamped her feet in frustration. 'Exactly what we didn't need,' she said. 'Come on, Upsall!'

Sue looked up at the vast black cloud that seemed to be growing thicker and sinking lower as if someone was filling it up with an enormous hose. The feeling of dread she'd experienced before was building inside her; she knew she should get out, run to higher ground, but in her heart, she was swallowed up by the football and the drama, and swept away by the team led by Daisy de Lowe, who blocked and tackled and encouraged her players to keep going with her relentless drive and skill and energy.

A heavy challenge sent Daisy flying. The crowd swayed and spilled onto the pitch.

The noise increased.

'That was late. Too damn late,' Isabella shouted, peeling off her scarf.

'Listen, Bells. Watch it,' Sue said firmly. 'You mustn't go nuts. You'll get expelled. I promised Solom—'

'It was deliberate and dirty—'

'**NO**, Isabella!' Sue snapped. 'Hold your tongue.' She grabbed her arm.

'But they're targeting Daisy exactly as Kemp said they would. They're going to kick her out of the game!'

Sue closed her eyes. Great, just what she needed; Isabella going out of control, again. She looked at her watch. Ten minutes to go. Isabella was already sizzling like a firework.

'What's that noise?' Isabella said.

'The gargantuan cloud should give you a clue.'

'Th... thunder?' Isabella said, momentarily removing her eyes from the action.

Sue nodded.

Some of the crowd started to leave; others were gesturing towards the sky and gathering themselves to go. This is it, she thought. This is where it starts—exactly as I saw in my nightmare. *It feels the same too*. I've got to tell Isabella. I've got to tell her NOW.

A ghastly feeling of panic prickled her. They should stop the game.

Her thoughts were interrupted as Daisy stole the ball and sprinted down the field. She skipped inside one tackle and then slowed, looking for support. The crowd roared their approval but, from nowhere, a couple of Chitbury boys smashed into her from opposite angles. All three lay on the ground as the ball was kicked away by another Chitbury player.

Play continued, but it was a poor decision.

'That's another foul. Yellow card,' yelled a senior boy. 'C'mon ref!'

The atmosphere turned. Late tackles and players being kicked indiscriminately out of sight of the referee.

Then one of the Chitbury strikers stole into the penalty area as a massive crash of thunder reverberated around them. At that exact moment, little Jimmy Nugent, chasing back, tapped the forward's foot and the player fell head-first into the turf.

The whistle shrilled.

'Penalty!' Isabella spat. 'I don't bloody believe it!'

The ball was placed on the spot.

'This is it,' Sue said quietly, 'the end of Daisy's dream... Bells, what on earth are you doing?'

Isabella was scribbling furiously in her notebook. 'Just watch for me a minute—you know, commentate like they do on telly.'

She didn't need to. The groan told her everything.

'What happened?'

'The ball trickled past Archie—he should have saved it. All he had to do was put his foot out. Ninety-nine times out of a hundred he'd have had that.'

Isabella stood up and thrust the paper into Sue's overcoat pocket. 'Ye of little faith, Sue Lowden,' she said. 'You'll see. Daisy will score again. I'll bet you a real barometer she does!'

Another roll of thunder boomed and cracked. More spectators headed off.

Sue's stomach lurched. It was now or never. She grabbed her friend and faced her. 'Bells, we must get out of here. I mean it. But listen to me first. If it starts raining, this pitch will be a river in less than ten minutes. It's important—'

'Please, Sue. Just shut up!' Isabella snapped as she turned back to the game. 'Get the ball to de Lowe,' she screamed. 'Give it to Daisy!'

She turned to Sue. 'Listen, hun, tell me whatever is so damn important at the end, OK. There's less than five minutes to go and it's two-all in the most important match of my brother and sister's life. Just give it a break for five minutes. Five minutes.'

And with that, Isabella sidled out onto the pitch, ran down the touchline and dived in among some spectators further down.

ARCHIE STOMPED around the penalty area, his face burning with shame.

For some reason, just before the Chitbury player stepped up to hit the penalty, it came to him; the person he'd seen way up on the steps heading into the alley was Kemp. For a start, his hair was a complete giveaway and secondly he was wearing a long coat—Cain's coat—that dragged along the floor.

Intense confusion filled him. He wanted was to run up there and find out what Kemp was up to.

In the very next instant, the ball trickled past him into the goal. The whistle shrilled and a collective groan eased around the ground. Daisy would be furious with him. Isabella's reaction didn't bear thinking about.

If Cain *was* there and Kemp had gone to find him, would Cain know? Would he care? But surely *he* was the one who was going to receive the power of a horse and strength of a lion, not Kemp.

He grabbed the upright and kicked the base of the post again. He felt he'd accomplished nothing—only given things away, like a vital goal and the opportunity for something extraordinary.

The more he thought it through, the more certain he was that Kemp was with the ghost. And the angrier it made him feel. All I ever do is look on hopelessly, he thought. When will I stop being so average and pathetic?

A slow-burning fury started moving through his body. It was an anger borne of frustration and annoyance and it was beginning to consume him.

'NOW, LOOK,' Kemp said pulling himself together. 'If you ask me, you need help.' He drew himself up, his confidence returning. 'All that forty days and nights rain stuff happened a very long time ago in this book called '*The Bible*'. But I don't see any ark or animals.'

'Look above you, Archie,' the ghost said.

'Yeah, right,' Kemp said. 'A few dark clouds. Big deal. Hey! Is that a lion?' He pointed down the alleyway. 'And look —two kangaroos and a couple of woolly mammoths. Excuse me, freak, but I'm outta—'

'No—you—are—not,' said the old man, spitting each word out so severely that Kemp fell back on the ground. 'Out of all the people on this puny planet, I've selected you. So be grateful, Archie de Lowe, because I'm giving you the chance to save your life. There is no other way.'

Kemp squealed and looked down the passage. What was holding him back? Why didn't he run? Why didn't he say that he wasn't Archie? But he felt oddly dizzy—as if a force was holding him against his will—like an elastic band stretched out only to rebound.

'You need convincing,' the old man said, his voice as smooth as honey once more. 'This has come as a shock, so I'm going to show you something to … reassure you. All I'm asking for is a little co-operation.' The old man took a step back. 'Please turn your attention towards the dark sky. Watch it closely.'

Kemp stood up, his knees barely able to hold him.

'You see, I'm going to tell you the story of what has happened so far and then I'm going to tell you what will happen next. Do you understand?'

Kemp nodded.

'Good. Firstly, let me tell you about that piece of paper in your pocket. Then I'll explain who you are and how you are going to help me.'

ARCHIE WAS ABOUT to kick short from the goal kick, but, from out of the corner of his eye, he saw Daisy in yards of space on the halfway line, catching her breath after the last attack. Could he reach her? It was worth a try. He pushed the ball ahead, ran up, and thumped it hard. The ball rose high into the air.

Daisy saw it and ran ahead, her eyes never leaving the ball. She took it down in her stride and, with a burst of speed, she tore past one player then another. Then she stopped so suddenly that another over-ran and she side-stepped one more who fell over. The crowd roared—this was Daisy at her best.

'*D-D-L, D-D-L, D-D-L—she will, she will—ROCK YOU!*' the crowd chanted.

Daisy side-stepped another and with a burst of speed headed towards the penalty area with real menace. Four Chitbury players lay sprawled on the floor, only one more to beat.

'Go on Daisy, you can do it,' Archie screamed.

Archie watched as the remaining defender was sold a beautiful dummy, which Daisy seemed to do with such ease it was laughable, and as she pushed the ball past and effortlessly made her way around him, the defender slid out a leg and tripped her—quite deliberately. Daisy stumbled and fell but she wasn't giving up. She crawled towards the ball and then, even as she lay on the ground, with the ball wedged between her knees, she somehow still managed to keep moving.

But a cry went up as three Chitbury players and the goal-keeper converged on Daisy. It felt as if Daisy had fallen into a trap as the Chitbury boys cocked their legs back and kicked out, striking more of Daisy than the ball. And then they kicked her again and again in a kind of frenzy, with Daisy refusing to give the ball up.

The crowd swayed and screamed and then fell silent. They could quite clearly see Daisy's face contorting as kick after kick rained in on her.

A boom of thunder echoed around the silent field as the crowd watched in startled amazement.

Archie couldn't believe it. Where was the referee? This wasn't football, it was violence.

He thumped the goalpost. He looked up. The giant, angry bruise in the sky now stretched above him like a vast, black, monstrous airship. It sagged so low he felt he could jump up and burst it as easily as pricking a balloon. Perhaps Isabella's experiments weren't so crazy after all.

The heady smell of damp filled his nostrils as another crack of thunder escaped. Archie felt the blood boiling inside him. Now there were five of them surrounding Daisy. She managed to stand, but one of them pushed her over.

That was the final straw. Anger flooded through him. No one, Archie seethed, does that to my sister.

He gritted his teeth, but he couldn't control himself. He found himself running down the pitch, the crowd baying, the referee shouting, desperately trying to separate the players, but everyone, it seemed, was fighting.

'NO! Don't retaliate, Archie—' he could hear someone yelling. But it was too late, he was already there and it seemed as if hell had broken loose.

One of the Chitbury boys was holding Daisy's hair and leering at her, screaming. Archie grabbed him by the collar and threw him away, as if he were a doll. The boy sailed through the air and landed in a heap on the ground. Then Archie punched another hard on the nose and he thought he heard crunching sounds, then found himself receiving blows but he couldn't feel them.

Blood coursed through his body and he felt strong and powerful—invincible. A couple of Chitbury boys jumped on him but he easily beat them off. Then he found another hitting Alexander. He smashed the boy hard in the stomach and threw him away like a piece of litter.

The whistle shrilled.

Finally a sharp, stern voice rose up out of the melee. Archie could see Isabella marching towards them. Uh-oh, he thought. He was in for it now.

Archie looked around and found a couple of Chitbury

boys and the referee staring at him with their eyes wide open. Were they looking at him in fear? It was a sensation he'd never really experienced before. He noticed the four boys he'd hit still lying in agony on the floor. Blimey, he'd done that.

Archie wiped his brow and allowed himself a smile. It felt strangely good.

FOR THE FIRST time in her life, Sue could feel the sensation of utter panic building up in her veins like a bubbling chemistry experiment. A series of flashes filled the sky, mirroring the extraordinary scenes of fighting on the pitch. Lightning fizzed and crackled in the dark cloud, forming—for a brief moment—a picture.

Sue gasped. A boy.

Then a thunderclap smashed overhead so loudly that the crowd cried out. Shrieks and screams filled the football field.

Sue fell to her knees, barely able to think, her body shaking. No! It can't be! It's not possible. It's... it's... Kemp's face—the lightning was Kemp's face super-imposed in the cloud. But how, how was it possible?

She looked around. Where was Isabella? Had she gone already; left her? Surely not. She followed the eyes of the crowd.

Oh NO! Isabella was striding towards the fighting on the pitch.

'STOP! ISABELLA, STOP!'

There was no reaction.

Without thinking, she took off after her. 'Isabella, LISTEN!' she screamed as she ran. '*It's you!*'

She ran on further.

'The dream is about your family, the de Lowes.' She sensed Isabella slowing down. 'You must ALL survive until sunset. Do you understand? SUNSET. YOU MUST STAY ALIVE.'

Her voice was petering out as she realised she was screaming herself hoarse. She sucked in a deep breath.

'Find clues in your house—Eden Cottage. *You must find the clues.*'

Sue coughed and then repeated the last part, adding, 'GO! GET HOME! NOW!'

She noted some of the crowd staring at her as if she was a madwoman. But she didn't care, not one little bit.

A LOUD ICE-CLEAR voice cut through the air: 'STOP IT—NOW!' It was Isabella's and she was striding towards the players with a sense of purpose.

The teams almost instantly ceased brawling. Isabella's direct approach had that effect on people.

'You're pathetic—all of you,' she shouted, pointing at various individuals. 'It's like a wrestling match for the Under 5s. Chitbury—especially you three—should be utterly ashamed of yourselves.'

Isabella scooped up the ball. 'And as for the refereeing—it's a disgraceful display. Twelve deliberate fouls by blue totally unaccounted for and you haven't even got the balls to book them, let alone send them off for repeated violent conduct.'

The football smacked into the referee's hands.

'What has the world come to when—?'

Before she had a chance to finish she was grabbed by Coach and Mr Bellwood who hauled her off her feet and away to the sidelines.

THE REFEREE RESPONDED by pointing rather belatedly at Isabella. 'GET HER OFF!' he yelled. 'You'll be dealt with later by the authorities.'

He blinked, trying hard to pull himself together. Why

couldn't he remember the procedure for dealing with a brawl? It felt as if his brain had emptied.

'And along with that madwoman, Upsall numbers one and eight, and blue players five, seven and four,' he said pointing at the Chitbury players. 'GET OFF THIS PITCH.'

The referee waved his red card at the players and scribbled in his book.

Another huge slap of thunder exploded almost directly overhead. A terrible feeling crept right up his back sending his hairs erect.

The ground shook.

'Direct free kick to red,' he said, quickly pointing to a spot just outside the penalty area. 'And the quicker we're out of here, the better.'

He studied his watch. Less than a minute to go, thank the Lord. The girl was right. It had been a dreadful performance. He couldn't think why. Maybe it was this huge cloud that was sitting bang on top of his back.

Whatever it was, by God, he wanted this game finished with.

ARCHIE SHRUGGED AND STARTED WALKING. Moments later he was running. He couldn't complain—more than anything, he had to find out what Kemp was up to—and fast. If he was right, there wouldn't be much more time left. His stomach churned as a darkness seeped into his bones that something terrible was about to happen.

The clouds crashed and boomed. Spectators began to flee to the school buildings. Without looking back, Archie sprinted off the pitch towards the steep bank that led up towards the town.

TWENTY-FOUR

THE PROPHECY

There was more, Sue thought, much more, but she'd said it; she finally said what needed to be said. Thank goodness she'd had the presence of mind to scribble down her dreams the moment she'd woken up. Now she had to get out of there—and fast.

'GO! Run!—run, all of you,' she yelled at the spectators. '*It's going to break. The storm's going to break.*' Thunder rolled out of the sky. She ran as fast as she could up the slope towards the buildings. She had to find a way out.

As she passed the top end of the ground she spied Gus leaning on the lamppost near to the kissing houses. She sprinted towards him. 'Gus. What are you doing?'

'Following Kemp—he's been acting weird all afternoon. Are we winning?'

'Listen Gus,' she said as she caught her breath. 'Rain … like you've never seen … you've got to get out of here and fast.' Her hand touched some paper in her pocket and she pulled out Isabella's note. 'You've got to believe me.'

Gus rolled his eyes. Had she gone completely doo-lally?

She started to read it out loud:

'*My best friend, Sue, there's a boat in the old shed. Key under a pot by door—oars on side. Canopy in cupboard … just in case. Love you. Be safe—Bells.*'

Sue kissed it in relief; clever, brilliant Isabella.

Gus grabbed the note. 'What's up with you two?'

'Look at the sky, Gus. When that 'thing' bursts it will rain harder than you can possibly imagine. In minutes the water will flash. I had a premonition—I'll tell you about it—'

'A premonition? Blimey. Cool. You sure?'

'Absolutely. No one has a chance. Can you drive? Do you have access to a car?'

'Of course I don't!'

'Nor me,' she fired back. 'Some of the kids have gone but I'm being picked up later, after the music.'

'Same,' Gus said, trying to keep pace with her.

'Then we're stuck, Gus,' she said. 'Screwed. There's no way out.'

'Stuck? What are you talking about? Why should we be stuck?'

'Look, Gus,' she said. 'I promise you I'm not crazy, I'm deadly serious and I'm right. This cloud isn't holding an ordinary storm, when it lets go it will be utterly catastrophic. Come on, keep up.'

Gus frowned. 'You really are serious, aren't you?' he said, the smile slipping off his face.

'Never more so.' She stopped to catch her breath again. 'Please, Gus, I need your help. Will you help me? Please?'

Gus scratched his nose. He liked Sue even if she was a bit of a nerd, not that it really bothered him; at least she was a pretty nerd. The person who bothered him was Kemp and, more than anything, he'd like to knock him down a peg or two. Gus carried on thinking; he had certainly never seen her quite so animated. 'OK. I think I'm going to have to trust you on this one. Where do we start?'

'Oh great! Thanks, Gus,' Sue said, moving in and hugging him. If she was going to do this, better to do it with big, strong Gus Williams than by herself. 'First off, provisions. Food; high-energy snack bars, chocolates, lemons, dried fruit, tinned food like tuna, baked beans, sweetcorn, a couple of lighters, bottled water,' Sue rattled off, 'blankets—if you can find any. Anything you can get hold of. Come on,' she urged him to keep up. 'You're the Scout leader, aren't you? So you know—stuff we can survive on.'

'To the shop, then,' Gus said, smiling his rather big, toothy smile and suddenly feeling rather important.

'I've got about eighteen pounds from the footie snacks and drinks. I'll pay it back later.' Sue did some calculations in her head. 'Actually, that's probably not enough. Have you got anything?'

Gus shoved his hands in his pockets and pulled out some change, 'Just short of four pounds.'

Sue grimaced. 'In that case, Gus, I hope you don't mind but you're going to have to steal—come on, there's not a minute to lose. When we get in there, grab some bags and start filling them. Don't hesitate or stop but don't be stupid about what you take. When it's done I'll drop the money on the counter and we run. Alright.'

'Blimey, Sue. What if we get stopped?'

'We won't. Oh, and if necessary, use force. Do you understand?'

Gus nodded and handed over his money. His eyes were bulging with surprise. 'Where are we going afterwards?'

'The boat shed.'

'Boat shed? What boat shed?'

'The old shed by the river.' She waved her hand in its rough direction. 'We should have time to sort out some kind of cover and find some survival things... then we're going to have to hope for the best. I don't know what we'll find when we get there but at the moment it's our only chance.'

ARCHIE SCAMPERED up the steep bank, pulling himself up on the longer tufts with his hands and using his studs to give him grip. At the top of the bank he caught his breath and looked about. A huge roll of thunder shook the ground as he watched Isabella being marched off the football pitch by a couple of adults. People were streaming away, pointing skywards.

Wow. What a mental couple of minutes. He couldn't believe his strength and the fact that he had actually *hit* someone and then thrown two guys two or three metres as easily as if they were pillows. He shook his head; Archie de Lowe, most laidback human on the planet, had hit someone. Archie smiled. And the odd thing was, it hadn't felt so bad. Was it the strange glass of water left by the ghost?

He spied the alleyway and ran over, the studs of his boots clacking on the stone beneath him.

This Cain, he thought, this ghost, couldn't really exist, could it? He peered down the alleyway and saw two shapes.

A sudden burst of lightning brought the pair to light and he could make out Kemp's red hair and another figure beside him bearing a long coat and a kind of trilby hat. Archie's heart pounded. They were making their way towards him.

OK. OMG. Wrongo. So what if Cain *did* exist and Kemp had got there first. Was this a good thing or a bad thing? Oh hell!

Archie shrank down, wondering what to do, and wiped the sweat off his forehead. As he urged his brain into action, Archie was struck by a thought. Cain was blind, wasn't he? He'd gone on about the fact that he didn't have any eyes— like the Ancient Woman. So, if Cain was talking to Kemp, perhaps Cain didn't know it was Kemp.

Archie stood up from behind the wheelie bin so that only his head might be seen. Kemp was about ten paces away and Archie could see that the figure next to him was a ghost by the simple fact that he didn't have any shoes on and his face was covered—rather oddly, he thought—by a scarf. A crackle of lightning fizzed above them and, from the light it threw out, Archie was able to see—just for a flash—Kemp's face. It was a picture of utter terror.

Archie's heart thumped like a drum.

Kemp's eyes widened, and for a brief moment their eyes met.

Kemp and Cain moved nearer and nearer. All the while Archie could discern the ghost's words like "power" and "magic" and "strength".

Archie was stunned; did Cain think Kemp was him?

A dark thought dashed into his mind: wouldn't Kemp be dying to get all of those things—power, strength and magic? Then Archie realised that the ghost was holding Kemp tightly around his left arm. Was Kemp moving them slowly out into the open, or was it the other way round? Who was moving who?

Archie listened harder as they stopped just the other side of the wheelie bin.

He heard Kemp's quivering voice. 'Tell me again about the Prophecy. I need to be absolutely certain before I make my final decision.'

Cain seemed unimpressed. 'Did you not listen, Archie?' he complained.

Archie gasped. Cain *did* think Kemp was him! So what was Kemp playing at? And why was he asking Cain to tell him about this Prophecy one more time. Was it for his benefit?

'I need to be perfectly sure,' Kemp replied.

'Very well.' Cain turned his head to the sky as though sniffing it. 'But a shorter version. We are running out of time.'

Archie stole another look at Kemp from around the corner of the wheelie bin. When he caught sight of Kemp's face, tears were streaming down his cheeks. Archie recoiled. Why? Why was Kemp crying? Was he trying to tell him something?

He crouched down and listened to Cain's deep, powerful voice. 'There is a great shift that occurs every now and then in the way of life, Archie,' the ghost began. 'Humans, who are at the top of this chain, evolve slowly but every now and then there is a big change. A change in physical attributes, a change in relation to surroundings, the infinite and beyond. The processes of these changes are shown in the form of dreams. The dreams that start this process have been given to you and your siblings. These dreams are the Prophecy of Eden, for you are the Heirs of Eden, the anointed ones.'

Archie's gut turned. JEEZ. Anointed ones! From their dreams. Why—why them? He remembered the strange creature above Daisy—he had been right all along—it *had* been giving her dreams. But it didn't make it any easier to understand.

The ghost coughed and carried on. 'It is complex—this is not the time to tell you the ways of the universe. All you need know is that the Heirs of Eden face fearsome challenges.' He turned his face to the sky. 'The first of which begins with a terrible storm aimed entirely at you. If any of you do not survive the storm, it will rage for forty days and forty nights and wash out the world, bit by bit.' Cain sucked in another lungful of air. 'When the waters recede there will be a different world with a new beginning.

'I tell you now. You children stand little chance—there is no ark to save you, nor any place you can go that you will not find yourselves shot at by lightning or washed out by torrents of rain. The earth will slip down hillsides, the rivers swell and trees crash down. There is nowhere you can hide. I do not tell you this with any joy, but the storm was designed when men were strong and lived long and knew how to fight with nature through other means, like magic. You are about to enter a time you are not equipped to cope with. Do you understand?'

Kemp nodded and his eyes bulged. 'Why?' he asked.

'Aha! Young man, the Prophecy is a measure—a test, if you like, to see if the people on this planet are ready to move into a new age, a new age of human enlightenment—the next step—if you like. The Prophecy was designed to test the strength, courage, intelligence and skill—to see if mankind is ready.' Cain stopped for a moment and chuckled. 'You and your sisters, the Heirs of Eden, must survive until sundown. On the absurdly small chance that you make it, the destructive force of the storm will cease...' Cain tilted his head skywards. 'There is no more time,' he barked. 'It will break in a few moments.'

Now, Archie was trembling. Everything Cain said rang true; he'd seen it all in his dreams, though of course it had meant nothing. And Isabella had been right all along!

Archie could hear Kemp's voice, strangely muffled saying, 'So … there's little hope for me and my sisters.'

'There is always hope, young man,' the ghost replied. 'But in comparison with the thickness of a rainbow, the chances that the three of you will survive are but an atom wide. You are a child. You have neither the strength nor the skills to combat what lies ahead. You know no magic and you do not understand nature. What chance do you have?' He paused for effect. 'None. That is why you must join me now, Archie. The world will be washed away, but I offer you the chance to escape through me. You have the opportunity, through me, to start again. All I need is the use of your body.'

'And will this help save your mother?' Kemp stammered.

The ghost seemed a little surprised. 'Yes, as I told you. You have seen her and you know that she holds a great secret within her that others seek to destroy. By joining me, Archie, she will be saved. I guarantee it.'

Cain was laying on the charm. His persuasion intoxicating. 'Here, the suffering will be great but together, Archie, we can build a new future. I am nearly useless without you and you are helpless without me.'

Kemp looked over at Archie whose terrified face had risen from the other side of the wheelie bin. 'But I still don't understand,' Kemp whimpered.

Cain growled. 'These things are beyond your understanding. Open your mind; you have seen it in your dreams.'

Suddenly, Kemp tried to make a run for it. He attempted to loosen the grip on his arm by charging at the wheelie bin. 'GO!' he screamed at Archie. 'RUN!' But the ghost held him tight and forced him to the floor. Kemp whimpered in pain.

The ghost moved into Archie's path in front of the entrance to the alleyway and began to unfurl the scarf that covered his face. 'I see,' he began. 'There is another one.' He sniffed the air. 'And one of you is Archie. You have tried to deceive me,' the ghost said, calmly.

'So there is a choice. Archie, if you choose to come with me, the world will be saved. My mother will be saved. You will be saved. If you run, you die.' He released Kemp who fell to the floor. 'Which will it be?'

Kemp looked utterly petrified—his face red, his cheeks streaked with tears. He caught Archie's eye, and stared at him —imploring him, begging him to understand. And then Kemp began to speak very slowly. 'Kemp, you are my only friend,' he said, 'and not long ago, I swore—on my life—that I would never hurt you or your family. I failed.' Kemp's eyes opened wide, desperate for him to understand.

Archie frowned. What *was* Kemp talking about? Had Kemp worked out that the ghost was blind?

Kemp began again, 'Run Kemp; save yourself. GO!'

'Uh?' Archie said, still confused.

'Yes, Kemp—you moron—get out of here! Get to safety.'

Archie stared back.

And then Kemp said it again. 'Look, Kemp, you great big oaf. Go now while there's still a chance. Leave this to me, but promise me one thing.'

'What?'

'Look after that fishing rod.'

'Fishing rod?'

Kemp couldn't believe Archie. 'Blimey Kemp, how stupid are you?' he said. 'Go! Now. Run you idiot—GO!'

Archie stared deep into Kemp's tear-stained eyes and could see a spark of light. Deep down, both suspected they were doomed, but Archie was sure that Kemp was trying to tell him that while there was even a tiny slither of a chance Archie had to try and make it through to dusk.

Archie curled his fist into a ball and punched his friend lightly on the shoulder. He winked and mouthed the words "Thank you".

'So long, Archie,' Archie said, 'see you in the next world.'

And taking a deep breath, he turned and ran for his life.

TWENTY-FIVE

CAIN'S BODY

D aisy dragged herself up and flicked a fleck of mud off her shorts.

What a crazy match; her being kicked to bits, Sue screaming at Isabella, Isabella going mad again and screaming at everyone else, Archie missing a total sitter and then beating up the opposition like a prize-fighter—and getting sent off—deafening thunder crashing overhead, lightning fizzing—everything so loud.

Her head was ringing.

She noted the ref looking at his watch. And now, with the last kick of the game, she had a chance to win the match. Boy, pressure kicks don't come much bigger than this, she thought. Better make it a good one. I'll curl it over the wall—the floodlights are so poor it's got every chance.

'Come on, Upsall. Come on, Daisy de Lowe, you can do it,' roared the small section of crowd still remaining before starting the repetitive chant of '*D-D-L, D-D-L, D-D-L*'.

Daisy bent down and rubbed her tired, bruised legs and drew her hands through her muddy blonde hair. She fixed her boots and as she did so she selected a slightly raised patch of turf on which she carefully placed the ball, which glowed like a full moon.

She stood back and studied her route to goal. Twenty,

twenty-three yards? Perfect—just as she'd practised time and time again with Archie. She rubbed her eyes and concentrated hard on the ball. It was now or never.

Everything she'd ever played for came down to this one shot.

She sucked in a large mouthful of air and blew it out, her eyes focusing on the ball so intently that she felt she could actually see the entire trajectory of the ball and the precise spot of where to kick it.

The whole atmosphere, the crowd and the rumbling sky for a moment seemed to disappear leaving a strange quiet.

The referee blew his whistle.

It was time to step up and smack it.

'IT HAS STARTED,' the ghost said, his hat angled upwards towards the sky. 'Something more powerful than you can possibly imagine has begun.' He raised an arm towards the lightning and thunder.

'If you want to see your friend for the last time, follow his path. I doubt he will last long. You too may run now, but you would be a fool, Archie.'

Kemp moved to the end of the alleyway, wondering if he should run for it. People were scattering everywhere even though the players were still on the pitch.

He watched as Archie hared towards the steep bank and went out of view as he vanished down it. He reappeared, running flat out, waving his hands in the air. By the way people were looking at him, it was as if he was screaming at the top of his voice. Now he was sprinting onto the football field.

Kemp shifted his gaze. Daisy was striking a free kick and…

CRACK!

With a deafening roar, a massive thunderbolt flashed out of the sky right on top of Archie. Kemp's heart missed a beat as he watched Archie fall to the floor like a ragdoll, his body spasming one moment, still the next.

Smoke drifted out of his friend.

Kemp recoiled and collapsed. Everything the ghost had said had happened; the sweet paper, the lightning in his own image in the cloud and now the thunderbolt aimed at Archie who lay dead on the ground.

Archie didn't deserve this; laidback Archie with his scruffy hair who was always late for everything. Archie who didn't really do anything; harmless, quiet Archie, his fishing pal, the only person he'd ever told about his parents. And he'd sent him to his death.

Kemp turned to find Cain directly behind him.

'I am nothing more than a sad ghost. I was stripped of my flesh and bones, but not my spirit. It means that I cannot move or touch with any great purpose, so I require flesh and blood to partially restore me. This is where you come in— where you can help me. I cannot do it alone.'

The ghost removed his clothing until all that was left was the overcoat that covered his body and the hat on his head. He sniffed the air around Kemp who felt a coldness on his face and stumbled; was he going to be … eaten, or have the life sucked out of him? He felt dizzy and sick and paralysed with fear.

'Rest assured,' the old man said softly, 'I know you are not Archie. I have no intention of taking your life, only *borrowing* it for a little while. When my work is done and my mother is saved, I will put you back near this very spot. That is my solemn promise. But nature's curse is upon us.'

The ghost took a step towards the quivering body of Kemp. 'You must freely decide if you will help me. You must choose now. I doubt you will get such an offer from the storm.'

KEMP FACED him head-on for the first time. All he could

see was a transparent gap beneath his hat. His teeth were chattering. 'If I don't—?'

'You will almost certainly die or be drowned in the rains or in the landslides or the tsunamis which will sweep through the land destroying everything—'

'Will you kill me?'

'Kill you?' the old man chuckled. 'No. As I said, I'm just going to *borrow* you for a while. Why would I kill you when my purpose is to save so many? You must *trust* me.'

Kemp looked up at the sky. It fizzed with electricity like an angry nest. A terrible boom rattled every bone in his body moments before a thunderbolt smashed into a nearby chimney pot. Terracotta splinters showered them.

His head shook.

He stared down the path, readying himself to run. But as his eyes focused on the dark shadows between the buildings, he found himself looking at a familiar face. It was Gus Williams laden with shopping bags! They locked eyes for several seconds before Williams simply ran off, as though someone had called him away in a hurry.

'Dreamspinner!' the ghost barked impatiently. 'Open up. It is time to go!'

'Wait,' Kemp croaked. 'What do I have to do?'

'Put on the coat and hat that covers me. Quickly.'

Kemp's mind was made up. In no time he threw both of his overcoats to the ground and moved in close. As he did, he felt a strange coolness wash over him.

'Ignore that I am here,' the ghost said, as Kemp fumbled. 'Put it on, like you would any other.'

Kemp grabbed the collar of the coat and pushed in his arm, amazed by the sudden intense freeze that enveloped it. Then his other arm slid in. Kemp had a wonderful feeling of enormous strength building up in him as though he was being filled with electric charge.

It started in his fingers, moved up his wrist, through his elbows, to his shoulders. All too soon it was spreading down through his loins and into his legs and feet. It was as if a thick liquid, like freezing treacle—stuffed full of power—was coursing through every vein, into every muscle and sinew.

Kemp drew the coat across his chest and the curious feeling leeched towards his heart and lungs.

Now, he cried out and stretched his arms wide as the ice-like treacle rushed into his vital organs and washed through his body. He shouted out a cry of pure ecstasy, his sounds echoing back off the old houses.

Kemp only had one more thing to do. He lifted up the hat and pulled it down over his head. Very quickly he could feel the cold charge oozing up his neck and through his mouth. For a few seconds, he shut his eyes, enjoying the extraordinary tingling sensations of the liquid ice entering his brain and slowly dispersing through the back of his skull, tickling parts he never knew existed.

Then the surge of power rounded the skull and headed towards his eyes. When it flowed into his eyes, everything changed.

With a rapidity that took him completely by surprise, Kemp felt a searing pain enter his head, and it grew like a balloon filling with air.

'What's happening?' he screamed. 'It's burning me... MY GOD, *my eyes*!'

He desperately tried to pull off the hat and wrestle out of the coat, but it was too late, they were stuck on. 'My head's being blown apart. What—have—you—done—to—me? Help me! *HELP*!'

The ghost chuckled as Kemp carried on screaming.

'Welcome to me,' Cain said, his voice laced with triumph. 'Welcome to the burnt-out body of Cain.'

TWENTY-SIX

THE STORM BEGINS

Confusion reigned as players and spectators ran hard towards the cars and houses above the football field. Screams filled the air.

Archie blinked, opened his eyes and tried to focus. His head pounded from the noise of the blast and he smelt burning hair. When his eyes focused, all he could see was a burning net and smouldering goalpost.

Daisy sprinted over. 'Archie! Winkle!' She kissed his forehead. 'Thank God!' she said, cradling him. 'I thought you were toast. Say something—are you hurt—can you move?!'

Archie smiled dumbly and mumbled several inaudible words. Then, very slowly he moved his arm and rubbed his eyes. His fingernails were black and smoking.

Daisy carefully pulled him into a sitting position. 'Your hair's gone all … all spiky—'

'ARCHIE!' Isabella screamed as she tore across the pitch to him. 'Please, Archie.' She ran directly over and placed her hand on his forehead. She felt for his temperature, then checked his pulse and inspected his tongue.

He smiled weakly.

'PHEW! I can't believe you're OK—you are OK, aren't you?'

Archie nodded, but his eyes were not focusing right.

'My strips must have saved you!'

'UH?'

'The strips I made you put on your boots.' She handed him a bottle of water. 'Daisy, why don't you get the tracksuits, while I make sure his internal organs are functioning.'

Isabella gave Archie a short examination and declared that Archie was well enough to take a couple of little sips. Daisy returned with their tracksuits and she slipped into hers before helping Archie into his.

'Victory!' Isabella said, 'You did it!'

'Don't be ridiculous,' Daisy scoffed as she pulled Archie's top over his odd hair.

'I'm not,' Isabella replied. 'The ball's in the net. It was blown into the goal. You scored!'

Daisy didn't know whether to hit her sister or cry. 'No,' she said furiously. 'I missed and Archie got fried. Look at him —it's a miracle he survived.' Daisy felt a dullness consume her; her limbs were tired, sore and defeated. She could hardly bear to look at her sister.

'He's fine, aren't you, Archie?' Isabella cried. 'Anyway you're wrong. Admittedly your shot was heading towards the corner flag but the lightning bolt deflected the ball into the goal—I swear it. The charge of particles must have generated a force to hit it in precisely the right spot to divert it without blowing it up. It's a miracle. It's the goal of the millennium—'

'Shut up! Please,' Daisy said, sharply. 'Stop it, Bells.'

Coach was running over towards them and he went straight to Archie where he spent some time checking him over.

'WOW-ee,' he whistled. 'That's one lucky escape, young man. I thought you were brown bread for a minute. It looks like the Gods spared you—you may feel a little groggy, but you're gonna be alright. Try standing if you can.'

With the aid of a person on each side, he stood up.

'How do you feel?'

He couldn't quite hear or see them, but he attempted a smile.

'That's the match-ball in the net, isn't it, Coach?' Isabella asked. 'I've taken a picture of it on my phone—for safe-keeping.'

Coach clapped his hands. 'You're right! Looks like we ruddy well won. We're only the bleedin' champions!' He slapped Daisy on the back, almost knocking her over. 'Quite amazing ...' But he stopped mid-sentence and turned to the sky, his tone serious once again. 'Listen, if you think you can make it, Arch—you'd better get off now up that funny track to your cottage. Otherwise I'll give you a lift back, via the school.'

'Don't worry, Coach. We'll get him back in one piece,' Isabella insisted. 'I promise—it's not so far. Anyway, you're not that bad are you, Archie?'

Coach eyed them. 'You sure? You'd better get going then. Best scarper before another of them thunderbolts gets us.' He patted them on their backs. 'And fast as you can! I reckon it's going to bloody piss down.'

Coach skipped off towards the car park singing loudly. Then he yelled back at them. 'Great goals, Daisy and bloody brilliant hairdo, Arch. You're legends!'

ARCHIE WAVERED a little and Daisy caught him. 'You really think we can get back home?'

Archie was trying to say something. But it came out slightly askew.

'What is it?' Isabella said softly.

'Storm! Go.'

Angry rolls of thunder boomed around them.

'Is anyone else finding this very loud?' Daisy asked. 'I've had to put tissue in my ears. Look!' And she pulled out the paper. Suddenly Daisy's face went pale.

Isabella spotted it. 'What is it?'

'I think there's another in-coming thunderbolt.'

'*What!*' Isabella said.

'RUN! NOW!'

They grabbed Archie round the shoulders and set off.

'I can hear the particles gathering in the cloud, I think. Sounds like a build-up of collisions.' Daisy stopped. 'DIVE!'

A moment later, a massive crack tore across the sky and unleashed a lightning bolt that smashed into the exact spot where, moments earlier, they had been huddled together. The ground smouldered.

'Bloody hell,' Isabella whispered, her knees buckling. 'That was close. It's like it's after us.'

'It is,' Archie mumbled. He closed his eyes and tried to work more saliva into his mouth. 'We have to survive... until dusk.'

'That's exactly what Sue was yelling about,' Isabella said. 'Survive till sunset.'

'Where do you get that nonsense from?' Daisy said. And then she twitched.

Isabella noticed. 'What is it, Daisy?'

'Another one—I think I can hear it!'

They reached the tree and slipped under the branches.

'We should be safer here.'

Daisy held her hands over her ears as a couple of tears rolled down her cheeks. 'My God. Here it comes!'

A lightning bolt crackled and smashed into the branches. The children screamed as a huge branch sheared off and crashed a couple of metres away.

They ran out hugging each other.

'**OH, NO!**' Daisy cried, her ears screaming in pain.

'What now!?'

'It's like... a power shower has just been switched on.'

A warm wind swirled and nearly blew them off their feet. Then the first few large rain drops like mini water balloons began to plummet out of the cloud.

'We need to move, NOW!' Isabella cried. 'This is the storm from hell we predicted—'

'*Predicted?*' Daisy yelled.

'Yeah, Sue and I ...' Isabella's voice trailed off. 'OMG,'

she said, 'we've got about five minutes before this playing field becomes a river.'

'Oh, well that is simply marvellous,' Daisy yelled.

Isabella and Daisy put their hands under Archie's armpits and folded his arms across their shoulders so he was properly supported.

'You've got to move your legs, Arch,' Isabella implored. 'HURRY!' she screamed, forcing the pace. The rain intensified as the wind blew in several directions at once. In no time, in front of them, on top of them, and behind them, a wall of water sluiced out of the heavens, pounding them, beating them hard on their heads and shoulders and backs. Isabella removed her coat and draped it over their heads. For the moment at least, it acted like a shelter.

'Where's the bridge?' Daisy shouted above the din of the rain. 'I can't see ANYTHING!'

Isabella slowed and stared at the ground. Water heads downhill, so it's got to be this way. If we get to the path, we'll find it. Without knowing why, she pointed her free arm ahead of her, closed her eyes and allowed it to guide her.

Soon the feel underfoot of soft wet turf made way for hard gravel. They followed it, but every step was tricky and they couldn't be sure exactly where they were going. Isabella rubbed the ground every so often with her foot to feel the hard path underneath. By the time they reached the bridge, the children were cold, soaked through and exhausted. And, more worryingly, water was spilling out of the river at an alarming rate—up to their ankles and rising fast.

'Bind—tighter—scrum!' Isabella yelled, 'We've got to move together, rhythmically, in time. I'll count.' She realised they couldn't hear her so she signed with her fingers: ONE, TWO... THREE and then she flicked out her thumb.

'Where's the bridge?!' Daisy screamed, before suddenly losing her footing. She screamed again as Archie hauled her to her feet.

Isabella shook her head, imploring her to keep going.

'DON'T FALL.' She turned to Archie to see if he understood. He nodded.

Isabella counted each agonising step, the force of the water gaining by the second, pushing hard at their legs. Every breath was a struggle and their heads were bowed from the pressure bearing down upon them.

Isabella had no idea where she was headed. She simply trusted her hands and, as if by a miracle, they guided her to the rail. She breathed a deep sigh of relief. They shuffled onto the bridge, still huddled together, their feet searching for the wooden boards.

Daisy suddenly went stiff, holding the others back. She turned to the others, her eyes bulging.

Collectively they realised what she meant.

'RUN!'

They scampered up to the brow of the bridge, Daisy leading the way holding Archie's hand on one side, when suddenly she dived, hauling Archie forward with all her might.

Bits of wood splintered around them, the noise deafening. Daisy picked herself out of the water, her feet grateful for the feeling of land, and discovered Archie next to her. He was fine; but where was Isabella?

Daisy called out but it was hopeless; she wouldn't be heard over the din. As she listened, the only thing she could hear was the roar of the rain and rushing water flushing everything downstream.

TWENTY-SEVEN
ISABELLA DISAPPEARS

I sabella found herself slipping and falling. The water took her as her world went blank. When she came to, her body was numb from the shock of the lightning bolt and, although she hadn't received a direct hit, every nerve and sinew tingled like a spectacular case of pins and needles.

She coughed and gasped for breath, spluttering and ejecting the water trapped in her lungs. Her hands and feet kicked, her arms and legs moving faster than she could have possibly imagined just to keep her head above the torrents. Already, her feet were unable to feel the bottom of the river— had the water climbed so high in such a short time?

The problem was finding enough oxygen to breathe. There wasn't a single bit of air anywhere. Her hand touched something and she grappled with it and tried to pull herself up. But it was a loose root and it fell away.

She plunged back under the surface and was pulled down river. When Isabella rose to the surface, she wondered how long she could keep floating helplessly like this and how far she had travelled.

She needed to touch down on the cottage side of the river. If she made land on the valley side, she was surely doomed— there would be little chance of crossing. Treading water as best as she could, she did a quick calculation: if the water was running from the moors down into the valley, she had to land on the right side as it flowed towards her. Isabella kicked hard until she could feel the water pushing her and then twisted to the right with all her strength, swimming at an angle into the current.

Moments later she touched on something that felt like a shrub. She put her feet down and was relieved to find herself waist high. She scrambled across the bush, her legs getting scratched to bits, and kept moving until her feet hit on solid ground.

Almost immediately, Isabella coughed and spluttered and then retched the water she'd swallowed. It felt as if her insides were coming out. She gasped for air and headed uphill for the cover of a nearby tree. She found one, leaned into it, put her head in her hands and breathed deeply.

She closed her eyes. And now it was exactly like her nightmare, except this time it was for real, the premonition she dreaded. Tears built up and for a moment they rolled freely down her cheeks. Daisy, Archie! They'll probably think I'm dead.

She imagined them waiting for her. Please, please, no; every minute spent waiting for her was a minute wasted.

And she wondered what had happened to Sue. Did she find the boat? In any case, would a little boat survive a storm like this? Never; it would fill with water and sink in minutes.

Isabella felt herself welling up, but a ripple of water washed against her shins. The water was rising fast. She had to keep going—finding the others was futile now—she was on her own. She'd head uphill, from tree to tree and use whatever cover she could find.

Only there would she find safety.

DAISY WAITED for what felt like hours, although she knew it

was little more than a few minutes. She shivered—grateful that the rain was not particularly cold. It was tepid—probably from being stuck up in that big cloud for so long, she thought. But Daisy knew that even warm rain quickly chills, and there was just so much of it endlessly pummelling them.

She ventured from side to side of the path as far as she dared, yelling and screaming for Isabella, but she knew it was hopeless; visibility was zero and she could hardly hear her own voice.

With every movement, her bones ached and her joints screamed out. If only she hadn't just played a game of football. She just didn't have the energy reserves for this kind of physical trial. If a thunderbolt didn't get her or the rains sweep her away, she'd surely succumb—eventually—to the cold.

She stamped her feet and jogged up and down. She concentrated hard on the water further down and for a moment she was sure that she could see, much further down on the river bank, a body, someone climbing out of the water. She shook her head—it was impossible, she must be seeing things—like a mirage in the desert.

She put a hand round Archie and hugged him close. His body warmth was like a hot water bottle. He seemed better—his eyes were clearer—maybe he was back to full strength—although she smiled as she touched his odd spiky hair—especially when hers was smeared all over her face and head like the tentacles of a jellyfish.

He seemed in shock. Numb, as though his tongue had been cut out. Was it the lightning strike, or was it something else?

What he had said earlier was very odd—that the storm would come after them until sunset. How did he know that? But she didn't need him like this, she needed him on full alert, thinking—helping. Perhaps, she thought, he needs another shock. She slapped him on the cheek as hard as she could.

'Blimey, Daisy!' he yelled rubbing it. 'What did you do that for?'

'Got you back,' she mouthed, kissing his forehead. 'I'm sorry—necessary.'

'There's no need to hit me,' he yelled.

But Daisy hugged him tight and spoke into his ear. 'Aw, but it did the trick. Keep moving, Archie—can't wait here much longer—freezing.'

Archie nodded and pointed towards the track.

'But what about Bells?' Daisy cried.

'She's a strong swimmer,' he said, and he drew Daisy's head in to his chest. 'She'll be fine.' But as he said it, he frowned. He looked at his watch. Only two-thirty. Jeez. What had Cain said: Nature will throw its full fury until sundown? Should he tell her that they had at least another two to three hours of this?

Even though they walked up and down the track almost every day—in winter, spring, summer and autumn, now, it was impossible to find.

At every turn, with the rain pounding on their heads, unable to see anything, they found themselves walking into the bank or into bushes or into trees. Eventually Archie discovered a section of fencing that had been washed up. He broke it up so they could use it on top of their heads but even then, keeping their arms in the air was exhausting and the rain stabbed at their fingers. At long last, Daisy recognised a big boulder that was just inside the bottom of the covered tree track.

A mini triumph, Daisy thought, as a long booming roll of thunder crackled gruesomely overhead. She covered her ears, wincing at the pain, but after only a few paces she realised there was a far bigger problem. She bound closely into Archie. 'Mud!' she yelled at Archie. 'Look—thick mud and stones—rushing down.'

Every step forward was like walking over barbed wire; the path was laced with branches, brambles and rock.

And, ever present, was the thick mud and water speeding down the narrow track. Worse still, the canopy that sheltered them was being smashed in by the rain, so that branches were falling down on them—not only twigs—but wood as thick as a man's wrist. Even though they'd only stepped a few metres in, it was becoming obvious that the canopy was close to breaking point.

Archie tried to skip over a large branch that was heading directly towards him. He slipped as he landed and cried out, the muddy water dragging him down the hill. He dug his fingers into the bank alongside, grabbed on to a root and managed to pull himself upright.

Daisy climbed up the side of the bank and waited for him. She looked down the track, and could see Archie struggling. For every two steps forward, he was pushed one step back.

'COME ON!' she screamed.

Archie hugged the side but found that every time he did, it simply folded in on him. Not only that, but his ankles were being stripped bare by the mud, stones and wood being flushed down. At last he made it to Daisy's position and climbed up next to her.

He gasped for breath and rubbed his badly scratched ankles covered in blood. 'We're never going to make it. Not like this.'

'We have to!' Daisy replied. 'Do you think it'll be any easier out there, getting pummelled by the rain?'

'But it's acting like a ditch,' Archie complained. 'A gigantic storm drain; all the water is cascading down here. The branches are about to collapse, several are already breaking off. It's about as dangerous a place as you could wish.'

'Then what's your suggestion?' Daisy fired back at him.

Archie thought through his next move. 'Up the bank and crawl along the top,' he yelled.

'But it's over a mile of crawling—'

'I know. But that's one mile of not being swept away and dying, sis. And we can use the cover of the trees. There's no other choice.'

Using the roots of the big oak they were sitting on, they

climbed up the bank. On hands and knees they made their way slowly uphill, brushing aside branches and thorns which tore into them. After several minutes, Daisy collapsed under the cover of the next large tree.

She rubbed her body, which was pierced by blackthorn and dog rose. 'Great idea, Archie!'

'Look at the track!' he replied.

Through the veil of rain, she could just make out a moving torrent of mud and branches halfway up the bank. It was flushing downhill at great speed.

'OK, OK. *Good* decision.' Daisy drew in her breath. 'How far up the track are we?'

'Keep going and we'll come to the big oak with the swing rope. We can rest there.' Archie had no idea, but he knew he must give her a goal. He could see she was struggling by the way her eyes kept closing.

Another huge boom of thunder clapped overhead, followed by a lightning bolt that crashed down nearby.

They crawled on. The foliage was thinning and once again the rain smashed down, beating on their backs. Archie led, with Daisy closely behind. But, after a short while, when he turned, there was no Daisy.

He backtracked and found her, hanging halfway down the bank, which had quite simply subsided into the water. Only the thick tendril of a rose and a large bush that was slipping into the mud was holding her. She was dangling above the muddy, rushing waters. He needed to act fast.

He grabbed the base of the rose and tried to swing it. But the huge old rose was near to breaking point and sinking under the pressure of the rain. Thorns dug into the flesh on his hands.

There had to be a better way. He shuffled to a nearby hedge and saw a small tree. That was it! He bent down, put his hands around the trunk and pulled with all his might. The roots started coming away. One more heave and it broke free. Archie turned it round, ripped off some branches and lowered it to Daisy. She grabbed hold and Archie tugged her out.

They moved under a nearby tree and gasped for breath.

'OK, so we've learnt two things from that,' Daisy yelled between gasps. 'The first is that the bank is collapsing and the second is that you've been working out without anyone knowing.'

Archie shrugged and looked at the small tree. For a boy of his age it was a seriously impressive show of strength.

Taking a wider berth away from the track, they continued crawling.

The rain did not cease for one moment and, as they inched forward, they were consumed with dread. Danger surrounded them: danger from branches snapping and falling, the dreaded thunderbolts, landslides, mudslides or simply being washed down onto the track and down the hill.

They came across a badger sett, which was now a huge hole and had to be circumnavigated. Eventually they struggled up to the large oak, the one they loved to play on, the one with the rope, which now dangled down.

Archie pushed Daisy on and up she went, her hands gripping one after the other as though her life depended on it. Archie was right beneath her, shouting encouragement.

The rope was tied around the thickest branch which hung over the lane. Where the branch met the trunk, a huge bough seemed to curve over, like a mini cave and, for the first time in ages, it offered them almost complete protection from the rain. Archie sat with his back against the trunk and Daisy sat in front of him, leaning back. They both took deep breaths and shut their eyes.

In no time, Daisy, through sheer exhaustion, fell asleep.

Archie didn't mind. He looked at his watch. It felt as if they had been crawling and sliding and fighting for days, let alone hours. And yet there was still an hour or so to go. If only he could remember what time the sun went down.

The problem with being stationary was the cold. The sheer amount of water made it feel like they were in a fridge.

He wrapped his arms around his sister. Her body rattled like a spluttering engine. A rest was a good idea, but at some point they were going to have to keep going, whether they liked it or not.

TWENTY-EIGHT

OLD MAN WOOD FINDS A CLUE

As the morning wore on, Old Man Wood was consumed by a feeling of utter dread, as if a toxic stew was brewing in his stomach and a splinter was stuck in his heart. Whatever he did, it would not go away.

He marched around the house looking for something, anything, that would alleviate this terrible feeling. He studied the carvings on his wall and traced his fingers over the rich detail in the wood panelling in his room. He inspected the old pictures for a clue. Anything that might not only shed some light on the nightmares he'd had, but also cure the interminable worry that filled him from the top of his head to the tips of his toes.

The pictures and carvings had been there since he could remember. Didn't they mean something? If so, *what*? He knew there was a vital clue missing and it was probably staring him in the face. The more he played with this notion, the greater and deeper the feeling of despair grew, like a slow-growing cancer.

Old Man Wood headed outside to see if his brain might clear from a walk up to his cattle. He wondered for a moment if he shouldn't go down to the school and watch the football match, but it didn't seem right. The children would tell him what happened in detail later, not that he understood much of it. Besides, he didn't like to show himself in public, he'd been around too long for that. Instead, he headed up to the ruin to check on the sheep and cattle.

They seemed quiet and tetchy, jumpy—like him, he thought, and wondered if they, too, sensed something unusual. He made sure that the shelter built from old rocks was sound in case the storm broke, and he counted them: eleven sheep, three cows, six bullocks and Himsworth the bull. He'd tried to milk the cows at their usual time, the crack of dawn, but their milk had stopped. Were they sick?

Old Man Wood sat down on a grey boulder at the head of the ruin and looked out across the vale. In front of him was a sheer drop of solid rock that disappeared down to thick forest for seventy metres or so before reaching the valley floor. He could just make out the river curving around the rock face and, from there, it slipped around the corner and along and up into the moors.

Old Man Wood shuffled his boot in the dirt. He was too old for this; too old for riddles and memories. His brain couldn't cope. He shook his head as he wondered what it all meant. Why the dreams every night—what were they trying to tell him? And why did he have a strong feeling in his bones about something that he hadn't felt for ages? He stood up as a deep roll of thunder boomed and crackled through the valley. He kicked a stone which flew off the ledge and sailed through the air before crashing into the canopy of the trees way below.

He could make out the school buildings in the distance although the top of the tower was smothered by the deep black cloud that sat directly overhead. He was lost in his thoughts when a lightning bolt shot out of the sky right into the heart of the village, and then another and another. Each one with a blast of light so bright and crack so loud that he covered his ears.

Then a searing pain walloped into his chest. For a moment he thought it was a heart attack. He bent over and cried out. The sky fizzed with lightning as another huge bolt crashed out of the sky directly onto the playing field. This time the pain was unbearable and he crouched low, clutching his chest, struggling for breath.

There was no danger of dying, he was absolutely certain of that. In fact there was no danger of him ever dying. So was this pain linked to the storm? Perhaps it was telling him something important. Whatever it was, he needed to lie down.

Old Man Wood straightened up as best he could and tottered back down the pathway, stopping occasionally to view the storm playing out over the school. Wasn't it funny, he thought, how the storm seemed to focus only on the school? He had a stirring inside him that the children might be in terrible danger. And, as he concentrated on this, the feeling began to grow and grow. He hurried back, certain that rain would follow. By the time he opened the door he was drenched from head to toe. He couldn't remember anything like it; torrents of water literally pouring out of the sky.

He lay on his bed and massaged his heart, trying hard to understand this feeling, when another thought crossed his mind. How would they get back? The river would be swollen in no time and the track would act like a storm drain. What if they got swept away? He dabbed his handkerchief on his forehead. He had to *do* something.

Just as he was preparing to get up, Old Man Wood felt a yawn wash over him and a powerful urge to close his eyes. His head fell back into his large pillows and a moment later he was snoring.

GAIA THE DREAMSPINNER appeared in Old Man Wood's room and found him lying on the bed.

Had he forgotten so much? Had he forgotten his entire reason for being there in the first place? How, when the children needed him so badly, could he be so utterly hopeless?

Old Man Wood hadn't reacted to any of the dreams given to him and Gaia worried that if Old Man Wood could not understand and believe his dreams, what chance would the children have with theirs? Were the dreams too complex, too terrifying? Was the approach wrong? Were the dreams too old, suitable for a different time? Perhaps their dreams needed to be more obvious, like action sequences linked together.

She dipped a leg in her maghole. Did the Heirs of Eden have any idea what they were up against? Did they stand a chance? No, probably not, she thought. They were mere children, unprepared for this onslaught that was designed for the best of men. And years ago those men would have used additional powers.

Gaia rubbed a couple of claws together. This wasn't the time for reflection—that would come later—and anyway, the children were alive, for the time being at least. The storm would not relent until sundown, so, if Old Man Wood could find them, then surely they would have a greater chance of survival.

She would give him a dream of action, and in it the old man would be struck by lightning. Yes, that was it. Perhaps it would re-energise him, get his brain working, jog his memory. She would not consider defeat, not yet; there was still too much to play for.

In no time, Gaia was over the old man, spinning a sleeping draft directly into his mouth. It worked fast. Moments later the dreamspinner was plucking tiny specks of dream powders out of her maghole and feeding them to the old man as he breathed in. Gaia added an ending—a reminder of a potion Old Man Wood had stored away a long, long time ago. Perhaps the old man would find it, perhaps not, but it was worth a try and it was the very best she could do.

As soon as it was done, Gaia stared down at the old man. She desperately hoped it would do the trick. Then she flashed inside her maghole and vanished.

OLD MAN WOOD tossed and turned as the dream filled his head.

He looked down and found himself wearing a pair of shorts and he was running. It was a lovely feeling, the air filling his lungs. And he had hair! How wonderful. He dragged his hands through it and it was silky. He felt young, like a child, the same age as the twins. His skin was smooth and his mind was... alert.

On his feet he wore a pair of football boots, just like Archie's. He looked up. A football was flying towards him and his immediate reaction was to run out of the way. But out of the corner of his eye he spotted Daisy yelling at him. What was she saying? Pass it? He went towards the ball but it was too fast and bounced off his boot straight to an opponent. This wasn't as easy as it looked.

Daisy swore and chivvied him to chase the player.

He took off and was moving at speed. Much to his delight, Old Man Wood found himself gaining. He lunged for the ball but tripped the player.

The whistle blew. 'Do that once more and you'll be in the book,' the referee said.

Old Man Wood caught his breath and brushed the mud off his knees.

Daisy was there in an instant. 'What do you think you're playing at?' she said. 'There's hardly any time to go. Don't make stupid fouls like that. We've got to win or we're never playing again.'

The other team lined up a shot and the ball was cruising towards the goal. But Archie danced into the path of the ball and caught it smartly. In a flash he punted the ball wide.

One of his players passed it to him. This time he managed to control it and he slipped a neat pass through to Daisy. Daisy, now on the halfway line, jinked past one, and then sped past another, her blonde hair bobbing up and down as she went. Boy, she was quick. He found himself sprinting just to keep up with her.

A defender forced her wide and she played the ball inside

to him. Looking up, he passed it to Isabella on the other flank. He couldn't remember Isabella ever liking football but she neatly passed it back to him just as she was clattered by an opposition player. He couldn't help laughing at the horrified expression on her face.

Now Daisy was screaming for the ball.

But Old Man Wood found himself running with it and it felt brilliant. He did a jink—just as Daisy had—beating the man in front of him. He knocked the ball forward, finding Daisy, who held off a challenge and stood with the ball under her feet.

In a flash she turned on a sixpence, the ball rolling under her other foot, totally foxing the defender. and headed towards the goal. Old Man Wood felt himself sprinting into the area as Daisy smashed a shot at the goal. Old Man Wood held his breath as the ball whacked against the post and rebounded directly into his path. Out of the corner of his eye he could see a defender running towards the ball. He had to get there first. He sprinted harder, cocked his leg back and kicked the ball as hard as he could.

The ball screamed into the roof of the net, tearing a hole in the netting, and was still rising just as the defender crunched into his foot.

A heartbeat later and a lightning bolt smashed out of the sky directly into him. A surge of energy fizzed through his entire body, through every sinew and fibre of his being.

It took his breath away and when at last the sensation wore off, he peered down to find a bottle of gold liquid on his lap.

And then he woke up.

OLD MAN WOOD opened his eyes and thumped the air.

'What a goal!' he shouted, and then, 'Ouch!' He stared up at the ceiling, a big smile on his face, his head sizzling as though a rocket had gone off in it and his body was tingling like mad. 'What a marvel-tastic dream,' he said out loud to the empty room.

His foot throbbed. He looked down and found he'd walloped the end of his bed. Must have been when he scored that amazing goal. He looked a little more closely and found a hole in the wooden sheet that covered the bed-end. He studied it, pulling a few of the fragments away and chuckling at the absurdity of it all—he'd certainly struck the ball with awesome power.

Old Man Wood wiggled his toes, grateful that he'd lain on his bed with his shoes on. As far as he could tell, nothing was broken or too badly bruised. Then, he heard the rain pounding outside and his heart sank. His earlier worries flew back at him. He kicked the broken piece of wood as though recreating the goal might lift his spirits. But it wasn't the same.

He climbed off his bed and peered out of the window, but the rain was so heavy he could barely see out. Were the children safely tucked away in the school?

His heart filled with heaviness. If something happened to them, he was responsible, but what could he do? There was no way of knowing where they might be. With no answers, Old Man Wood walked slowly back to his bed and lay down.

He looked at the hole in the wooden panel. A tiny flicker of light, like a dim torch whose batteries were running low, seemed to leech out from behind it. Now wasn't that strange, he thought. Maybe it was a trick of the light. But none of the house lights were working—he'd already tried them.

Maybe he should crank up the generator—at least it would give him something to do. He swung his feet off the bed and as he did the light from behind the wooden panel intensified.

He inspected the hole a little closer and found that there was indeed a faint glow emanating from behind it. He prised it open with his fingers and, feeling more than a little intrigued, began to wrestle with the wooden surround that covered the large bed-end. But it was stubbornly attached. He found a torch, switched it on and rushed out of his room past the wide staircase to the tool cupboard, where he selected a crowbar before returning to his room.

Moments later, Old Man Wood wedged the crowbar in behind the panel and was attempting to lever the wood away by leaning on it as gently—but firmly—as he thought necessary. But whatever angle he tried, the panel would not budge. Furthermore, he was conscious that if he was too heavy handed he might damage his beautiful bed carvings.

He scratched his head and slipped out of the room, returning moments later with a flat head screwdriver and a hammer. Old Man Wood thrust the flat head into the tiniest of gaps and gave the end a smart whack with the hammer. The nails securing the panel lifted, just a fraction.

Placing the crowbar in the new gap, he levered it once more and after a few more whacks, the panel popped off.

He rubbed his chin. 'Well, I'll be blowed,' he said, as he ran his fingers over the three panels that now stared back at him. 'What in the apples do we have here?'

In front of him were three beautifully inlaid panels that seemed to glow like three small monitors—rather like the children's computers. The difference was that these ones were inlaid into the bed itself and surrounded by carvings that matched those on the bed.

He stared at them for a while, his face a picture of confusion, the wrinkles on his forehead deeply pronounced. Every now and then the images in the panels moved and, when they did, Old Man Wood could feel his heart racing. And it kept on happening with all three panels, randomly. Was he was seeing things, he wondered?

He noticed that the overlying image was hazy—like looking through heavy rain. Maybe it was mirroring the weather right now, he thought, as if it were in some way, however ludicrous, a weather forecasting unit. As he became more accustomed to the panels, the images on them became a little clearer. On each panel was a figure. Three panels, three figures, one on each "screen". And why did each one look so familiar?

He studied the carvings to the sides of the screens. The first was an ornate pointer in the shape of an arrow. He touched one that faced away from the first panel. To his astonishment, the panel seemed to move the image out, exactly like a zoom on a camera. He did the same with the next panel, this time pressing on the arrow that turned in. Once again the picture moved, but this time closer. He studied it with increased fascination.

The person he was looking at appeared to be drenched and walking up something—tripping every now and then—as though trying to negotiate a pathway, but the image was still so hazy. He rubbed his hand over another carved icon adjacent to the arrow, which he thought looked rather like a cloud. He pressed it and magically the picture transformed, removing the rain.

Old Man Wood gasped as he stared at the new image. That balance and gait could only belong to one person, and that person was Daisy. He pressed the inward arrow a couple of times and he could now see her in quite extraordinary detail.

A thrill passed through him. He was looking at the children, right now, in real-time, and he realised that, if he could determine which buttons to press, he'd be able to see exactly where they were. He did the same to the panel on the right, this time pressing the cloud and zooming out with the away arrow.

He clapped his hands. It was Archie, definitely Archie, with a kind of spiky hat on his head—and he was standing right next to Daisy. And, just like her, he was trying to walk through something and that something, he concluded, was not in the slightest bit helpful. It was like a river of goo sliding towards them. So, where were they? He pulled out and saw an image of a gully with low branches bending down.

The track! It must be the track. He clenched his fists. But where? He pulled out even further. Apples alive! At the bottom! His heart sank. At least the twins were together, but what about Isabella?

He scoured the left panel and sighed with relief as he saw her outline. He honed in and pressed the cloud icon. It cleared the screen. He pressed the outward arrow to try and work out her position.

She was heading towards a large object with a sheer face, pushing past bushes and through trees. He zoomed out. Behind her, he could see something creeping up on her. Was it water? It had to be. My goodness it was flooding fast. He thought quickly. The only sheer rock he could think of was... was underneath the ruin. So how come she was separated from the others?

It didn't matter. She was where she was.

Old Man Wood breathed a sigh of relief. They were alive. He looked at his clock. How long was it since he'd been out for a walk? Two hours? He trembled.

Had the children been out in this for that long? Goodness gracious. Not much would survive in that.

His heart thumped. He needed to find them before they were battered and drowned in all that rain.

TWENTY-NINE

LIGHTNING BOLTS

Daisy dozed, her head resting on Archie's chest. Her mind swam. She dreamt fleetingly of the cottage, of Old Man Wood and their parents. She dreamt of scoring a goal with a sensational bicycle-kick and Archie making a flying, fingertip save. The storm seemed a million miles away.

Suddenly she woke. A noise had clicked in her brain. She studied it, her eyes shut tight. Then she realised what it was.

'MOVE!' she screamed at Archie.

Archie opened his eyes. 'Eh? What?'

'Incoming. I can hear it. MOVE!'

'Where?'

The noise was building somewhere miles above them.

'Down the branch. NOW!'

Archie did what he was told and shuffled his bottom as fast as he could, the rain smashing down on them once more.

'Further,' she screamed. 'As far as you can.' She was skimming along, almost bouncing when she stopped, wrapped her hands and legs around the thick branch, and hugged her body into the wood. She hoped for the best.

Archie continued on, oblivious to Daisy's action. From out of nowhere, a terrific surge of power smashed into the tree. The branch was severed like a head being cut off by an axe and it crashed down, bridging the track just above the flowing mud. Archie flew into the air and came down into the torrent. He sank underneath the waterline.

Daisy convulsed with electricity and was filled with pain, particularly her ears. She uncurled her body from around the branch as the rain crashed onto her back and head.

Regaining her composure, she turned round. Where was Archie?

She tried to call out his name but not a single sound came from her mouth. She knew it was hopeless. Even if she could scream for help, he'd never hear her. She scanned the area. Suddenly she saw a hand struggling to grip the end of the branch. And then it fell away, caught in the torrent.

She shrieked and desperately fished her hand down into the water but felt nothing but twigs and leaves and the occasional bush flashing beneath her.

Daisy thumped the branch, tears streaming from her eyes, blending with the rain. How much more she could take? Her eyes dipped.

And now she was all on her own.

ARCHIE FELT his body being whipped away. He battled with all his might and when he surfaced, the huge branch now straddled the track.

His lungs burned.

He reached up, but however hard he tried, he couldn't get a hold on the bark and after several attempts he felt a pain as though the nails on his fingers were starting to detach. The force of the water was so great that he had simply no option but to give in. He let go and was swept away. He desperately needed to breathe. He struggled to keep his head up and every time he did, it was battered down again by the rain. And all the while he searched for buoyancy—a branch or a tree he could grab that might keep him afloat.

He thrashed out with his feet like a madman, kicking the water beneath him in a last massive effort. Something caught around his left leg, possibly a root. He succumbed, shattered and beaten. He smiled ironically as he let himself go, Cain's words coming to him as he floated away: if it wasn't the thunderbolts and it wasn't the rain, it was the landslides.

But, much to his surprise, he remained bound by this thing that had snared around his leg. The current pushed him towards the bank and he made a grab for a protruding root, twisting his body round and keeping his head up. He sucked in air, coughing water out of his lungs. He gave his foot a yank and found it unyielding.

He tried again, this time holding the root on the bank with his other hand. It moved! Now there was just enough slack to allow him to climb up. He bent forward to see what was around his ankle and felt into the water, pulling his left leg towards him.

He touched something coarse and thick. Archie's mind was working overtime. Then it struck him. It was the swinging rope attached to the big branch.

He pulled harder, knowing that if Daisy was still attached to the tree trunk she couldn't possibly know it was him. The rope came away a little more. Now there was enough slack for him to try and untie it. He reached down and figured that the end had knotted around his ankle. It wasn't the trickiest knot he'd ever seen, but the rope was thick and the current was pulling him and the rain beating down and every time he thought he had it, the slack was withdrawn and he was back to where he started. He gave the rope an even bigger tug. The whole branch moved. This time the rope gave and slipped off his foot. He grabbed it, and tied it around his waist.

And then he heard a scream. Even above the roar of the rain and the torrent, it couldn't be mistaken.

It was Daisy, screaming;

'IN-COMING!'

Archie knew exactly what he had to do.

Daisy was still on the branch—he was sure of it. He tugged with all his might and felt the branch yield. He pulled again and again. Slowly the branch twisted off the bank and slid towards the torrent below. There couldn't be much more time. One more pull was all it needed.

He harnessed the rope around his shoulders and yelled out, pulling like crazy. Suddenly the branch broke free and shot forward, just as a thunderbolt crashed into exactly the place it had been resting. Archie wondered if he'd done enough—if Daisy had managed to get out of the way. But he had no time to think, for the big branch began slipping down the slope, joining the torrent that was flushing down the lane.

Archie was whipped away behind it, trying desperately to keep himself above water, holding on for dear life as the branch joined the main body of the river. As it did, he pulled himself closer and put his left leg out, using it as a rudder. It seemed to work and the great branch pitched towards what he hoped was the bank on the left hand side.

Archie pulled himself up onto the log, shut his eyes and gritted his teeth. The rain slammed down on his back and head as if it was beating him to death, slowly and surely, with blunt nails, like Chinese torture.

Maybe he should slip back into the water to take the pressure off his body. But what if he did that and was swept away? It wasn't worth it. He didn't know if either Daisy or Isabella were still alive. If they were, it was a miracle. How much longer could he last? He felt his eyes closing and he thought he heard a voice. Was it Old Man Wood? No, similar but different. Cain? Archie lifted his head and swore he could see something sitting near him on the branch. 'Daisy—Daisy,' he groaned.

'Come with me,' a voice said. 'You can be saved, Archie.'

'Saved,' Archie repeated. It was the best offer he'd had for a while.

'I can lose this other boy. Say yes, and it will be done.'

Was it Cain? With Kemp? Everything Cain had said was true - what did he have to lose?

His brain swam. All he could think of was his sisters and nothing else. The branch jolted and snapped him out of his trance.

No. Archie knew he had to get Daisy off the log and find Isabella. There was no other way. They'd die together. But better to die together trying to save the world than not to try at all.

'I'd rather be with my sisters than join with you,' he spoke into the rain.

The voice laughed back at him, 'I will return, Archie. You may need me yet.'

THIRTY

ISABELLA GETS TRAPPED

For every step Isabella took forward, she seemed to slide back two more. And when she was out in the open she found herself pushing blindly through sheets of water with no idea where she was heading.

She needed guidance and wondered if she could find the strange sensation in her hands that she'd felt when helping them to the bridge. She extended her hands in front of her and felt a gentle pull, one way and then the other. With each step, her feet touched on harder ground. Sometimes her hands swung her at right angles and every so often she had to backtrack. But she trusted in it, for it was the only thing she had.

The one thing that terrified her was the thunderbolts.

Daisy had been able to hear them forming—or so she said —and it was true. Every time Daisy screamed and they ran, a thunderbolt crashed onto the spot where they had just been. But now there was no Daisy, Isabella sensed that it was only a matter of time before another would come. And she had a deathly feeling in her gut that it would come directly at her out of the blue.

She moved forward, all the while waiting for the crack or the blast. And, as fast as she went, the trickle of water around her ankles kept gaining on her, so that for every surge she made forward, in no time it had caught up with her, sometimes as high as her knees. She scrambled on.

Isabella had a sense of a thunderbolt generating in the clouds above. She didn't know why, it was simply a terrible, stomach-wrenching fear that filled her.

She crawled fast, scampering over fallen branches and through brambles up to the base of a large tree that offered her decent protection from the rain. Almost immediately Isabella stretched her hands into the air above her head, her palms facing outwards, her fingers touching. She channelled every ounce of energy into protecting herself. She didn't know why, but it felt as if her hands were her only hope.

She closed her eyes and waited and waited. Sure enough, and only moments before Isabella was thinking of putting them down, a thunderbolt sliced out of the sky directly upon her. A fraction of a second after she heard it break, Isabella slammed back at it.

She could feel its power pushing her into the ground as the immense voltage made to slam into her head. She gritted her teeth and pushed out harder, her hands red hot as if burning rods of molten iron were being welded into them.

And then it was over.

Isabella's body slumped to the ground, her hands smoking, her eyes closed, a look of peace fixed on her face.

IT WAS the water licking at her lips that brought her back.

Isabella opened her eyes and shivered. The thunderbolt! She'd survived! How long had she been out, five minutes—half an hour? She pulled her hands up to her eyes. Even in the dim light she could make out large black circles, like burn marks, on her palms. Her body tingled, the electrical charge still running through her. How—how had she done it? It didn't make any sense. By rights, she should be frizzled.

She checked her limbs one by one. They worked, but her

whole body ached like crazy and her head felt as if it was full of wire wool.

'Keep going,' she heard. 'Move, now.'

It was as if someone was with her, egging her on, trying to lift her. Was this her spirit, begging her not to give in?

She forced herself forward and fell flat on her face. Again, she heard the voice. She picked herself up and wondered who or what it could be. She crawled on, finding a steady rhythm that made her progress faster than before. Soon she was above the waterline and she kept on going until she cracked her head on a large black rock.

'OW!' she cried, as she rubbed her head. She noted that the rain had ceased pummelling her. It was a sheltered spot under a rock shelf and, for the first time in ages, she felt a little safer. She sat back, stretched out her legs and cradled her head in her hands. Where would the next meal come from, she wondered—that's if she remained alive long enough. She was lonely, terrified, lost and starving.

Isabella pulled herself together and tried to take some bearings. She was pretty sure she was on the cottage side of the river but she could be anywhere—who could tell how far she'd drifted—and the hills carried on for miles and miles. She picked up a rock. At the very least she could narrow it down by working out where rocks like these came from.

Moments later there was a terrible explosion of noise, like the sound of a train smashing and crunching into another right above her. The sound got closer and closer until it was right next to her and all around her. She shut her eyes and put her hands over her ears.

Out of the sky, a deadly surge washed over the rock. Isabella shook. She didn't have the strength to put her hands up to protect herself, but if she had, it would have been useless. Through the veil of water something else was pouring out of the sky—darker, and deadlier—directly onto the area from where she had crawled.

It took a while for Isabella to work it out. It was a land-slide. Even above the noise of the water she could hear cracking and crushing and splintering sounds as everything in its path was obliterated.

For several seconds the cascade rattled on. Isabella's heart thumped; she wouldn't have stood a chance. Eventually, the cacophony ceased. She ventured out into the rain and, only a couple of metres from where she had been sheltering, she encountered a vast pile of boulders, rock, mud and splintered wood.

She slunk back to her sheltered position as a terrible thought began to wash over her.

If she was underneath a cliff face the chances were that it was either a landslip off the top of a hill or, and she thought this more likely, a section of the cliff face had simply fallen away. That would explain the boulders. The only place she knew where that had happened before was below the ruin.

In her mind, she pictured the geography of the area and the position of the cliff face. She knew from several attempts to climb it that surrounding her probable position was a ledge and, above this, a sheer wall of pure rock.

And then, like a thought one doesn't want to think about but cannot avoid, she realised that she was completely and utterly trapped.

THIRTY-ONE

GUS' CANOPY

Gus was sure he'd seen Kemp and that he looked nothing less than terrified. And who was that odd chap he was with? Oh well, what the hell. Whatever he was up to, Kemp was probably best left to his own devices. Right now he had more pressing things to be getting on with.

He hurried after Sue, his arms nearly dropping off with the weight of the shopping bags. It had been so embarrassing. In the shop he'd rushed round and shovelled everything he could find—pretty much the entire contents of two shelves—into three carrier bags, much to the shopkeeper's increasing curiosity. Sue was the other side doing the same, before running up to the counter and literally throwing money at the shopkeeper. The notes fluttered in the air and the coins sprayed like confetti all over the counter. She spun on her heel and fled out of the door with Gus right behind her.

'Stop! Thieves!' the shopkeeper yelled out, but even though Gus turned round and shrugged his shoulders as a sort of apology, he'd run away as fast as his legs could carry him, down the hill. And when he took a little breather, that's where he'd seen Kemp.

The boathouse was clad in old weatherboard wooden planks with big, square, open windows at either end. Gus thought it looked like a mini wooden barn. On the river side, the shed had a section removed with just enough room for a boat to be pulled in and out.

Sue was trembling so much she couldn't lift the plant pot under which the key sat, and eventually Gus put his bags down and calmly did it for her. The key was old and rusty and got stuck in the lock, turning only fractionally. He forced it first one way and then the other, loosening it gradually until it clicked and fell around. If that was the condition of the lock, he thought, then what sort of condition will the boat be in?

The door whined as it opened, as another crash of thunder and lightning crackled in the sky overhead. Gus shivered and brushed a few old cobwebs out of the way.

'When was the last time this was used?' he asked.

'No idea,' Sue replied, searching for a light. She pushed the switch and a solitary dangling light bulb flickered into life.

In the middle, and covered by a tarpaulin, was the boat, which sat on two large pieces of wood on the dry ground. It was a rowing boat with three bench seats and Gus reckoned it was probably twelve feet in length and four feet wide. He laughed. 'And this piece of junk is going to save us? It should be in a museum!'

He dragged off the tarp and shook it. Dust flew everywhere. 'Help me fold this up and stow it,' he said. They opened it to find that it appeared to be twice the size of the boat. They folded it quickly and nestled it inside the boat. Gus whistled as he inspected the vessel. Layers of varnish had peeled off and the wood was covered in a thick layer of dust. He wondered how much weight it would take.

'We need to build a canopy,' Sue said.

'Why?' Gus quizzed.

'So the boat doesn't fill with rainwater and we don't spend the entire time bailing it out, that's why.'

Gus pulled the oars off the wall and nestled them in the rowlocks before searching the boathouse for wood. He found a few decent lengths of 2 inch by 4 inch cut timber.

'How long did you say we would be stuck in this?'

Sue shrugged. 'How should I know? A day, a week—'

'A week?'

'Maybe a month?'

'Jeez. A month.' For the first time, Gus was taking their situation seriously and he sprang into overdrive. He ran round the room finding things that might be useful and tossed them into the boat; rope, bits of wood, a couple of buckets, a crabbing line and a fishing net. He found a handy looking wooden box and a plastic container with a sealed lid. He told Sue to give it a quick clean before putting in the matches and anything else that needed to be kept dry.

Then he had a thought. How would they anchor down the canopy? And what would they sleep on? And what would they drink? He yelled over to Sue who was still busy cramming the tarpaulin under a seat. 'Really, a month! You think so?'

A huge crack of thunder smashed overhead.

She put her hands out. 'How long is a piece of string?'

Gus spied four fifty-litre plastic containers. He ran over and smelled them. No foul odours. Good. He took two to the tap, rinsed each one out and filled them before heaving them up onto the boat, which creaked ominously under the weight. He hoped the wood was sound.

'Make room for these,' he instructed Sue, 'one at each end.'

Gus tied the two empty ones to either side to act as bumpers or emergency buoys.

With this task complete, Gus stood up. As he did, the rain suddenly started to cascade out of the sky, thumping like a carnival on the tin roof. Within moments water was spilling through the cracks. Gus wished he had a bit more time. He spotted a couple of loose planks on the far wall. He marched over and, without hesitating, began levering the first one off. As it fell to the floor Gus stared in disbelief at the rain. Holy moley, he thought, she really is right. Rain was falling out of the sky like a sheet.

He pulled two more weatherboards away and slipped

them into the boat. 'Hammer and nails,' he yelled out. 'Have you seen any?' He mimed hammering a nail.

Sue pointed in the direction of an old workbench.

It was a long shot but if there were any it might make all the difference. He went through the drawers and cupboards, finding paint and rags and paintbrushes and sandpaper. He dragged out a thick canopy and laid it aside. But there was nothing suitable for attaching it. To the right was another pile of bits and bobs covered in two large, old dust sheets. He picked them up, shook them out and handed them to Sue.

Beneath this was a selection of woodworking tools. Gus thumped the air. What an astonishing stroke of luck. Clearly someone had set out to repair the building and left everything.

Right, Gus thought. I reckon I've got approximately fifteen minutes to build a world class, life-saving canopy.

Gus stretched the canopy, which in truth was a thick, heavy-duty plastic sheet, the length of the boat from bow to stern. It fitted perfectly. To make the main beam, he placed a long length of wood under one side and a matching length above it, so that it sandwiched the plastic sheet. He used two 2 inch by 4 inch sections, about four feet long, to connect to the main beam—one at each end. Then he nailed in two more sections at each end from the side rim of the boat to the main post, which levered the canopy up to form a tent shape.

It was a tad uneven, Gus thought, but it would do. He listened to the downpour. It needed to be super strong. He'd take more wood and prop up the mid section if he had time later, once they were underway.

Next, he nailed two rough planks on both the port and starboard sides, leaving a gap in the middle for the oars. As fast as he could, he nailed a baton to the side of the canopy on the outside of the boat. He repeated this on the other side so that, in no time, the boat was covered in a tight tent and better still—if it worked—water would run off the canopy and out of the boat, not into it.

Sue looked on in awe. Gus didn't come across as the

brightest spark in school, but my goodness he was practical. He was a credit to the woodwork department. She ran round pulling bits of the canopy tight while Gus hammered and sawed and stretched the plastic sheeting. So immersed in their project were they, that they hardly noticed the water seeping in and over the floor.

'Almost time to batten down the hatches,' Gus cried, smiling.

Sue ran up and hugged him. 'I couldn't have done this without you,' she said, and she genuinely meant it. Sue climbed into the boat and sat under the canopy as a deep sense of foreboding filled her. She desperately hoped she was doing the right thing. And she hoped like anything that Isabella and the twins had got away safely.

Gus slipped a few remaining planks into the boat and a couple more of the 2 inch by 4 inch sections, grabbed the remaining nails, the hammer, a saw, a small axe and a chisel and threw them in the box. Just before the water covered the whole floor, he scanned the shed looking for anything else; Sue's umbrella for starters, a couple of old empty paint pots with lids. More rope, string, a whole reel of strimmer cord, another large dust sheet, this one neatly folded. He rummaged through the cupboards like a man possessed and found an untouched bag of barbecue briquettes. He threw them in. When they landed, they'd need fire.

Sue packed them away. Then with a few last minute alterations as the water reached the upper limits of his boots he clambered in, praying like mad there were no holes in the boat. And he prayed that with their weight and the fresh water and the timber, they wouldn't drop through the bottom.

Slowly, the boat rose with the rising water level. It creaked, but so far so good. No holes nor rotten timbers—as far as he could tell. Sue shook as thunder and lightning blazed outside. It felt as if they were waiting in the depths of the Coliseum before being fed to the lions in front of an angry, screaming crowd. The boat rose further still before finding its buoyancy. Then it started to drift.

'Here we go,' Gus yelled. 'Hold on tight.'

But, a moment later, the boat clunked into something. Gus looked confused and squeezed past Sue to the bow. He looked out and muttered something under his breath.

'What is it?' Sue cried. 'Is there a problem?'

'Technical difficulty,' he said, scratching his chin. 'Pass me the axe.'

Sue scrabbled around in the box and handed it over.

Gus disappeared and set about trying to smash the weatherboards. A short while later and Gus' banging stopped. 'It appears,' said Gus, popping his head back under the canopy, 'that the water has risen higher than the gap the boat was meant to squeeze out of. In short, we're stuck!' and he smiled his toothy grin again.

'For crying out loud,' Sue howled. 'Can't you get the boards off?'

'What do you think I've been doing? Knitting?'

She rolled her eyes. 'So, how are we going to get out?'

'There's a window directly above, so panic ye not. I've got an idea,' he said. 'Pass me the saw, and move to the other end —please.'

Gus took the saw and stood on the seat right at the prow of the boat. He began sawing as fast as he could through the timbers surrounding the window, the boat sloshing from side to side.

After several minutes of sawing and whacking, Gus put his drenched head back under the canopy. 'Don't think that's going to work, either.' He smiled again. 'Rain's quite warm, so that's cool.'

Sue looked appalled. 'What are we going to do?'

Gus stretched out his legs, closed his eyes and took a deep breath. 'We wait.'

'Wait!' Sue roared. 'You must be joking. We'll drown if we stay in here. Can't you see that?'

Gus ignored her and smiled toothily again. It seemed to act as an anger-deflecting shield. 'You know what we haven't done?' he said, his large eyes sparkling.

'What?' Sue snapped.

'Named our vessel.'

Sue eyed him warily. 'Seriously, Gus, before we start thinking up names, do you actually think we'll get out of here?'

Gus raised his eyebrows and nodded.

'How?' Sue said, raising her eyebrows back at him. Getting a straight answer out of Gus was proving to be a bit of a nightmare.

Gus pointed upwards.

'God?' she yelled, sarcastically.

Gus laughed and his whole body galloped up and down. He moved close to her so they could hear each other without yelling. 'No, you banana-cake; through the roof. So long as the water continues to rise,' he peered out of the end of the boat, 'and it is, just as you said it would, then we go up.'

Sue grimaced. 'Really? You sure it'll work?'

'Oh yeah. Far easier this way. There's corrugated iron sheeting up there, they'll lift off and then, whoosh—away we go.'

Sue couldn't help but admire his confidence, although she wasn't entirely convinced. Wasn't corrugated sheeting incredibly heavy? 'So what do we do now?'

'Well, let's see. We could start by naming our boat. It's definitely good luck before a maiden voyage. You got any ideas?'

'Not really. You?'

'Yeah,' and he smiled his big smile again.

'Oh no, what is it?'

Gus opened his eyes wide. 'I think we should call it the "The Joan Of".

'That's it?' Sue said. She looked mystified. 'The Joan of … what? What does that mean? It doesn't make any sense. That's not a name for a boat.'

Gus feigned a look of shock. 'Now, come along, brainbox. This little teaser shouldn't be difficult for a super-smart girl like you.'

THIRTY-TWO

TO THE RESCUE

Old Man Wood hadn't taken his eyes off the panels. It was impossible. But increasingly he knew in his bones that he absolutely had to do something. More than anything, he was amazed and thrilled that the children were alive. He couldn't fathom how they'd managed it. How could children so young survive the tumult out there? 'They're only little', he said, as tears formed in his eyes.

He knew Daisy was tough and had a very high pain tolerance —the purple bruises she wore after football matches gave him the proof of that. But Isabella? Archie? No. No chance. They were soft—like all the children he'd ever known of that age.

What could he do? He felt helpless and, worse still, he wasn't even sure if he could help. He viewed the screen; Daisy and Archie were sitting in each other's arms up a tree. Now that was clever—keeping warm, out of the rain. He clapped his hands together. If they stay just as they are, they'll be fine —he'd go and find them.

In a second it changed.

He saw them shuffling up the branch as though something was coming to get them.

He zoomed out.

Was it a predator, a big cat or... ? He scratched his chin.

Suddenly a huge flash burst onto the screen. Old Man Wood fell back. Lightning? Sweet apples! His skin prickled with a cold sweat. Daisy lay on the branch as it crashed into the bank—where was Archie?

He watched the scene unfurl: Daisy hanging on for dear life—Archie being swept away. Archie held up by something and, as though in a huge panic, straining on the rope with all his might while Daisy lay on the branch. What was she doing? Screaming? He couldn't take his eyes off the scene. Then another flash struck directly at Daisy.

Old Man Wood shrieked and felt for his heart. He could hardly bear it. Then he watched as the entire branch of the tree hurtled down the makeshift drain towards the swollen river, Archie dragged behind, under the water.

Old Man Wood yelped and clasped his head in his hands. Much to his astonishment, Archie resurfaced and climbed onto the log. How did he have the strength?—he must be possessed.

Daisy lay still, just as she had before. She hadn't moved since she'd screamed. Her screen flickered, as though it was faulty. Old Man Wood gave it a pat, as if that might restore it. But it flickered again, little lines cutting through the clear picture.

A terrible feeling rushed over him and the colour drained from his face.

'NO!' he yelled out. 'Don't give up, Daisy. Whatever you do, DO NOT EVER GIVE UP!'

Old Man Wood was spurred into action. He had to get down there and fast. What should he take? He turned on the torch and shot off towards the shed. His heart and mind racing, he grabbed a rope, a small axe and his hard helmet with a built-in torch on the front. He dashed into his cold room where he stored his huge variety of apples. He selected eight rather small ones from the special box he kept far from the door.

In the cloakroom, he found his long, waterproof coat and

walking boots, which he slipped on to his large feet as fast as he could.

He returned to the bedroom and stared at the screens.

Archie was cradling Daisy, he could see that. Tears were running down his face. 'Oh you poor things,' Old Man Wood cried. 'Keep her warm and speak to her, little Arch—don't let her drift off.'

At least they had found somewhere to disembark. It was on what looked like a huge pile of rocks. And Daisy's monitor was back to normal, for the moment at least.

'Now, where was Isabella?' He furrowed his brow. 'Well, she's in a funny place. Bang next to a rock face surrounded by boulders. And she's shivering, crying. No wonder. How did she get there?' He zoomed out and pressed the cloud button which cleared away the rain.

'Apples alive!' he said. 'They're on either side of the same great heap of rocks. With all that rain they'll never discover one another, unless it's by chance!'

He zoomed out further on Isabella's monitor. 'I know where it is!' he exclaimed, his eyes almost bulging out of his head in excitement. He checked his watch. Ten minutes before four o'clock or thereabouts. Just over an hour before nightfall.

He darted out of his room, bursting with an energy and purpose he hadn't felt in years, when an idea shot into his head. He turned on his helmet light, made a detour and skipped down the cellar stairs. 'Now, which one was it?'

He headed along a very musty brick corridor that smelled of old wet rags and stopped outside a low, thick wooden door laced with metal studs right at the end. Cut into it were the Roman Numeral markings for cellar No. 2.

But, he thought, how did the door open? There wasn't a key, he was sure of that—it was something smarter; keys could be lost or discovered by nosey children or unwanted guests. He strained his brain trying to work out what it might be. 'Aaarghh,' he cried. 'Why does my head always go blank at times like this?' In his frustration he thumped his fist on the wall. One of the bricks shifted. His eyes darted up and he groped about, pushing the bricks to see if anything would happen.

Nothing.

He screwed his eyes up. He couldn't even remember the last time he'd been down here. From the corner of his eye he spotted a piece of stone protruding from the wall. Maybe that was it. He pushed it.

Again, nothing.

He left his hand there as he tapped his forehead on the wall in utter frustration. The stone moved! He pulled it further and heard a soft click. He twisted the metal ring on the door and the latch came free. He was in.

Inside, it looked exactly like a room which had been forgotten about for centuries. It smelled of dust and linseed oil. Old Man Wood brushed past the cobwebs that drooped from the ceiling and shone his helmet torch around. There, lying on shelves surrounding the walls, were hundreds upon hundreds of glass bottles and jars filled with liquids, each one covered in a thick layer of dust.

Starting at one end, he picked each one up and blew the dust off to reveal the writing, which was neatly etched into the glass. 'Spindle Sap, Ogre Blood, Wood Ox, Willow Potion and Oak Spit.' He hoped like mad that when he saw it, he'd know.

A flood of memories rushed in, almost overwhelming him. These were his bottles. HIS! From a time … well, from a time he'd lost, a time he'd forgotten. He continued along the row, reading out the names as he went until he found what he was looking for. Three full bottles with the words "Resplendix Mix" pronounced in bold writing on each. He pulled one off the shelf and brushed it down. In the torchlight, the colour was like liquid gold, and as it moved, little sparkles of light, like diamonds, danced within it.

His heart was beating like mad. Maybe he really could save them.

Old Man Wood closed the back door and was instantly set

upon by the water. He breathed a sigh of relief that he'd found the hard hat with the light to protect his bald head.

Every step he took involved wading through shin-deep water. What was the best way to the bottom of the cliff, he wondered. He scratched his chin. The lane was impassable - maybe he could lower a rope from the ruin and let himself down. He felt the coils bound around his torso. But he knew the rope wasn't long enough and anyway, what if he was swept off the top?

No, it would have to be though the woods and then somehow up and onto the ledge.

THIRTY-THREE
CAIN RETURNS

After the euphoric sensation of the icy power sluicing through his every sinew, Kemp experienced a pain like he had never felt before. His whole body raged with fire, the burning excruciating but, as he dissolved into Cain, Kemp kept repeating his name and his birthday, and his mother's and father's names and his school and his favourite colours and everything happy that he could ever remember.

The last thing he remembered was diving head-first towards the electric body of a weird spidery creature and then being sucked into a void. He must have passed out.

When he opened his eyes it was as though he was seeing through a grey filter. He could see shapes and objects, but nothing clearly; no detail.

He sensed he was lying on a bed. He shut his eyes, and tried to see if he could lose the pain—a constant, driving, nagging ache. He could sense that he was in a body that was gently rising and falling—his body—but it was surrounded by something else. Ash? Soot?

Cain was sleeping. He was sure of it. Kemp felt woozy and weak, and utterly helpless. Nothing he did seemed to make any difference. He had no control, but maybe he could use this time to think—as himself—while Cain slept.

Now Cain was stirring. Suddenly Kemp felt his entire

body taken over and his brain and eyes and everything seemed to be fading away, like a gas lamp being extinguished.

FOR THE FIRST time in ages, Cain woke feeling like a different person.

What a wonder, he thought, rubbing his non-existent eyes. Sleep. I had forgotten how invigorating it is. I feel marvellous and now I am hungry. The boy inside me needs sustaining.

'Food!' he yelled out. 'Schmerger, I require food. WHERE IS MY FOOD?'

From the door, Cain could make out a shape which stopped at a respectable distance and bowed. 'Your Lordship,' the bent figure of Schmerger said, 'you haven't eaten for thousands of years. Are you yourself today?'

Cain picked himself off the bed and marched up to the servant. 'I require food, immediately; a huge feast.'

The servant had a look of shock and confusion on his usually featureless face. 'There is no kitchen,' he replied.

'NO KITCHEN?! What kind of palace is this?'

Schmerger was completely taken by surprise. 'May I be so bold and say that ever since I was assigned to your highness, there has never been a kitchen. Your highness banned them.'

Cain thrust out his arm, picked the man up by the throat and threw him at a table which splintered over the floor. 'Is that so?'

The servant held his throat and, in shock, wondered how Cain had acquired his new-found strength.

Cain drew up to him. 'How and *where* do you eat, Schmerger? Show me.'

The servant bowed and led the ghost down the wide main staircase through a corridor and several doors before entering a small room.

Cain followed, delighted that for once he could see outlines of people and rooms and his bed and even his dim profile in the mirror. And though it was a shame he couldn't see with any detail, it was a great deal better than nothing at all.

Schmerger picked up a wicker basket. 'From Mrs Schmerger, Sire.'

'Tell me,' Cain quizzed, 'what is in it?'

Schmerger thought this was quite ridiculous. 'It was my lunch, Sire,' he lied. 'There is no more.'

'Do you take me for a fool?' Cain said, as he thrust his hand into the basket. He pulled out something black and stodgy and, without hesitation, stuffed it in his mouth. For the first time in ages he chewed, although he had to admit it wasn't really for him. Aside from a tingle in his mouth, it tasted like soot. But he was sure the boy found it favourable.

Schmerger backed out of the room, trembling, leaving it to Cain.

Cain pulled another piece of food and popped it in his mouth. This time, it crunched and splintered. Cain spat it out. 'Schmerger,' he yelled, 'what is that?'

'It is the leg of a bird,' the servant said. 'One does not ordinarily eat the bones.'

Cain crashed his fist down on the table. 'What is there to drink?'

'There is nothing but water, Sire,' Schmerger said. 'Your Majesty has never had a requirement for any.'

'I do now. Bring me some this instant. I have a thirst.' Cain marched out of the room. 'Let me see this palace of mine. Bring the drink to me, and more food.'

Cain crashed through the doors and found himself at the foot of the grand staircase. Then he had an idea. 'Dreamspinner, dreamspinner, dreamspinner,' he called out. It was their agreed way of contact.

Moments later Asgard appeared, his maghole tingling as usual with electrical current.

For the first time, Cain could just about make out his outline. 'Let us see how the Heirs of Eden are surviving. And let me try and persuade Archie to come with me.'

Asgard opened the hole and Cain bent down and dived through.

Asgard took him to the big log that straddled the track and, as he emerged, he surveyed the scene. Cain was frankly amazed that the Heirs of Eden were still hanging on to life.

They looked desperate, pathetic. He could tell their struggle was nearly over. Their bodies could not take much more of a pounding. And where was the old man? Ha! He didn't even know what was going on. Sad. Truly.

Cain realised that this was possibly the last chance to tempt Archie to go with him. He could lose the one inside him and have Archie instead. In one easy step it would resolve this theatre, this charade, that these puny Heirs of Eden might survive.

He would put them out of their misery and everything would be resolved.

THIRTY-FOUR

HOLDING ON

A rchie stared at his watch: gone four. When was sunset, five, half five?

He crawled over to Daisy and cradled her in his arms. 'Come on, Daisy,' he whispered as he sheltered her face. 'Don't give up on me. There's only a little while to go, you know. And I'm going to keep you alive, if it's the last thing I do.' He put his cold hands on her face. He was cold but she was icy.

Gently, he massaged her heart, he didn't know why, but it just seemed the right thing to do. 'Please, Daisy, you've got to come back. Don't you dare back out now; I don't know what I'd do without you. And if you go, we've all had it; everyone, not just us.' Her eyes flickered and he saw the corners of her cut lips turn up.

Thank goodness, he thought, a spark of life.

He'd keep talking and somehow he had to keep her listening. 'Right, here's what we're going to do,' he said, quite aware that there was probably no way she could hear him. 'I'm going to pick you up and start carrying you over these rocks and stuff, OK?'

Very gently, he tried to find a foothold in the debris. He took one step and then another, swaying each time to keep his balance. Every so often he studied her face to make sure she was still with him and carried on, leaping from one rock to the next, disregarding the rain, disregarding his own discomfort, worrying only about each step and the wellbeing of his sister.

As he climbed, he carried on talking. He talked about what was going to happen and how safe they were going to be in only a little while and anything else he could think of. When he ran out of things to say, he started singing. The first song that came into his head was a song their mother taught them when they were young. With chattering teeth, he sang it as best as he could. When he forgot the words, he hummed it, his voice shaking with cold.

After a few minutes of this, Daisy's eyes flashed open. He looked down at her and smiled, trying to hold back his tears and continued his humming. But he could feel her tensing. Now her eyes were wide open, as though telling him something. What was it? Her eyes rolled back.

Archie tensed. 'Oh no. It can't be. NOT ANOTHER ONE!'

Instantly, Archie threw Daisy over his shoulder in a fireman's lift, which helped to centre his balance. He reached the top of a boulder and tried to see beyond it, but there was nothing but the steady veil of rain. 'Daisy!' he cried out, 'I've got to jump and I don't know where we'll end up. If this goes badly, just remember that I love you.' He had no more time.

Archie sucked in as much air as he could and closed his eyes. He bent his knees and jumped as high and as far as he possibly could—into the dark unknown.

ISABELLA COULD REMEMBER IT WELL. It was her first skiing trip, high up in the Alps a couple of years ago, and the day had been beautifully hot with a bright blue sky. At lunch, she stripped off her jacket, threw off her hat and ditched her long johns giving them all to her mother who crammed them into her rucksack. Then, they'd jumped on a chairlift that headed right to the top of the mountain. Halfway up, it stopped and swung in the air. They stayed like that for ages—an hour, maybe more. Then the weather changed.

First the clouds blew in, followed by an icy, biting wind and after that, snow. She sat there freezing, with nothing but her father's arm around her to protect her while, in the seat behind, her mother was holding the bag with her clothes in. An hour later as they skied off, every bone in her body, from the top of her head to the tip of her toes, ached with cold. She remembered how it took two hot chocolates before she could move her jaw enough to say anything. What she would give for a hot chocolate now.

What had her father said? *Keep moving, girl.* That was it. *And if you can't keep moving, hug someone. Hug them nice and tight.* A warm feeling filled her as she remembered how Archie thought this was the perfect excuse to go round hugging people and everyone had thought him rather cute, even Daisy.

Isabella tried to smile - she needed to move. Using her hands as a guide along the face of the stone, she felt for jagged bits or protruding rock so that she might get a decent foothold. She found one, lifted herself up and then felt for another further up. She'd done enough climbing to know that planning a route up and making sure one's feet were stable was the key. The problem was that she couldn't see and there was so much water and she was so numb that she couldn't feel if her grip was true or not. She slipped back and landed with a wet thud on the ground.

Isabella shook her hands vigorously in front of her and slowly the blood began to return. She jogged on the spot, her wet trousers sticking to her legs, and rolled her head on her shoulders. She needed to search further along.

Once again she followed the face of the rock, guided by her hands, her legs now knee-deep in the water. A little further on—to her right this time—she found the perfect spot: an outcrop of stone concealed by bushes.

Moving them aside, she found not one but two easy steps.

She pulled herself up, placing her foot carefully on the first and making sure it was solid. Then, hugging the rock, she tested her weight slowly on the next. It felt solid, like a step, and she wondered if it had been purposely carved out of the rocks.

Her arms searched around in the rain trying to find another. She found it and levered herself up. She did the same again, noting that the steps curved around the rock face. She found another, and then another, and as she reached out for another, she realised she was on a flat ledge.

With the rain driving at her, she had lost her sense of direction. She sat on the ledge trying to fathom the angle of the steps in relation to the rock face. She crawled on her hands and knees in the direction of the cliff face, scanning for any sudden gaps or boulders. Aside from pebbles, it felt smooth. She crawled on further before she realised the rain was subsiding a little. Then it stopped altogether. She was under the cliff face itself! She wiped the water from her face, and leaned into a big, round rock behind her. Isabella felt strangely elated, as if she'd completed a task.

In the dim light she could make out that what she was leaning on was a huge round rock. She examined it and figured that it sat directly under the cliff face. The question was, how would she get out from here? The logical answer was to head out to the right—above which their cottage sat. But she wasn't sure if it was such a clever idea. The light was failing fast and the rain wasn't letting up. Maybe she'd have to stay put until the morning. At least she'd be dry and safe from the water. It couldn't rise this far, could it?

And anyway, what had Archie said right at the start? That the storm would go at them until sunset, or something like that. She dismissed it, stood up and stretched her back.

And then they came out of the sky.

She hardly had a chance to react—just to duck down.

Two lightning bolts smashed into the rocks near to where she'd just been.

Oh my God. What if there's one for each of us! In a

heartbeat she knew exactly what she had to do and she threw herself off the ledge. As she went, a huge bolt spat out of the sky and smashed into the exact spot she'd been standing on.

Isabella tumbled into the water, her heart beating like crazy. She sank down as low as she could go, amazed at how much the water had risen. But Isabella knew that this section of water was secured by the boulders of the landslide.

It was now a deep pool where the current wouldn't whisk her away.

She stayed underneath as long as her lungs could hold her, hugging the cliff face as splinters of rock and stone punched the pool like deadly shrapnel.

THIRTY-FIVE

THE BOAT HEADS OUT

'Oh, *ARK*!' Sue exclaimed. 'As in, *Joan of Arc*.'

Gus nodded. 'Blimey. At long last. Remind me never to partner you in a pub quiz. Ever.'

'You mean,' Sue said, 'you've actually been to a pub quiz?'

'Of course; every Friday night with my dad.'

'Really? My mum would never do that kind of thing. What's it like?'

Gus wondered if he should make it sound really exciting. 'Well, it's OK. Actually it's quite nerdy—you'd probably do pretty well.'

Sue's eyes sparkled. Gus was full of surprises. Just goes to show, she thought, you really can't tell a book by its cover. 'So, what subjects are you good at?'

Gus pulled his brainiest face, which made him look pretty stupid. 'Particle physics, geography, English history from 1066, current world affairs and, er, yeah, modern American history.'

'You're joking me!'

'Try me. Go on,' Gus said, looking like a dog after a bone.

Sue didn't know what to think. She screwed up her face as though deep in thought and asked: 'Which President of the

United States of America wrote the American Declaration of Independence?'

Gus scratched his chin and made lots of quite odd-looking faces. 'Abraham Lincoln—'

'Ha, wrong—'

'Won the Civil War,' Gus continued, ignoring her. 'Thomas Jefferson was the main author of the Declaration of Independence.' He tried very hard not to smile. But he did raise his eyebrows. And they were very big eyebrows.

Sue couldn't believe it. 'Correct,' she said, trying to think of another question. 'Name the English monarch who came after William Rufus?'

'You can do better than that, sexy Sue.' He pulled a serious face. 'William Rufus, heir of William the Conqueror. Shot by an arrow by a noble who thought he was a total nob-end. Succeeded by Henry, as in Henry One, also a son of the Conqueror, who sat on the throne for a middle-age marathon of thirty-five years.'

Sue shrieked. She couldn't believe it. 'Gus, you're brilliant at this. Why are you such an idiot in class?'

Gus shrugged. 'Low tolerance to teachers—'

A loud clunk stopped them in their tracks. Gus raced up to the bow step. 'The Joan Of has hit the roof,' he yelled. 'Here we go.' Gus ducked his head inside the canopy. 'I hope you're ready for this. Pass me that long bit of wood and sit at the end. And Sue...'

'Yes.'

'Whatever you do, please don't scream—it really won't help.'

Gus had never really expected the water to rise quite so high, nor so fast. In fact he was pretty sure they'd stay in the boathouse quite safe from anything outside. Now, it was very different. He grappled with the piece of wood, eventually holding its base, and thrust it up towards the corrugated sheeting directly above. Come on, you little beauty, you've got to move. Nothing happened. He changed his tack, trying to lever the roofing off. Move, you little sod, he murmured, as he pushed the wood with all his might.

But, as he pushed, he noticed that the entire building had begun to move of its own accord. Gus stopped hammering on the roof and watched as the shed began to lift up and drift off into the flooding all on its own. He couldn't believe it. He wondered if, incredibly, the buoyancy of their boat had given buoyancy to the whole building—and now it had gone adrift with them inside it. That, or he was suddenly immensely strong.

The only thing he knew for sure was that the whole unit was moving very quickly into the swollen floodwaters. As far as he could tell, they were safe. In fact, he rather suspected they were safer than any place they could otherwise have expected to end up in—so long as The Joan Of wasn't rotten. He ducked down under the canopy. Sue was crying hysterically.

'Everything ship-shape and dandy, Capitan,' he said, saluting.

Sue looked confused. 'What's happening, Gus, I'm scared.'

'I pushed the roof and the entire shed came away. Funny thing is, I always suspected I had superpowers.'

'Is it … safe?'

Gus looked at her blankly. 'Truthfully? I've no idea, but so far, so good. Now, how about another brainteaser.' He sat down and put his legs up again. 'Can't wait all day.'

Sue peered up at him. She simply couldn't believe his brazen attitude to the disaster unfolding around them. The boat lurched and her eyes widened. But Gus rubbed his eyes and yawned.

'You are ridiculous, Gus Williams. I don't know how you do it.' She took a couple of very deep breaths as if to control herself. 'We're on the verge of plunging into Armageddon and you want another teaser, Gus?'

Gus nodded. 'Yeah. Absolutely.'

'Good Lord.' She took a deep breath. 'OK. Physics question—you said you were good at physics, right?' He nodded. A question popped into her head. 'Where does bad light end up?'

Gus put his feet up on the seat in front, confidently, grinning like mad, which Sue later discovered was a sign that his brain was working. 'OK,' he began, cagily, 'either it's in an ohm?' Sue giggled but shook her head. 'OR,' and there was quite a long pause. He clicked his fingers, 'In a prism?'

Sue clapped her hands. 'Brilliant! You big strapping genius.'

Gus was bursting with pride. Big, strapping and genius— in the same sentence—from delicious, sexy Sue; he hardly dare tell her he'd read the answers in a magazine at the dentist. 'One for you,' he said. 'What did the male magnet say to the female magnet?'

Sue burst out laughing. 'I'm seriously attracted to you?' She turned purple on the spot.

Gus caught her eye. 'Not bad. Want another try?'

Sue shook her head. 'Go on, tell me.'

Gus looked quite serious. 'From your backside,' he began. 'I thought you were repulsive. However, from the front I find you rather attractive.'

Sue clapped her hands and laughed as Gus punched the air.

Suddenly, a terrible noise, like the body of a car scraping along a road silenced them.

Gus slipped out at the front. Then he dived back in and dashed toward Sue at the rear. 'Move up front,' he ordered.

Sue shuffled up as Gus headed out of the canopy at the bow.

Seconds later, he reappeared and, without hesitating, sat in the middle of the boat and grabbed the oars. He started to row, pushing the oars in to go backwards, as fast as he could.

'What's going on?' Sue cried.

'Our time has come. The Joan Of has landed.'

With a terrible crunching noise, the back end of the shed began to lever high into the air as if the nose had plunged in to the water. Gus took a deep breath. 'We're on our own. Let's pray that The Joan Of holds together.'

With a massive effort, Gus continued to row the little boat backwards, creeping under the raised end and out into the river. For the first time, the rain whammed into the canopy and the boat rocked in the water. The sound was deafening. Sue screamed.

After a couple of minutes, Sue bravely put her head out as far as she dared and tried to survey the scene. But the only things she could see were faint outlines of cars, wood and sections of plastic, bobbing along beside them.

She ducked under the canopy, her face ashen.

'Everything alright?' Gus yelled, noting the distress in her face.

'Isabella, Daisy and Archie are in this—with no protection,' she yelled back. 'They haven't got a hope.'

'They'll be fine,' he yelled back. He looked down. 'Sue,' he screamed, his voice only just heard above the sound of the rain smacking down on the canopy. 'Get a bucket and start bailing!'

THIRTY-SIX

A LEAP OF FAITH

When Isabella surfaced she noticed a big difference. The water level was near to the ledge and it was almost dark. She pulled herself out and sat down, her feet dangling in the pool. She shivered and stretched her hands out in front of her.

There was something else and she couldn't think what it was. Then it struck her. The rain had almost stopped! It was like a miracle and she smiled through chattering teeth.

The remains of her clothes stuck to her like cold, soggy slime and she still had to make it through the night. How was she going to do that? The temperature would drop—it always did at about this time of year—and there was no hope of a warming fire.

In the next breath, her thoughts turned to Daisy and Archie. There had been three huge thunderbolts, one designed for each of them. Why, she had no idea, but it seemed right, even if it was absurdly illogical and absolutely terrifying.

She shuffled along in the darkness and called out their names.

'Archie. Daisy—are you there?'

She listened, but heard only the swishing sounds of the running water beyond.

Again and again she called out and listened.
But no reply was forthcoming.

ARCHIE HAD no idea what he might land on: rock, mud, a piece of wood, an old section of metal? But a broken leg was preferable to being fried to death by a lightning bolt.

To his shock—and relief—Archie, with Daisy over his shoulder, had landed in a pool and sank down to the very bottom at the exact moment two lightning bolts smashed into their previous position. The brutal force of the energy sent shards, pebbles and larger stones flying towards them, shaking everything to the core. Archie stayed down, holding Daisy, cradling her head for as long as he dared until her eyes opened wide as if she was on her last reserve of oxygen.

Archie winced as the first stone hit him on the shoulder. Then he felt himself being peppered, but he had to get to the surface to breathe, to get Daisy out. As he rose to the surface, a rock whacked him on the head. He fell back into the pool and saw stars.

With a last effort, he pulled himself over towards the rocks and, feeling his feet touch firm ground, he pushed Daisy up as far as he could. Her body slumped and fell on what he desperately hoped was a safe place.

Now his head spun so fast that in no time he felt himself go, his body slipping away to a place of softness and light. A feeling of great calm washed over him, a warmth—a comfort —like a cuddle brimming with love in the arms of someone who truly adores you.

With his last breath of consciousness, Archie had the wherewithal to reach up and grasp a hand-hold. And then his mind slid into the darkness of a black and deep abyss.

ISABELLA WOULDN'T GIVE UP. Deep within her, she

sensed they were near, but it was so hard. She was so tired, so cold, so hungry. She knew she had to pull herself together. Come on, she told herself, no time to be lazy; look for them. A thought kept returning: what if they were a few feet away and died in the night because she couldn't be bothered?

She crawled along the ledge as far as she dared, all the while making sure she kept a firm grip of the surface, and calling out for them in turn, '*Daisy*, *Archie*'. Then she listened, but every time, there was nothing, just the lapping of water splashing up against the rocks.

Had Daisy and Archie been blasted to smithereens by the bolt? Had they been swept away? What if they had never been close but found their way home? She knew that was impossible. She ran her hand through the water and then through her hair, removing the strands that were stuck to her face. With defeat threatening to overwhelm her, she dragged her aching body to the rock face, out of the drizzling rain.

The problem now was survival. She had all night to wait out until the dawn of a new day.

She shivered, her lips quivering involuntarily as she stared out into the darkness. Occasionally she heard a sound like a groan but it was hard to tell if it was the crunching of metal on metal, like cars or sheds being washed down the river and colliding with each other, or whether it was from people or animals. Tears built up and an overwhelming sense of sadness began to leach into her, her feeling of helplessness almost complete.

As if in response to her cries, a tiny sliver of light appeared on the lip of the horizon and threw a grey light over the water. Isabella peered at it and, for a short while, thought that she must be dreaming. It looked so beautiful, like the gentle sparkle of light catching the rim of a silver bracelet. She blinked and shook her head. The moon? It was moonlight!

Now, instead of the pitch darkness, she could distinguish the outlines of the boulders and the ledge and, looking up, the rock face curved above her. She scoured the valley and was struck by a curious sight; a dull, watery reflection, gently flickering, which extended on and on in front of her.

As the moon rose, its brightness lifted her spirits further; now she could walk where before only crawling was possible. A renewed sense of hope swept through her—maybe she'd be able to find a way out. She scoured the ledge. The round boulder she had leant on before the lightning struck was reduced to rubble, save for several large chunks that had been hewn into rough, awkward shapes. But the area behind it seemed unnaturally dark.

She approached. With every footstep, she grew more curious, her feet crunching through the debris. Was there something behind it, something hollow and open, or was her mind playing tricks on her again?

She sidled closer, until she found herself peering up at the perfectly symmetrical entrance of a cave.

Without hesitating, she placed one foot ahead of the other and made her way in.

A breeze was blowing out of it, and for a moment she caught it on her face—warmth? Hot air?

Cautiously, she took another step, hoping that her eyes would adjust to the moonlight. Oh, how lovely and warm it was, like being in front of a hairdryer. But how come? This bit of rock wasn't thermal, like a volcano—or was it?

Isabella was about to take a further step in when she heard a strange cry from near the ledge. Her heart skipped a beat. Daisy? Archie?

She scanned the area but found that the ledge was only just higher than the river and it was hard to tell where one stopped and the other started. She heard it again, a groan followed by a cry and a tiny cough.

Her heart beat faster as she scoured the ledge again. She concentrated, feeling that if she could find one of them, she might very well find the other.

She ran to the right, urging her eyes to peer deeper into the night sky.

Nothing.

She walked cautiously to the left.

Nothing.

In front of her, all she could make out was a blob. A blob, almost black in colour, like so many of the other rocks and bits of debris. As she approached it, the blob stirred. Isabella's heart leapt. She was there in a second.

The body was barely covered by clothes. It was smeared in dirt intermingled with bloody cuts and angry bruises. The legs and arms were as white as a sheet. Isabella's heart sank. As she turned the body over, the arms folded round limply and splashed helplessly in a puddle.

The eyes were closed.

Isabella screamed. It was as if someone had ripped her heart out. She had never seen anyone look deader.

It was Daisy.

THIRTY-SEVEN

STUCK ON THE CLIFF

At every step, Old Man Wood was forced to hold on for fear of being pulled down and swept away. Twice he lost his footing only to slide fortuitously into a nearby tree. And on another occasion he thrust his axe out and wedged it into a tree trunk. He pulled himself up and hugged the tree like a long lost brother who had saved his life.

Every so often, Old Man Wood stumbled into a rock he was familiar with or a tree he knew, even when the tree had been uprooted. And from these small signs, he was able to gauge his direction towards the cliff face beneath the ruin.

The problem building in his mind was getting up on to the ledge. Usually it was done by means of some steps at the base of the cliff. Why they were there, he had no idea, but he knew that by now they had to be submerged. He'd make his way along a rocky seam further up and see if he could climb across and downwards.

Before long, Old Man Wood was at the point where he needed to start down the steeper, sharper cliff face.

Old Man Wood faced the rock and shuffled along, happier in his step where the mud gave way to stone. As he angled across the cliff face there were sections that sheltered him from the downpour, while other parts showered him with mud and loose rock. He dug his fingers into every tight crevice and small hole—moving along as carefully, yet as fast, as he dared—unclear of his position, but hoping like mad he hadn't started too high.

Shortly, he was able to take stock of his position under a deep overhang where he found a decent foothold. He gulped in huge mouthfuls of air as he leant into the stone. Should he drive a bolt into a suitable crevice so he could attach the rope —just in case?

He found a hole, delved into his pocket, found a quick release bolt and thrust it in. It expanded instantly and fastened into the rock. He put his weight on it and it held. Good. He tied the rope to the end, and attached the rest around his body.

As he turned to inspect his next foothold, a huge electrical pulse flashed out of the sky below and to the left of him. He looked on in shock. Then a second bright charge, the noise piercing his eardrums.

The valley lit up and he saw everything move like a huge grey beast. 'Apples-alive,' he muttered under his breath, as his heart raced. He was too high above the ledge.

He checked his footing and tested his grip but, in the very next moment, a huge thunderbolt smashed out of the sky directly into the cliff face beneath him.

For a second Old Man Wood held on for dear life.

There they were!

He could see the children.

Isabella diving into a pool, Daisy further round, and Archie.

He had to get down there fast.

If he tried to scramble down, the overhanging rock extended too far over on one side and there was every chance he'd suffer serious injury on the sharp edges.

'No, it will have to be a far more radical route,' he mumbled to himself. He climbed along as fast as he could, letting the rope out behind him. After several metres he tensioned the rope and started to descend, being careful not to slip and fall. The old man sucked in his cheeks.

'Right, here we go; nothing like a bit of adventure,' he said.

He pushed out with his feet and the rope swung out. Old Man Wood was flying through the air, rain smashing into his face.

He began preparing himself for the landing. It was going to hurt, he thought. Rather a lot.

The rope swung out again, this time gaining speed. Moments later, he was back to his starting position, like a pendulum. This time, as he reached the limit of his arc, he noted that the rain had suddenly stopped.

The shock at the lack of rain, and the fact that the moon now offered just enough light to see below, forced him to hold on and he let his momentum take him out one more time. He was ready to jump. But as he looked down, he could see Isabella directly below him.

He swung back, holding on for dear life—but it was one swing too many. The bolt disengaged from the rock, and the rope and Old Man Wood hurtled downwards.

As he landed, a pain shot into his ankle and his back. He attempted a parachute roll, but instead, he skidded and smacked into a large rock.

He lay in a heap, his breath knocked clean out of him. The old man tried to pick himself up using the rock as a prop. But the burning sensation in his ankle meant that the joint was refusing to take any weight.

He watched Isabella walking out and bending down. He heard her scream. Then muffled cries. Was he too late? Had she found one of the children? Daisy?

Old Man Wood couldn't believe it. Had he come this far only to fail? Oh apples alive, he cursed, how could he be so hopeless. He summoned his strength, trying to ignore the searing pain that coursed through his legs.

He urged himself on, but his body would not co-operate. He slumped back down and pulled up his trouser legs. Already his ankle was swollen—full of blood, huge and tender, like a juicy summer pudding.

His eyes watered as his fingers probed the swollen flesh. Was it a tear or a break? Had it twisted on landing? He wondered if his back was equally shot. He turned his head and his back screamed out as if a knife was stabbing at his vertebrae.

Even his hands were hurting. He studied them and found that blood was pouring from a cut in the middle of his left palm.

What a pathetic, hopeless disaster. What had he been thinking? Swinging on ropes at his age, he wasn't a child who was able to play football. He couldn't even bring himself to laugh at the madness of it.

And now his body was beginning to shut down. It was in shock—Old Man Wood knew it well. Then it struck him—how come he hadn't thought of it earlier? Resplendix Mix! Of course! He'd self-medicate.

With his swollen hand he reached into his pocket. There it was. He attempted to open it. Did it twist off?

Old Man Wood set the bottle down and attempted to hold and turn, but when nothing happened apart from his hand slipping round the rim, he inspected it.

No lid.

Harrumph. Maybe it needed a sharp pull, so he tried, but there was nothing to pull on.

Old Man Wood shook his head in frustration. No shaking or twisting or pulling or yelling would make it open.

He felt his eyelids becoming heavy and struggled to keep them open. He wondered if he shouldn't try and break the top off by smashing it on a rock. But his thoughts vanished like vapour on a window as a deeper yearning for sleep filled his mind.

He tried to fight back, but it was hopeless.

And then his mind slipped away.

THIRTY-EIGHT

BAILING FOR THEIR LIVES

Sue felt like she'd scooped out enough water to fill an Olympic-sized swimming pool three times over. Her arms ached so much she thought they might simply drop off.

Every so often, the boat would bash into something solid, like a wall or a car, and they would be thrown forward. It was at these moments that both of them knew the strength of the boat would be tested. All it would take was a crack or a small hole and that would be the end of it. At other times, The Joan Of seemed to grind against something, or spin as it diverted off an object, the water tossing the boat one way and then the other.

Several times, Gus managed to lever the boat away with an oar, pitching it back into the swell. Gus would hold her, or stare into her eyes reassuringly—his wide eyes not so much in fear, she thought, but more in excitement. To her, Gus was having the time of his life.

When he started singing a hearty sea shanty as he tossed the water out with his bucket, his singing got louder and louder until it was in direct competition with the rain. Sue didn't know whether to laugh, cry, join in, or hit him. But, for a while, at least it stopped her thinking about the disaster and her friends.

After three hours, Gus pointed upwards. 'I think we've

moved away from the main rain belt.' She nodded in agreement. 'Problem is—how far do you reckon we've gone?'

'No idea,' she said. It was impossible to tell.

Gus put his head out of the canopy. 'Still can't see a thing,' he reported back, 'apart from muddy water. Fancy some grub?'

Sue was starving. Gus opened a tin of tuna and a bag of salt and vinegar crisps and took a swig of water. When they'd finished, he had an idea.

'Look, Sue,' he began, 'one of us had better have a kip— we're going to need to sleep at some point and there's not much room. If we do it this way, the other can keep look-out.'

Sue hadn't thought of this. 'Good idea, brain-box. On sailing boats, I think they do four hours on and four hours off. Want to give it a try?'

'Sure,' Gus said. 'It's five-fifty now. Have a sleep till half nine—if you can. Then I'll look out till one and do the early morning shift at four or five. Sound OK?'

With a bit of a shuffle, Gus pulled the planks he'd stowed from the bottom of the boat and made up a bed—of sorts— where at least one of them could lie down. Gus unfolded a plastic sheet and laid it on top of the boards so they wouldn't lie in the wet. Sue lay down and he spread the dust sheets over her. It wasn't great, but it would have to do.

Sue closed her eyes. She didn't really feel like sleeping, but having a rest now after all that bailing out was welcome. And Gus was right, one of them needed to be on look-out—especially if there was a place they could land—and it would be a disaster if they were to miss out while they slept.

GUS MOVED out to the bow of the boat and breathed a big sigh of relief. Quite amazingly, it seemed, they had got over the worst and the makeshift canopy he'd erected had saved their lives. He laughed. He'd have won the DT prize for that; just goes to show what you can do when the pressure's on. He wondered if Sue had any idea how close it had been, and then he thought of his mum and dad. Mum would be worried sick, but his dad would be chuffed to bits with him, he reckoned. He hoped they hadn't gone looking for him—there was nothing he could do about it if they had. Anyway, what a surprise it would be when he got home.

At least they had food and water and could keep dry. And so long as the boat held together they had every chance. Plus they made a good team. He took a deep breath as the last gasps of daylight started to eke away. Yeah, they made a very good team.

If only they had some way of telling where they were. He thought for a minute if it wouldn't be worth dropping the oars and trying to make it to land by rowing hard to one side. Or maybe he could drop an oar at the back and use it as a rudder. But, then again, what if he didn't have the strength to handle it and dropped the oar into the water. No, it wasn't worth the risk. He wiped the rain, which was now bearable for more than a minute, off his face. Best keep on and hope the boat might bank somewhere where they could make off to safety.

He ducked inside and, as Sue dozed, he slipped past her, grabbed a bucket and started the process of bailing the water out all over again. How long would the rain continue? Perhaps they were over the worst, but what if the deluge came back? He shivered. They had been lucky—astonishingly lucky, he'd never seen anything like it—but he didn't fancy their chances if it happened again.

At the change-over, the boat continued to float freely, bumping into driftwood and other debris being washed out. Occasionally, The Joan Of spun and pitched, but not with the same force as earlier. Gus wondered what they were going to eat for supper, before resisting the temptation to devour a Mars Bar. He headed to the front of the boat where, every so often through the drizzle, he imagined he could see a spark of a light in the distance.

When Sue woke, they tucked into a cold pork pie and

shared a few pieces of chocolate. Gus was very strict on the rations, stating that until they had some idea where they were, they needed to conserve every morsel. Sue complained bitterly, but Gus made it quite clear that this was non-negotiable. By the time they had given each other a few more teasers, and told each other stories about their childhoods, it was ten o'clock. Gus reluctantly lay down on the planks while Sue kept look-out.

At midnight, Sue was frozen. And she was bored of looking out onto the dark sky and being spat on by the rain while the boat bobbed along. She climbed under the canopy and, instinctively, she lay down next to Gus, who was fast asleep. She nestled up to his warm body, rearranging the dust covers over herself and inhaling the boyish smell of his clothes.

Staring at his peaceful face, she moved in and planted a small kiss on his cheek.

THIRTY-NINE
BETRAYAL

Gaia, the dreamspinner, flashed back to see Old Man Wood as regularly as she thought appropriate, returning as near to the old man as she dared. Once she understood what the old man was doing, or not doing, she inverted into her maghole so that her movements would not be seen, nor her presence missed.

Gaia knew it was nearly impossible for one dreamspinner to follow another, simply because each one went wherever they chose by simply thinking about their destination and flipping through their magholes to get there. So unless another dreamspinner had access to her thoughts she was safe enough, but in these strange times, who knew who was checking up on who?

Every dreamspinner, Gaia sensed, fully understood the events playing out with Isabella, Archie and Daisy. And they knew that what happened now would affect them. It wasn't a game, it wasn't coincidence, and it wasn't something they could ignore.

She sensed a strange atmosphere of nervousness around the Great Atrium—the vast chamber where the last specks of dream powders were stored. On top of this was another sensation that she was not familiar with at all. She wondered if this was the feeling humans called *fear*?

Dreamspinners knew their purpose was threatened. Would they now spin only bland dreams and nightmares, filling the world with dreams of anguish and sorrow and mediocrity?

Wasn't the point of dreaming to let the dreamer reach out to something magic or beautiful or bewitching or out of the ordinary? Wasn't it another way of understanding the universe and the complexities of life?

But, then again, if they had no more dreams to give, what would become of them?

Gaia flicked a couple of her legs. The story of the Prophecy was commonplace. The dreamspinners knew of the loss of Archie's gift of courage, and whispers abounded that the Heirs of Eden were not really the Heirs of Eden at all, but just three children who happened to be in Eden Cottage with the old man. Gaia had put them right. They were the Heirs of Eden alright—it was their birthright.

As for the old man, well, Old Man Wood had never expected to live so long. He might be doddery but he was the only one who could help them. And, with any luck, he still would.

The trouble was, Gaia thought, that dreamspinners had never meddled in the lives of others, however terrible the mess, however easy it would be to make a situation better—or worse. And, they never toyed with the consequences.

As Gaia thought about this, she crossed and re-crossed her long, slender legs, occasionally dipping one in her maghole. Now that the dreamspinners understood how perilous their situation was, would their approach change? Were dreamspinners evolving?

Gaia wondered what Asgard was up to. She sniffed the air and reached out into the cosmos. It was a long-shot. She'd have to feel the vibrations of a physical place where a dreamspinner might be.

Strong feelings came to her from Cain's palace in Havilah, particularly from the roof of the ballroom - perhaps the fireplace. Dreamspinners loved fireplaces.

Gaia needed to act fast.

Moments later she reappeared on the ceiling of Cain's ballroom. Had she done enough to camouflage her body? She wondered whether the white powder rubbed over her dark parts masked her deep-grey age-lines. She'd have to see.

Young dreamspinners acknowledged the senior ones by means of a simple, subtle and quick movement, a nod of the head, the flick of a leg or a flaring of the mouth. In return, the senior dreamspinner would return the gesture.

Gaia reminded herself that, now she looked a thousand years younger, she would have to remember to do this first rather than in return. If only she still felt as slight and as fast.

There — a tiny flicker of light. And now she looked closely, masses of dots of light, like faint pinpricks, flashed by the huge, open hearth of the great fireplace.

Was this an organised gathering?

She plotted a course for the vast chimney and inverted. Inside, it was crammed full of dreamspinners.

'Friends,' said a familiar low vibration. It was Asgard, just as she suspected. 'I trust you have not given yourselves away?' A shared vibration went round and Gaia had no option but to hold it and pass it on. Each dreamspinner sent a vibration back. Gaia tried to guess how many there were, three hundred, a thousand—more? She wondered if her vibration would be picked up. Her physical disguise was not so bad, but she hadn't thought to conceal her vibrations. She tried to muffle them, hoping they would slip through unnoticed.

Asgard's vibrations continued. 'There are many here, so shrink your bodies. Now, I will tell you the bitter truth.'

More arrived. Gaia retracted her maghole.

'The Heirs of Eden,' Asgard vibrated solemnly, 'are on a course to fail.' Gasps shot around the chimney.

'You know this, Asgard? You have proof?'

'Are they dead?' another quizzed. The air was humming.

'There is not long to go,' Asgard began. 'Reports come to me regularly.'

'How can you be certain?' said another.

'It takes just one of them to die,' Asgard continued. 'I am informed that two of them are on the brink of expiring.'

In vibration terms, the chimney exploded into an uproar. Gaia stuck a leg out and heard a few, feeling the expressions of shock and anguish and worry, but she kept her head down, and hidden. She needed to find out what Asgard had planned.

'I know how you feel,' Asgard said, his vibrations rising up above the clamour. 'The chance to open up the Garden of Eden once more—after so long—is slipping away like the lives of those children. The new time we hoped for will not be. The heirs have failed, and failed at the very first test.

'A child of man is never going to be strong enough to survive the ravages of nature, let alone the three great tasks. I told this to the great Genesis who ignored my pleas. But I have been proved right, as I knew I would. Perhaps in her great age she is no longer in touch.'

Uneasy vibrations flew around.

'Be sure of this, dreamspinners,' Asgard continued. 'There is nothing I would desire more than for their success, but by this time tomorrow there will be no dream powders to inspire man, no dreams of wonder or evolution—'

'Then what do you suggest?' came a vibration.

'What I suggest is that it is time to regard our options. Do we wait until the time of the next Tripodean Dream? And who knows how long that might be—a hundred days, a thousand years, or a million years? It may never happen, and if this is the case we dreamspinners probably won't even exist. Perhaps, then, we should join with Cain here in Havilah and spin the dreams from the spider webs of Havilah in the hope that a route into the Garden of Eden is found in the meantime.'

The chimney exploded.

'An alliance? With Cain, never!' cried one.

'We are independent,' shouted another.

A strong vibration shot down from near the top. 'We will never do the bidding of others. Never!'

'Do we wish,' said a loud vibration from the side, 'to spin nightmares and painful dreams for the rest of our days?'

'What has it come to if we do this?' said a deeper vibration.

Asgard waited until the furore had calmed down. 'If this is what you believe, then you had better consider my words.' The chimney fell silent. 'You are here because each one of you is fearful for the future. Has it not once entered your mind that perhaps now is OUR time?'

'Time for what, exactly, Asgard?'

'Time to evolve, dreamspinners.'

Vibrations of both agreement and disagreement shot back and forth.

'We dreamspinners are the only species ever created who have neither reached forward nor plunged back. We have never needed to embrace change, either by desire or necessity. The failure of the Heirs of Eden is, perhaps, a sign that we *must* alter our ways.' A series of strong vibrations shot out in agreement. 'If not, we will end up with no purpose. And we all know what happens to creatures that have no worth.' Silence filled the room. 'Don't we?'

Asgard could feel opinion shifting towards his position. 'And that is why I am helping Cain, because at the end of this, he is the one who will surely come out on top. The dreams of Havilah will be the only ones left for us to spin.'

Angry vibrations shot out once more.

Gaia was bursting with rage. 'But they are not dead yet,' she seethed, 'and dusk is falling. If they are alive—if there is but a *murmur* of a heartbeat in them, the heirs will have prevented the destruction of the land. You are fools to write them off.'

'Who speaks so?'

Before Asgard could find out, there was a tiny flash and one of the dreamspinners had vanished.

'That dreamspinner has made the wrong choice,' Asgard vibrated. 'Be sure you do not make the same mistake.'

INSTANTLY, Gaia was above the battered body of Old Man Wood, who was desperately trying to prise open the lid of a bottle. In no time, she was spinning the old man a dream. Seconds later Old Man Wood was fast asleep.

Good, she thought, the powders are working fast.

So, it was Asgard who had betrayed them, just as she suspected—and he had brazenly admitted it! "Helping Cain!" he'd said it, just like that—as though it was the most natural thing in the world. Traitor! Gaia poked a leg in her maghole. In which case, she was going to add balance to the drama.

She needed Old Man Wood to wake up. The dream-spinner hovered around the body of Old Man Wood, waiting —for there was nothing physical she could do to aid his recovery. Shortly, the old man stretched his arms out wide and yawned. Then he screamed in pain. Gaia watched as the old man shuffled, his face contorting in surprise as he found the Resplendix Mix. Then he studied it as he realised exactly what it was.

Now let us see how he does it this time. Gaia watched as the old man placed the bottle top to his lips, closed his eyes and kissed it. Instantly the top of the bottle opened.

Excellent, Gaia thought. *It worked.*

FORTY

A CRY FOR HELP

O ld Man Wood took a couple of drops, barely wetting his lips.

Immediately, a heat like the glow of a hot fire and the burning sensation of eating hot chillies, coursed through him. Those parts that were damaged or hurt burned with more savagery, the heat intense like a soldering iron welding him back together. He gritted his teeth as the Resplendix Mix set to work.

Shortly, now the heat was bearable, he had the urge to stand. He rolled his head and breathed deeply, the air filling his lungs like bellows. Aside from the glow of the Resplendix Mix, he felt wonderfully well and invigorated. He coiled up the rope and scoured the moonlit ledge.

Where were they? Isabella—he'd seen her directly below him on the rope. There she was, bent over … holding something. A body?

Old Man Wood scampered over. As he neared, a terrible wailing noise was coming from her. He prepared himself and coughed as he approached.

'Looks like you could do with a hand,' he said solemnly.

Isabella turned. 'Old Man Wood!' she flung her arms around him. 'Am I glad to see you? Look! It's Daisy—I think she's, she's…'

'Oh, little 'Bella, let's see what we have.' Old Man Wood bent down and ran a hand over Daisy's brow. He felt only coldness. He searched for signs of breathing, nothing. 'My goodness, she's had a terrible beating,' he said, trying to locate the Resplendix Mix in his pocket. He noted how her lips were a pale crimson—bloody pink—against her white skin. He felt for a pulse and his heart nearly stopped: he couldn't feel one. If it was there, it had all but gone. He could sense Isabella staring at him, searching his face for answers.

'Now, Isabella, there is only one thing I can do.' He showed her the bottle. 'She needs just a couple of drops from this bottle of Resplendix Mix. I'll tell you about it another time, but all you need know is that it's a very old remedy of mine for healing. Thing is,' he continued, a deep frown filling his forehead, 'the bottle will only open if the potion within can heal the person whose lips it touches.'

Isabella frowned. It didn't make sense. 'Anything, Old Man Wood—hurry!'

Old Man Wood lowered the bottle to Daisy's mouth and pressed the top against her lips.

'Why don't you just open it?' Isabella growled, mostly in frustration.

'As I said, I can't. The bottle will open if it can heal—otherwise I am afraid we have lost her.'

He shook his head.

'What is it?' Isabella cried.

Old Man Wood's lips trembled. 'I'm so sorry, but I fear it isn't going to work.' A tear rolled out of his eye and landed on Daisy's cheek. He wiped it off, and inspected the top of the bottle, which remained closed. 'I am too late.'

He picked himself up onto his knees, his eyes watery. 'I'm so sorry, little Daisy. So terribly sorry.' Another tear dropped out. Old Man Wood was bent over, dumb with shock.

Isabella stared numbly at her lifeless sister as a feeling of intense anger rushed into her. She directed her hands towards Daisy, closed her eyes and screamed:

'STOP BEING SO STUPID, DAISY DE LOWE, YOU

WILL NOT DIE ON ME. IS THAT PERFECTLY CLEAR? I WILL NOT ALLOW IT!'

A strange, pink glow emanated from her hands, cocooning Daisy's body.

'YOU WILL NOT GIVE IN!'

Daisy's eye's flickered.

Isabella reeled. *Blimey*, she thought, *it worked*. What had she done? Had her words really had that effect?

Whatever she'd done, she suddenly felt desperately tired. She stumbled and collapsed to the ground.

Old Man Wood put the bottle to Daisy's lips and found that it opened. He gasped. 'Come on now, just a drop is all you need.' Moments later, they could see the colour in Daisy's cheeks returning.

Isabella smiled weakly and tried to hide a huge yawn.

'I think you could do with a drop of this too,' and he applied the Resplendix Mix to Isabella's lips. 'Is there any shelter?'

Isabella pointed towards the rock.

Old Man Wood scooped Daisy off the rocks and carried her in to the cave. Isabella followed. As soon as she stepped inside, the warmth made her feel drowsy and tired and hungry. She sat down and closed her eyes.

Old Man Wood shone his torch around the chamber and gasped. The whole place was covered in paintings that seemed familiar—as if he'd seen them somewhere before, a long time ago.

In the middle he found a small, circular recess—like a large fire pit, but empty. It seemed a good place to rest and, more importantly, as he stepped inside to inspect it, it was deliciously cosy and warm, a covering of a soft, sandy, dust-like substance on the bottom that was as fine as talcum and soft as a mattress.

He lowered Daisy in, making sure her head was propped up, and started back out of the cave. From the corner of his eye he spotted Isabella, slumped and fast asleep on the floor. He moved her into the same pit. It seemed the right thing to do—a place where they were warm and away from danger, where they might sleep—while he searched for a way out.

Two were alive by the skin of their teeth. Now, he had to find Archie.

ARCHIE SOARED LIKE A BIRD, swooping first one way then another. He shot high into the air, twisting as he went, enjoying the marvellous sensation of weightlessness. Each gust of wind caressed his body and he cried out at the freedom and the speed. Now he was diving, and flying fast, as fast as an arrow. He screwed left and found himself heading, at breakneck speed, towards a rock face, a large boulder, as if he *was* a bolt of lightning. *Maybe he was a bolt of lightning.* He couldn't stop, he couldn't turn fast enough and there wasn't enough room for him to manoeuvre. But he wasn't afraid. He would wallop into it with his head. That's right—it wouldn't hurt at all.

BANG! The rock shattered into several pieces.

In place of the boulder was the entrance to a cave. He looked inside. Isabella and Daisy were there, with Old Man Wood. They were so excited and wanted to tell him something. They beckoned him, teasing him to step in and join them. They were laughing and smiling and looked so happy and content.

He raised his foot and carried on through the entrance. But as he did he felt the anger of Cain smash into him and he fell to the ground. Cain started kicking him—smashing him in the ribs, in the chest, and then to his face.

He gasped, struggling for air.

Why would Cain want to hurt him? They were on the same side, right? He felt air leaking out of him like a balloon with a small hole that was getting bigger all the time. He gulped. He needed to breathe so badly, so badly it hurt, like his body was crying out...

Archie surfaced and thrashed the water, desperate to find

a hold. His fingers touched on a rock. He pulled himself up. He felt sick. He vomited, expelling the water from his gut— but it felt as though he'd swallowed a full bathtub and he retched and hacked until it felt as though his internal organs might come out as well.

He lay panting on a stone. His head throbbed like crazy. He could feel drops of rain on his face, though not as hard as before. He shivered. *Daisy? Isabella?* He couldn't see anyone close by, in fact, he couldn't see anything at all.

He shuffled out of the water, and slowly up onto a boulder where he pulled his legs into his body. *Cold, so cold.*

In his mind he wondered if he could hear things. 'Help,' he called out. But he had no way of telling if the word was coming out as a sound.

He wanted to yell out for one of his sisters, for Old Man Wood, but instead, he knew there was only one person who could help him.

Cain.

'*Cain!*' he yelled. 'CAIN, HELP ME!'

And through the cracks in his eyes, he swore he could see someone approaching.

FORTY-ONE

LOST

The Joan Of rocked gently one minute and then seemed to climb up a bank and skid down. For a minute, Gus thought he might be at a funfair. But what was that terrible noise? He yawned, opened his eyes and found himself looking into Sue's sleeping face. He smiled; what a very pleasant way to wake up, even if she was snoring.

And then he wondered what his breath must be like. *Probably gross.* Heck.

Trying not to disturb her, he shuffled down to the end of the boat, popped his head out, closed his eyes, stretched his arms and took a huge lungful of fresh air.

He opened one eye. Then the other.

OK, so this was interesting.

He pulled himself right out of the boat, and stood on the step while leaning on the canopy. Then he whistled.

Sue was stirring inside the boat and Gus could hear her yawns.

'Good morning, Captain Sue.'

'Oh, morning, Gus,' she said, rubbing the sleep out of her eyes. 'Everything alright?'

He popped his head down. 'Fine and dandy-ish.'

'Any idea where we are yet?'

'Ab-so-lute-ly none. Have a peek for yourself.'

251

Sue crept down to the other end and leant out.

'Oh!' she said, calmly. A moment later she ducked her head inside, her eyes wide open and her face as pale as milk.

'Oh? Is that it?' Gus said.

'Yes, Oh!'

'We're miles out to sea with no way of knowing where on earth we might be and all you can say is "Oh".'

'Yes, oh,' Sue began. She took a deep breath. 'Right, Gus. I've never sworn at anything or anyone before in my life—but I've heard my mum do it and I think this is the perfect time to finally give it a proper go.'

Gus looked a little confused. 'Oh?' he said.

'You see,' Sue continued, 'every time she swears, it always begins with, "Oh".'

Gus raised his bushy eyebrows. 'Oh,' he said again.

And with that, Sue returned out of the canopy and screamed at the very top of her voice. '**OH $*%@!**'

FORTY-TWO

WHY CAIN?

O ld Man Wood sat on the edge of the pit and studied the children who lay sleeping in the strange soft substance in the base of it. The sound of their gentle breathing was the sweetest music he had ever heard. He reflected on his extraordinary fortune. It was a miracle that he'd found them, he had the curious bed panel to thank for that, and then there was the amazing re-discovery of the Resplendix Mix.

He whistled. The torrential rain, the lightning, the mud slides and the cold. Old Man Wood shook his head. How, in all the apples in the world, were they alive? And how had Daisy come back when he'd felt no pulse. Had Isabella clawed her back from death's door, or had Daisy done it through sheer bloody determination?

And what about Archie? He'd seen a body at the other end of the ledge on top of a rock. As he approached, his heart had fallen; the boy was delirious, curled up and shivering, his mouth foaming and his eyes staring wildly in different directions. His body was battered to bits.

But what was so strange was that, with his first glance, he could have sworn it wasn't Archie at all, it was his friend—the one with the ginger hair who was always so unpleasant to the girls. That's right, the boy Archie liked to go fishing with. The boy called Kemp. He wondered if he'd been washed up on the shoreline—the first of many, he presumed.

He'd rubbed his eyes and looked out over the water. In the next blink of his eye it was Archie. And Archie was calling out '*Cain, Cain,*' over and over again. But who on earth was this Cain, and why did that name strike a chord deep within him that was not at all pleasant?

Old Man Wood searched his memory. Why did Cain seem so important to Archie and, oddly, to him as well? That one name, *Cain*, dredged up a confusing sense of love and anger and it didn't feel comfortable at all.

Now the children were asleep, he lowered himself into the pit and studied them in more detail. The bruises and cuts on their bodies were quite simply astonishing. On each he found signs of terrible burns; no doubt from the lightning bolts.

Daisy's legs were entirely black and blue, criss-crossed with cuts—some deep and some sharp, like punctures, and others raked by thorns. Her fingernails were black, and on her ring finger and index finger the entire nail had detached leaving only bare, raw skin. Her shoes had long gone and her feet looked as though they had been forced through a blender. Her tracksuit bottoms were almost non-existent apart from the elastic, and one of her football stockings was attached by a few threads and it flapped off her bright red and raw shin.

Old Man Wood wondered if he should give her some more Resplendix Mix. But, then again, he knew deep down that any more so soon wouldn't be a wise idea. Resplendix Mix was powerful stuff, and powerful potions, he suspected, needed careful portioning.

But as he thought about it, his attention drifted back to Archie. Like Daisy, the boy had been battered, beaten and pulped to within a millimetre of death. But there was one significant alteration to his appearance; Archie's hair stood on end in spikes, like a medieval mace club, exactly as he'd seen in the panels, when he'd thought it was a hat. He ran his hand across Archie's head and found that the spiky parts were fused together as if worked on by superglue or a whole pot of

Daisy's hair gel. Old Man Wood couldn't understand it. He tried to bend a section of hair but it was set tight.

He inspected Archie's hands. They, too, were terribly cut and bruised. He suspected a broken finger or two by the way his digits were angled. And on his palms there was a raw streak, like burning—probably from pulling the rope, he thought. His head bore the blows of rocks as did his body—as if he'd been sprayed by a rock gun. Some of his cuts seeped, others had congealed already. Old Man Wood sucked in a deep breath. How on earth had he survived?

Most extraordinary of all, perhaps even odder than Archie's hair, were Isabella's hands. The palm of each bore a hole that looked as if they had been burnt through as though punctured by a red hot poker, so that he could see light coming through on the other side. Old Man Wood stared at them for some time and shook his head.

They'd be safe enough here for a while but how would they get home? In the light of morning he'd give them another drop of Resplendix Mix. Then, he would have to find a way out. He climbed out of the pit and headed towards the cave entrance, grateful for the gentle light of the moon. The water reached near to the top of the stone ledge in front of him, lapping at the edges.

He pulled himself up onto a higher rock to the side and sat back, trying to envisage how far the water must extend; two hundred, three hundred metres, perhaps more—a mile or two? And everything in its path destroyed in the space of a few hours—just like that. The power and the fury of nature, he thought.

Why did he feel so especially linked to it?

Before long, Old Man Wood found himself falling into a deep sleep punctuated by dreams, his mind racing from Archie's shouts about someone called Cain, to the boy with the red hair, to the terrible injuries of the children. And then his dream flashed to the curious bed panels and his old cellar and the strange pictures on the cave walls.

FORTY-THREE

THE BUBBLING POOL

Old Man Wood was awoken by a fizzing, gurgling noise. He opened his eyes and immediately wondered how long he'd been asleep. He checked the sky, and the moon had disappeared behind a cloud higher up. Rain was falling again, slightly harder than the drizzle earlier and, as he jumped down, he plunged into water. His heart missed a beat. Apples alive, he thought, how had the water level risen so high so fast?

The children! He'd left them in the pit!

He waded to the entrance from where the peculiar sound was coming. A strange mist floated out, like a huge, billowing steam cloud. Cautiously, he peered in, his face a picture of confusion.

The cave was dry inside and water flowed rapidly along a neat, straight channel that led, he presumed, directly into the pit. Old Man Wood's heartbeat raced. He followed the channel on his hands and knees through the thick mist. As he crept closer the colour of the water changed from blue to pink and it was gently bubbling.

He leant over the edge of the pit, his heart thumping. Were they still alive?

Then he heard a voice. Or was it laughter?

'What on earth are you doing?' Daisy said.

Old Man Wood reeled.

Daisy giggled. 'Hey, why don't you get in?'

Old Man Wood felt himself choking up. 'Goodness me. Daisy!' he cried. 'Is that you? Is that really you? I can't see you.'

'Yeah, it's me alright. Come on in. It's gorgeous and warm and fantastic,' she replied. 'And it smells delicious, like lavender and pine needles.'

'Are you alright in there?'

'We're absolutely fine,' Isabella said. 'Come on in—see for yourself.'

Old Man Wood was confused. 'Are ALL of you fine, I mean, *well*, in there? Isabella, Archie?'

Old Man Wood heard a splashing noise and Archie's strange head popped out. 'Yeah. You?'

'Apples alive!'

Archie smiled. 'Well, it's good to see you too. How long have you been here?'

'Your head?'

'Yeah, I know. Something's happened to my hair. I think it was a lightning bolt.' And he patted his spikes before drifting back into the steam.

Old Man Wood's heart leapt for joy. 'Right then, you lot, I'm coming in.'

He could hear them laughing. 'About time too, there's masses of room!' Daisy said. 'And watch yourself as you get in or Archie will puncture you with his ridiculous hairdo.'

Old Man Wood dipped his foot in the water, which felt like a winning combination of champagne and cream.

Ever so slowly, he lowered his body into the pool and the water bubbled up around him. He closed his eyes and let himself drift under. Almost immediately, he felt the bubbles caress his aches and pains, as though targeting each one individually. When he resurfaced and opened his eyes, the children were beaming at him.

Old Man Wood laughed. 'You did it, you survived! HOW

in apples' name… how? And are you better—Daisy, Archie —truly?'

The children floated over and hugged him.

Old Man Wood inspected Archie, looking for the cuts and bruises on his head and on his hands and body. He did the same with Daisy, but their skin was clear and smooth. It was as if the battle through the storm had never happened.

'I can't believe it. I simply can't believe it,' he repeated. 'In all the world I thought you were as good as dead, you twins. Battered to bits you were and now look at you. It's a miracle.'

The children looked at each other blankly. It was indeed strange that their cuts and bruises had all but gone, but maybe they hadn't been hurt that badly. Anyway, wasn't that what thermal springs did, heal? This one, they decided, must be a pretty good one.

Isabella asked. 'So, how did you find us?'

Old Man Wood hesitated as he tried to work out how much he should tell them. 'I was up at the cottage watching the storm blasting out of the sky and thinking to myself that if you were trying to get home you'd be in a spot of trouble. There wasn't a word from the school so I thought I'd better try and, er, find you. It took a while, mind, slipping and sliding. By the looks of you lot when I found you—you know exactly what I mean.'

'I can't remember much,' Daisy said, playing with her hair, 'apart from being very cold and very tired. That's it really. Oh and holding on to a branch for dear life and some big, nasty flashes.' Her eyes sparkled. 'Did we win the football?'

Isabella laughed. 'Really, Daisy, of all the questions. You don't remember?'

Daisy shook her head.

'Well, I'll tell you. With the last kick of the game, you hit possibly the worst free kick the world has ever known,' she raised her eyebrows. 'Still not ringing any bells? Fortunately for you, the ball was deflected by a thunderbolt into the goal and, in the process, fractionally away from Archie's brain, short-circuiting his hair.'

The four of them roared with laughter, while Archie tried to bend his new strange mace-like follicles.

'Daisy,' Archie said, a tone of uneasiness in his voice, 'could you really hear the thunderbolts coming?'

'Yeah,' Daisy said. 'Couldn't you?'

The others shook their heads.

'Oh.' She seemed genuinely surprised. 'It was a funny crackling noise miles up in the sky, the sort of noise you get when you put wet leaves on a roaring bonfire. It was quite easy to recognise after a while. Are you *sure* you couldn't hear it?'

There was a small silence.

'Anyway,' Isabella continued, trying to sound a little more cheerful. 'I can remember seeing you, Old Man Wood. After that I must have fallen asleep. And, when I woke up, I was sitting in a wonderful thermal bath with you guys. I thought we'd arrived, you know, in Heaven.' The children laughed. 'All my aches and cuts and bruises had vanished.' She opened the palms of her hands. 'Apart from these.'

The black burn marks had gone, but the indents were still there with the hole through the middle.

'Ow!' Daisy said. 'How did you get that?'

Isabella winced. 'I think I managed to deflect a lightning bolt.'

'*You did what?* But that would have killed you.'

'I know, I put my hands up to protect me and…' Isabella was confused. It didn't make sense to her, and furthermore, she didn't want to elaborate. 'Anyway, we haven't heard from you, Archie, what happened to you?'

'I honestly don't remember a great deal,' he said as a cheeky smile grew on his face. 'Did I really punch one of the Chitbury players?'

'Punch?' Daisy said, her eyes wide, 'yeah, big time, you went bonkers, like you were possessed.'

'Blimey.' He fell quiet. 'I've never hit anyone before.'

As he tried to recall the moment, the image of Kemp and Cain came flashing back and a dark scowl crept over his face. 'Can't remember much more—apart from pulling that massive branch off the lane and getting tangled up in the rope, and then I think I got whacked in the head. Feels fine now.'

Archie ducked under the bubbles and when he re-emerged he blew the water out of his mouth at Daisy. She retaliated by flicking water at him and a water fight developed, which was a welcome break from telling their awkward survival stories.

But there was one thing Daisy wanted to know. 'Archie, do you remember you said just before the storm broke—that it was going to come at us and wouldn't stop until the sun went down? How did you know? I mean, that's exactly what happened. All those thunderbolts came at us, didn't they? And Isabella told us the heavy rain stopped just as the sun disappeared.'

Isabella leant in. It had been playing on her mind too.

Archie felt pretty uncomfortable. Thinking about it made him go cold. How could he explain it without sounding like an idiot? Maybe he'd tell them later. He just wanted to eat something and go to sleep. He yawned. 'I dunno,' he said and shrugged his shoulders. 'Just a hunch, I suppose. I'm starving.'

'You're hiding something, aren't you, winkle?'

'I hate it when you call me that,' he said, and splashed his twin with water.

But the girls knew there was something he wasn't telling them.

OLD MAN WOOD LISTENED ATTENTIVELY, noting that they had survived direct strikes from lightning bolts. It was impossible—so how had they done it? There must be something rather special about them, just as he suspected. And what was it about the awkwardness in Archie's face—the exact expression he'd seen when he handed him the coat. And what about this "Cain" person he'd called out for?

He remembered the apples. 'I've got just the thing,' he announced, rummaging in his coat pocket. 'You must be starving, so I took the liberty of bringing you something. Afterwards, it'd be a good idea to grab some rest. After all, we've still got to figure out how we're going to get out of here.'

Archie cupped some of the water. 'The delicious water in here's filled me up a bit,' he said, 'but a nice chocolate brownie—preferably with chocolate custard—would hit the spot.'

'Or a massive plate of Peking duck pancakes with plum sauce, cucumber and spring onions,' Daisy said.

'Or a wedge of banoffee pie, with thick cream,' Isabella added, licking her lips.

Old Man Wood pulled out the apples. He noted the disappointed looks on their faces.

'Now, before you start complaining, these are my special apples, so make sure you eat the whole thing, understand. Pips and all. They'll fill you up. Trust me. Don't know why or how, but they will.'

He threw an apple at each one of them. They all bit in hard and were rewarded with the taste of golden syrup, honey, apple pie and raspberries flooding their mouths.

The children pulled themselves out of the pit and wrung-out their tattered clothes. The cave was beautifully warm and their bodies—now devoid of cuts and bruises—quickly began to dry. From the multicoloured glow of the water, which seemed to generate its own soft light, the children searched for somewhere to sleep. It soon became evident that there were four ledges, like stone benches, off the floor, as though individually made for them.

Daisy sat down heavily on the one in front of her and, in the next movement, she pulled her legs up and lay down. 'Mmm. lovely,' she announced, scrunching her hand in the soft velvety texture. Before long, she was snoring loudly.

The others did the same, and they too experienced the blissful sensation of the warm silky powder, softer than feathers, that moulded perfectly around their bodies.

Within moments, the Heirs of Eden and Old Man Wood were sound asleep, their adventures forgotten.

To be continued…

Get Book Two, Spider Web Powder, here.

A LITTLE HELP...

Dear Reader,

If you enjoyed my book, a review would not only help me in my quest to find new readers (and being able to market the book to them), but it's a help for new readers to see what you may (or may not) have liked about it!

Please, spare a moment to give THE POWER AND THE FURY an honest REVIEW from the online version of the store where you purchased it!

I'm working on several new projects right now. By leaving a review it will spur me on to finish the series.

Thank you.

JKE

AUDIOBOOKS

Listen to the Eden Chronicles books which are brought to life quite brilliantly by award-nominated voice artist Rory Barnett.

The Power and The Fury is now available at all digital outlets:

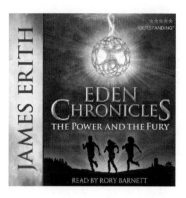

The Power and The Fury, narrated by Rory Barnett

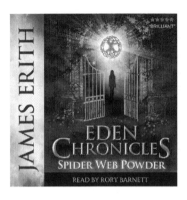

Spider Web Powder - COMING SOON!

ALSO BY JAMES ERITH

The EDEN CHRONICLES series:

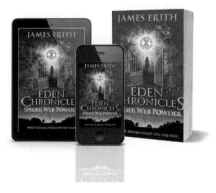

Spider Web Powder - Eden Chronicles, Book Two (ISBN: 9781910134108)

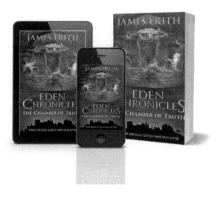

The Chamber of Truth - Eden Chronicles, Book Three (ISBN: 9781910134115)

The Dragon's Game - Eden Chronicles, Book
Four (ISBN:9781910134245)

ABOUT THE AUTHOR

James was born in Suffolk in the UK. After travelling the world extensively, James worked as a journalist in the 1990's and then turned to his passion for the great outdoors, designing and building gardens for several years before returning to writing.

James moved to North Yorkshire where he lived between the Yorkshire Dales and the Yorkshire Moors. It inspired him to use these beautiful areas as the location for the **EDEN CHRONICLES** series.

In 2013 James rowed across the English Channel and the length of the Thames to raise money for MND and Breakthrough Breast Cancer.

www.jameserith.com
james@jericopress.com

facebook.com/JamesErithAuthor

twitter.com/jameserith

instagram.com/edenchronicles

goodreads.com/jameserith

pinterest.com/jameserith

amazon.com/author/jameserith

EDEN TEAM

If you'd like to join my closed "Eden" group, on Facebook, go to Facebook, look up "EDEN TEAM" and request to join.

Or, send me an email.

NOTE: This is only for those of you who'd like early access to new releases in exchange for feedback and reviews. If you fancy being part of my publishing process, here's your chance to be an advanced reader, give feedback and just be a rather cool supporter when new books come out!

To join, I would expect you to have reviewed one book and preferably to have read at least one other…

No sweat if this isn't for you, drop by my Author Facebook page—James Erith Author—and give it a like!

My website is: www.jameserith.com

I look forward, very much, to seeing you there.

James

Printed in Great Britain
by Amazon